"*Hattie's story comes out of the heart and soul of what it means to be human in a sometimes inhuman world. It is an extraordinary journey through the depths of human struggle, the heights of human triumph, and the ways in which they are vital and intimate partners in a courageous and transcendent life. HATTIE is exuberant with insight and awareness, and there is not a false moment in it. This beautifully realized novel teaches us about life, love, and longing, and we are humbled and glorified in the process. HATTIE is a terrific read and a life-lasting experience.*"

—Janet Thomas, author of *Day Breaks Over Dharamsala*

"*Like sitting with a friend telling me stories by the fireside, I was riveted by the mystical, haunting tale of this quietly courageous woman. Hattie's voice is warm, wise, and totally engaging.*"

—Heather Summerhayes Cariou, author of *Sixtyfive Roses*

"*HATTIE is about a tragic journey from survival to relationship to wisdom. Like a quilt, the novel is skillfully sewn together into a rich narrative, and Bowen weaves the snippets and stories of Hattie's life with a deft touch. Each section of cloth has its own history, its own story; come together there is a wonderful wholeness. As Hattie tells her stories one cannot help but remember one's own. It's in the telling and the sharing that hearts connect, and you will come to know Hattie and yourself more deeply.*"

—Richard Poletunow, psychotherapist and adjunct faculty, St. Vincent's College, Bridgeport, Connecticut

"*Anna—you are someone who could lead us to our communal soul.*"

—Thomas Moore, author of *Care of the Soul in Medicine*

HATTIE

HATTIE

Anna Bozena Bowen

Cover photo by Amanda Huye
Author photo by Doug Bowen

Designed by Kristen Sund

ISBN 978-1-937650-16-2
Library of Congress Control Number: 2012946880

SMALL
BATCH
BOOKS

493 SOUTH PLEASANT STREET
AMHERST, MASSACHUSETTS 01002
413.230.3943
SMALLBATCHBOOKS.COM

To the Universe—
It has held me, guided me,
taught me, and never let me down.

Contents

PART 3 ~ THROUGH THE WOODS

"It's funny how the world can be as small as the flesh around you or as large as the winds your voice travels upon."

—*Hattie*

The Beginning

*I*f someone had happened to look out over the lake that one day in late spring, all they would have seen were a few bubbles breaking through the surface. Air, no longer trapped, being whisked up by the waves of a breeze sweeping the water. At first she struggled. The terror of impending death had instinctively gripped her. Her lips clenched. The pressure of tightly held air mounted until searing pain tore through her chest. Her lungs felt on fire. To hold back what was inevitable, her throat and face hardened like a stone dam. Her body twisted in agony. Her face distorted. Her hands clawed.

One last thought fought its way through the terror. "Not like this." She didn't want agony. She didn't want to look deformed. And she knew she was going to die. So she made the last choice she was ever going to make. She stopped struggling. Slowly her body began to untwist. Her arms and legs loosened and let the water hold them. Her face softened. She parted her lips and opened her mouth. Her throat relaxed. The cool clear water of Willow Lake flowed into her. She stopped struggling for air that wasn't there and the fire in her lungs was soothed. There was no more pain. No more struggle. As she drifted downward, her eyes gazed upward and watched

1

one last bubble of air be set free. One last whisper of life. She saw it floating away from her. Further and further toward the surface. Toward the sun's light glistening far above her.

Now I can tell my story, for at least you know how I died. I drowned. Though I had known many terrors up to that point, the terror of death that seized me surprised me. But I have to say, once I accepted death and was able to choose to release that last bubble of air, I felt a peace I had never known in my entire life.

Part 1

In the Meadow

She Fit Just So

My voice never traveled very far. And so my world stayed very small. It was the kitchen and the washtub that drowned my arms from morning 'til night. My fingers were raw from scrubbing. My upper arms heavy with muscle. And my elbows crooked from the bent motion I found myself in. I washed for the Rosens across the road. I had the washtub. He had no wife but many children. So I scrubbed for us and for him and for others who would come by and say, "Please, Hattie?"

I hated the word please.

More than that, I hated myself for not saying no.

My husband Harry worked in the mines. He'd be gone weeks, months at a time. I never knew when or if he'd come strolling home. He was a man whose home was a place to stop off at if there was no better place to be. He'd come wandering in and say, "Hey Hattie, I've come home to you." And I'd think, "Big deal." He would paw at me in the night until we were both wet, then insist that I meant everything to him. That I was his woman.

I gave up crying a long time before, but on those occasions I would almost remember how to cry. I could almost taste the relief that comes with warm full tears like the drops of mother's milk that flow from the breast and bring release to the heaviness a woman is meant to carry. But I never quite remembered that feeling of crying again. It was canned away in me. Somewhere deep inside where only God could find it and even He would have trouble looking. One time Harry never did come back. Even then I didn't cry. I just kept on bending my arms and drowning them in the washtub.

My youngins, they were real little. And they stayed little 'cause all they had was a lost Pa and a washtub Ma. Jeremy, my firstborn, asked me once where the butterflies that he ran after but never caught went. Over the fumes of lye soap I said, "Does it matter, son?" That night as I was pulling the quilt over his shoulders I whispered in his ear, "They fly to where they want to go and then they die. And then they die." He rolled over just then and his child scent crept up my nose and I almost found a way to cry. Almost, but not quite.

Ellie, my baby girl, was as soft and pretty as the petals of a full-bloomed flower. The kind of flower that suddenly awakens one morning, looking pretty and delicate under the early sun, and then as quickly dies. Ellie. Oh God. I hate to remember. Yet I have to remember. I have to remember because she reminds me of the joys of mothering. She brought me to a point of feeling glory in life. Not just being happy, but the kind of joy that reminds me of the trumpets of heaven. Ellie smiled every day of her short hard life. The crooked elbows that I held her in were nothing compared to her bent little body. She clung to me with her curled little fingers, and I clung to her. I did not want her to leave me. But she did leave me.

No one loved her like I did. No one saw her like I did. They saw her like a tadpole. Meant to be a form but not quite one yet. Harry did not touch her before and did not touch her after she died. I cradled her in my bent arms. She fit just so in them. It's as if they were meant to be that way. As if washing was meant to form my arms so I could hold my child the way she needed me to.

A woman thinks silly things when given the time. Holding Ellie I was given the time. In her two short years, my crippled child gave me more time to think than any one family would have given me by not sending me their dirty clothes. When she died I held her as long as my arms could bear and my heart could stand. Then I, only I, for I would not have anyone accompany me, carried her up through the gentle slopes of the meadow. I found a spot where the sun seemed warmest. It was as if the light pointed to that spot in the earth where the soil yielded easily. I could have dug it with my hands. I laid my baby in that shallow grave. I didn't put a marker there. I would always remember the spot and no one else needed to know. Harry didn't care. He was gone when she was born and he was gone when she smiled her last, sweet, toothless smile.

Odd how mothers think. Somehow I knew that she wouldn't be with me long. Youngins start teething when they are, oh, six or eight months old. Ellie never cried from gum pains. Nothing pearly white ever pushed through those pink little hills. I would put my fingers into her mouth and Ellie would frown from the bitter taste of lye soap that was always on my hands. I would rub her gums searching for the firm point of a tooth. I never found one and she never grew any. No teeth was a sign to me of a short life. My baby girl would not need to chew food.

At first she drank my milk. Then I gave her goats' milk. Mrs. Osgood, from down the road a ways, took pity on Ellie in a kind, neighborly way and brought us milk from her goats. Ellie swallowed like a sparrow but seemed to enjoy every swallow. She smiled after each one. Ellie didn't have teeth and she never talked and she never walked, but she always smiled.

Jeremy and his sister were twins. God only knows how two babies born from the same womb on the same day could be so different. Mother's love, many a day I asked God how mother's love could be so different. My children were both very dear to me, but Ellie needed me more. Jeremy must have felt her need for me 'cause he never asked for anything. Never, except when he asked me where the butterflies went. But I was so tired from caring and washing and never saying no to anyone that I didn't give him the answer he hoped for. That look in his big brown eyes—

distant eyes like Harry's—searched for something. Something that was gone like his pa most of the days.

Jeremy suckled my breast, but his teeth hurt me and he weaned early. I remember the clinking sound the metal cup made when he lifted it to his mouth in the hurried fashion a youngin does when he's learning something new. Sometimes he would cry if the cup pinched his lip against his front teeth. I'd glance over at him while Ellie gurgled and smiled, milk drooling from her mouth. The cup against his teeth sounded like a rattle, so I came up with this silly plan. When he got bigger, and his baby teeth fell out to let new big white teeth grow in, well, we would save those little teeth. We'd put them in a tin can and use it as a rattle for Ellie to play with.

Jeremy never asked why he had teeth and Ellie didn't. He never asked why I held Ellie so much and not him. He would watch her, curled up, crooked, not growing bigger, lying in the wooden box we used for her bed, and he never said anything. When Ellie left us, he laid down in her box, curled himself up to fit in it, and slept. He slept in that wooden box each night for a week. After that he took all the bedding out of it and used it for playing.

One day, as I sat in my wooden straight-back chair, my arms resting on my lap, Jeremy came up to me. He climbed up on my lap, curled into the folds of my elbows, and asked, "Like Ellie, Ma? Do I feel like Ellie?" I had no answer for him. But I held him and rocked him and loved him. I so wanted to make up for all the moments he needed me when I had held Ellie. For all the times that cup clinked against his teeth instead of having the soft firmness of his mother's breast against his cheek. I wanted to make up for everything. But life doesn't hold us in debt for making up things missed in the past. They are gone like the breath caught in the passing wind.

Naming

I am somewhat mixed about what happened next. Believe me when I say that when I again found myself full with child I wondered how it happened. I did not remember Harry coming home. He must have sneaked in with the evening breeze. Maybe it was when my soul was grieving Ellie and it paid him no mind. He must have come and gone very quickly. To this day I don't remember how it happened, and to be truthful I'm glad I don't.

Jeremy was three years old when the new baby was born. Poor Jeremy. He always found himself shying up against a quiet corner and looking at his ma holding some other youngin. This one was a boy. Straight, long, and cold. He had steel-blue eyes. Stark eyes. He would arch his back and scream. His sound was not the cry of a baby. It was a scream of resistance. He rejected me from the moment of his birth. He nursed only for survival. He fought any comfort I offered. And he never smiled. Maybe he was not Harry's. Maybe a demon had crept into my night and taken advantage of me as I slept. God only knows. And He's not telling.

When Jeremy and Ellie were born, I named them

quickly and with ease. I looked deep into their little wrinkled faces and saw their names. For a long time I just could not name this child. At first I called him "baby." Then I called him "your little brother." Finally, out of complete frustration, I named him Zak. It was for no good reason at all. It was a name I saw in a newspaper that happened to be at the bottom of Irma Dumas's laundry basket. She came by one day and dropped off her washing. After taking out the last of her dirty clothes, I found a page of newsprint. "Zak Emery's Pig Farm Sold," it read. So I said, "Child, Zak is as good a name as any I can think of." That day I christened him Zak. There was no preacher in our town. He lived in the next town over. He came through our town about as often as Harry stopped by. I had little use for either of them.

When Zak was three months old, Harry came home. "Woman," he said as he towered over the child. "You're crazier than I thought giving him a dumb name like Zak." "Husband," I said. "Go to hell."

I often wished that at that moment my arms had been sunk deep in the washtub. Maybe then he would not have heard my words above the sloshing sound of water and cloth against the washboard. Instead, there I was, standing face to face with him. Even though my words weren't loud enough to be carried by the winds past my world, they were loud enough to brush against the oversized ears that stuck out from Harry's head. He was not a good-looking man. To be honest, he was almost ugly, but too stupid looking to be ugly.

His mother Beatrice, God rest her soul, once said to me, "Hattie, Harry's a good man. Remember looks ain't everything. God passed him by when he was making masterpieces, but he gave him a strong body to work hard. He will take good care of you."

Mothers can be so wrong in seeing their sons. Oh yes, he had a strong body. On our wedding night he nearly suffocated me with his weight. He was bearing down—pushing, rocking back and forth like he was trying to hoist a wagon stuck in mud—forgetting that I was alive under him. When I cried out, gasping for breath, he thought I was crying in ecstasy. Such a stupid man!

His arms were strong enough to hoist huge buckets of rock out of the mines he worked, but never strong enough to hold the youngins. That day, standing there next to him, I felt his arm—just one mind you—come away from his side and fling me clean across the room. I found myself in the corner with Jeremy. There I sat, looking foolish. My print dress had popped a couple buttons and the skirt lay open over my thighs. What went through my head as my eyes lifted up to his made me shudder. He's thinking about having me.

As much as I wanted to pull my dress together and cover myself up, it would have been letting him know that I knew what was going through his mind. So I did nothing. Above Jeremy's silent terror and Zak's screams, he came toward me. His thick hand fisted around the neckline of my dress. Without effort he pulled me off the floor and lifted me up so that my eyes met his cold, heartless stare.

My face felt his hot breath seeping over it as he said, "Woman, I forgive you for saying such a thing." Then his big, callused hand patted my cheek with enough pressure to make my head feel the wall behind it.

Snippet

I can only tell you what I remember, but it is not in any order. My life was not in any order. I slept when I was tired, but only so tired that keeping my eyes open was impossible. Yet even though my life seemed driven only to the ripples on the washboard, I felt that somewhere, somehow there was a way to change the little world around me.

Letter Writing

Isabelle was a woman I met later on in my life. It was an unusual circumstance. I got to know her through her sister Miss Jean, who lived in town up the road a bit from my house. Miss Jean would ask me to come by and write letters for her to Isabelle. Whenever she received a letter from her sister—sometimes two or more arrived together—I would sit and read them to her. Then I would listen to Miss Jean as she carefully spoke her words, and write a letter in return. After a while, I got to know Isabelle from the letters the sisters shared. She seemed like a fine woman. She was caring of her family. She was educated. And for me she held a certain mystery. I felt something weaving itself between the words of her letters. I didn't know what it was, but I felt it had meaning for me and my life.

Even though Miss Jean told me what to write, I made the letters even longer. I added bits of news about the weather or the town or what Miss Jean did over that week. This gave me more time to be in a place where I was something other than a washwoman. As the letters came and went, I began putting bits of myself into them, too. I was curious about Isabelle and hoped she would be a little curious about me. Usually, at the end of each letter, she would write a short note thanking me for being such a help to her sister.

One day though, and it took me by surprise, Isabelle started her letter with a question about me. Well, I'll tell you, nothing compared to the excitement that greeting brought to my heart. Of course, when I saw my name in the first sentence I tried not to show my jitters. I was afraid Miss Jean might take offense at being second in line. So, I fiddled with my glasses and fidgeted in the chair as if I was trying to get comfortable. All the while I was silently reading the part of the letter that was meant for me. It wasn't much. Just a few sentences. But in a way it was more than any man or woman had ever said to me. And it wasn't anything about my washing abilities. Miss Jean finally asked me what the holdup was so I told her my eyeglasses needed cleaning, and I pulled out my cloth and gave them a good rub to satisfy her. All the while I was smiling wider than I knew I could.

By this time I was pretty well known for being able to get even the deepest, most stubborn stains out of cloth. Sometimes I used secret formulas that somehow invented themselves as I needed them. One day though, I was frustrated by a spot the size of a fist in a pair of trousers I was laundering. It looked like blood. I could usually get rid of blood without a problem, but this stain just would not budge. Maybe it was real old blood that just refused to let go its hold, but there was no way of telling. In our town, no one ever asked what caused a spot of blood to appear on clothing. No one wanted to know the answer. I think they were afraid of it. So anyway, not knowing what I was trying to get rid of, I just kept at it. After trying a few different concoctions, I finally did manage to get most of that stubborn stain out. But that's a different story. I wanted to tell you about Lady Isabelle and what she wrote. I started calling her Lady Isabelle that day after I read her letter.

"Dear Hattie," she wrote. "I know little about you, but I believe in my intuition. My intuition tells me that you, my dear, are a gifted woman. Has anyone ever told you that? This sense I have about you comes through in the style of your penmanship. I hope that one day we have an opportunity to meet."

Sadly, the joy I felt from reading this was short-lived. The letter I wrote that day was the last letter I ever wrote for Miss Jean. Two weeks later, a drifter passing through our town invaded Miss Jean's home and killed her. He did not rob her. He did not rape her. He did not beat her. He just killed her. Slit her throat while she sat at her kitchen table doing her needlework. After he watched her blood drain over the piece of white linen—which was delicately embroidered with pink roses, tiny green leaves, and blue ribbons—and over the table, and down to the floor, he stepped outside. Then he hollered over to John Peacock, who happened, as usual, to be sitting in a chair leaned up against the front of the grocery.

"Hey mister, there's a dead woman in here. You best get some help and move her before her blood flows into the street and drowns this stinkin' town."

Then he laughed.

John Peacock later said that the laugh was so terrifying that he found himself glued to the chair. He could not move a bone in his body as he watched the stranger step down from Miss Jean's porch and walk away. He stayed that way, feeling as if he was "deaf, dumb, and blind," as he put it, until he saw the man disappear around the bend.

The townspeople were, of course, shocked by this vile act. They could not understand how a man could commit such a crime for no reason at all. What did I think about the whole thing? Well, I'll be honest. I knew something had happened before I ever heard the news. Having just washed a load of laundry for the Rosens, I stepped outside the house to empty my washtub. It was then that I saw a man walking down the road in my direction. He looked like any man might look, except for his eyes. His eyes were on fire. He had a look of evil satisfaction in them. It reminded me of the look that Harry would get after hitting me. Except this man's look was worse. It didn't stop. From the moment my eyes caught sight of him, I felt locked within my stare. I knew he held evil and that it held him. I felt it coming at me. It stopped the breeze that was cooling off the beads of sweat scattered over my forehead, between my swollen breasts, and under my arms. It pierced my eyes. It tore into my heart. It made me sick to my stomach.

It was worse than the feeling that death brings. It was the terror of being defiled, of being torn apart, of being buried alive. I knew something awful had happened. And I knew that if I walked back along the tracks this man left, I would meet death at its worst. Face to face.

It took me days to find the courage and the words to write a letter to Miss Jean's sister. Things being the way they were in our town, no one wanted to talk about this to an outsider. No one else felt that they should deliver the "bad news." Bad news. What a way to describe what happened! How does one tell about something so terrible? Yet, I could not not do it. Lady Isabelle had to be told. The difference was that I was not writing a letter to her from Miss Jean. I was now writing from myself. Somehow—hard as it would be—I knew that with my words I would be able to paint her a picture about what happened to her sister.

It was so very difficult getting started. That was the hardest part. I sat in Miss Jean's kitchen, at the table where she bled, where her last breath was taken. In the chair that supported her body as her spirit left her so violently. From this spot, I knew I could write the letter and tell Miss Jean's story.

By now all her blood had been scrubbed away. Everyone knew that I could get stains out of anything. So of course, I had done the task. By the time I got there with my washtub, the needlework that had been Miss Jean's companion over the months was matted to the table in the dried blood. Gently I pried it up. I cried then. Oh yes, even though at one time I believed my tears would never flow, by this time in my life I had again learned to cry. But that is another one of my stories. Stories you will have your fill of when I am done. I picked up the piece of cloth, which was by then brownish-red and stiff, as if overstarched. I held it and ran my fingers across the little humps of pink flowers that Miss Jean somehow managed to stitch, though her eyesight was so very poor. Flowers that I could feel but no longer see.

I didn't admit to anyone that I didn't get the blood out of that needlework. I never even tried. I wrapped the blood-starched cloth in a dish towel, put it in her box of threads and other samplers, and took it home with me. When the day was right I buried it near to that spot where so long ago I had laid my dear Ellie.

When I finally started writing the letter, I got as far as the date and then my fingers would move the pen no further. What was I to write next? Up to that point every letter I had written for Miss Jean started with "My Dearest Isabelle." How was I to address Lady Isabelle now? I know that was a silly way to refer to her, yet that is how I saw her. She was a fine lady. Not only meaning that she was well groomed, wore fine dresses, and walked arm in arm with her husband. Lady Isabelle had grace and elegance, and a respect for other women. In her eyes, even women who were different, who were not like her, were worthy of being loved and respected and treated kindly. What was I to call her? Isabelle was too familiar. I did not know her well enough. After much time had passed and still not feeling I had the right words, I decided to begin with "Dear Mrs. Sanders."

Then, all of a sudden the rest of the words, as if attached by a thread, began to appear. In a strange way, this writing felt like sewing. It was as if the pen became a needle and the ink a thread, both helping me get through this horrible task. You see, though I was not sure about my writing, I could sew nearly as well as I could wash. And maybe Miss Jean was there too, helping me with her stitches.

Dear Mrs. Sanders,

I have a feeling you already know that this letter holds only sorrow. Yet there is no other way of telling you that which must be told, if only to allow Miss Jean's spirit peace. Yes, your dear sister has died. Worst of all, she left this world in a brutal way. If her death had been easy and quiet, like drifting away from the earth on a cloud, I may not have had to write this letter. I believe you would have felt her peaceful leaving and not needed explanations. But the violence that surrounded her last living moment has to be told.

Miss Jean, God rest her soul, was murdered by a man who happened into this town with a desire to revenge his woes on some innocent person. He chose to walk up the white steps of your sister's porch. He entered her home and slashed her throat with her letter opener and she never even saw his face. He took her by surprise as she worked on a piece of linen, embroidering pink flowers. It was an artful piece of work that she loved doing, especially while I sat with her writing her letters. She never screamed. She never even dropped the needle she held in her fingers. She just slumped over and died.

This may sound like a made up story. Like a tale someone tells that just can't be true. But aren't our lives full of stories? And though we may wish or want to believe that what is told is not the truth, believe me when I say that this happened. I don't tell tales. I tell the truth. Your sister was a warm, wonderful woman and she loved you in that special way that a sister loves her own. She was a good woman. And she helped me because she gave me reason to write.

My dearest Isabelle—please don't take offense at my calling you by your first name—my tears ran in puddles when I saw the evil act that man had committed. My heart felt branded by the sight of Miss Jean lying in her blood. Forgive me for having to share these details with you, but I felt you would want and need to know why and how she died. If I can be of any help in settling any of her matters, I will gladly do it for you. I will miss writing letters for her. They were a passage for me into another world.

Yours sincerely,
Hattie

So, from a stream of words smeared by my tears, I wrote this letter. I sent it off with hopes that Lady Isabelle would not think badly of me.

The Cauliflower Man

You may be wondering what happened to my youngins and to Harry. Those stories I will tell in time. Now I want to talk about the Cauliflower Man. I called him that sometimes. It was my nickname for him. His real name was Sam. Just Sam. The last name doesn't matter. This man came into our town looking for a place to stop for a while. By then I was living alone. I no longer had Harry bothering me, or myself bothering my two boys, Jeremy and Zak. They used to say, "Ma, quit botherin' us." Then one day they didn't have to say it anymore.

But back to the Cauliflower Man. He came tripping into town one day. I say tripping because as he walked along leading his mule, every few steps he would appear to stumble, though he never got as far as falling to the ground. He would catch himself, rise up, and stand tall over the mule one more time. I found out later that he had a trick knee that would fall out of line from the rest of him and cause him to have these stumbling steps. A few belongings hung over the animal's sides. Some of them clinked and clattered as Cauliflower Man and his mule came up to the house. His roll of clothing was no larger than a small sack.

Also hanging from the saddle was a collection of gardening tools. There was no rifle or other harmful object except for a small hatchet that he used for chopping branches from trees when he was in need of them.

As would happen, there was no room in the rooming house. Not so much because it was overflowing with visitors, but because many a person, who had at one point or another come passing through town, never left. I didn't understand why they would want to stay. But those that did somehow managed to talk Miss Huxby, who owned the rooming house, into letting them stay on indefinite-like. Indefinite. That word has a sort of fascination for me. It's what Harry said to me one of the times that I really believed would be the last time I laid eyes on his rotten face.

"Maybe Hattie," he said, while giving me one of his usual hard pats on the cheek, "maybe I'll be back some day. My plans, they're indefinite right about now." To this day I can't gather where he came up with a word like that, because Harry was not one for using big words.

Another time I remember hearing that word was the Sunday that Lincoln Avery, a minister who stopped off in our town for a few days, decided to hold a service. He made it quite clear that he was expecting everyone to attend. Well, so-and-so, I can't remember his name, couldn't come because he was busy with his cows. Some of them had passed through a broken fence around his pasture and ended up far off his property. Jesse Cowen couldn't come because she had a small fire in the kitchen and was busy cleaning up all the soot and ashes. Emma couldn't come because she had just birthed her ninth youngin. The list of who wasn't able to attend went on for a long while, leaving only a handful of people, Emma's husband being one of them, to show up at the service. I think he must've figured that listening to the preacher was better than being in a house full of crying youngins and a tired wife. I myself wasn't there because I received some unexpected laundry and was busy with my washtub. But, to tell you the truth, I wouldn't have gone anyway.

Well, the minister was mighty angry about the poor showing. So riled up by what he said was a lack of religious devotion in the townspeople, that he proceeded to give a very loud, angry sermon lasting most of two hours. Afterwards, I heard some of the townsfolk talking about the preacher and his sermon. They were saying how they thought he was going to go on preaching indefinitely. As they shared their complaints—talking about their tired feet, the hot sun, their thirst, and his raging voice—no one spoke about what he had actually said to those select few who had heeded his instructions and gone to the service. The fear I saw in their eyes told me that they were afraid to repeat the preacher's words. It was as if he had cursed the people of our town for being heathen-like. I myself didn't care what the preacher said. Curse or not, I had my own beliefs and didn't need him telling me what he thought I was doing wrong.

Indefinite was how I often felt when my arms would be lowering into the soapy water in the washtub. Inch by inch as my arms got covered with suds, and before my fingers would hit upon the bottom of that big metal tub, I would feel as if I could keep lowering them indefinitely. Like there was no end to the washtub. But then the picture of the rest of me following my shoulders down and being swallowed up by the dirty water would make me remember just how definite the bottom was. Do you know that in all the years of using that tub it never wore out? Never got a hole that would let some of the water escape and run over my kitchen floor. It lasted me all the years I used it as a washtub. Even when the day came that I was done using it for washing, it sat there in the kitchen as always, intact and waiting. But that is getting off the track again.

Let me get back to telling you about Sam the Cauliflower Man. Since the rooming house had no room for Sam, Miss Huxby suggested that he might inquire at my house. Imagine my surprise when this man, good looking I might add—he had a smile in his eyes, a soft gentle manner in his voice, a lean looking figure, and a not too long, straight, handsome nose—came up to my door and asked if I might be able to offer him a room to sleep in for a few days. He explained how Miss Huxby had mentioned that I, being a woman living alone, had an extra bedroom that I might be willing to rent out. Silently, I laughed to myself. In our town, a woman living alone and renting a bedroom to a male guest would usually be frowned upon. By now though, especially since I had found my footing at some of the worst times of my life, no one dared to frown upon me. Not that I believed the townsfolk had any real respect for me. I knew they didn't give me trouble because they needed me scrubbing their clothes clean for them. But whatever their reasons, they no longer dared judgment. At least not to my face.

I liked Sam right off. He was straightforward and honest and enjoyable. I had never before thought of renting the boys' room to anyone because, even though I knew different, I somehow thought they'd be back. I wanted to see them there, sleeping under the quilt I had sewn. I even dreamt about them laying there, the tops of their heads peaking out from the covers. But the big bed, neat and unwrinkled, stood empty. So I figured, if for no other purpose than to give me a reason to launder them sheets, why not take a boarder for a week or two?

One month later, when Sam and I were sitting in one of my favorite spots on the hill by the meadow, and my neighbors were starting to complain because I had slacked off using my washtub—a couple of times I hadn't even gotten a simple stain out of a shirt or apron—I was thinking how I liked the feeling of being in the company of this man. He made my heart feel like it was fluttering, lifting up in my chest, wanting to float up, up into the air, into that beautiful blue sky. I often imagined and hoped that this was the feeling Ellie's spirit had when it left her little twisted body and went to heaven.

Sam and I had just come from the spot where I had buried her. A place where the grass grew thick and lush with blue flowers scattered like raindrops over it. I never thought that anyone except me would want to go to that spot of earth. I never thought I would want to lead anyone to Ellie's grave. But one morning I told Sam about Ellie. I told him how she was a miracle in my life. After that he asked me if I would take him to where Ellie was buried. Well, at first, I couldn't even think. No one had ever asked that of me. But Sam did, and his question opened up a gate in my head. I began to think thoughts I didn't know existed. Thoughts and pictures I must have tried to bury with Ellie. I didn't want to feel or see or think any of them. "Close the gate. Close the gate," I heard in my head. But some things inside me were changing. In the end, I thought about what Ellie would have liked and I said, "Yes, Sam, I will take you to that spot of earth where the sun is so warm and the earth so rich."

The day Sam arrived on my doorstep, it was about three in the afternoon, he found me tired and sweaty and smelling of dirty laundry. I had just finished washing Mr. Rosen's filthy clothes. It seemed the longer I did their laundry the dirtier the clothes were every time I got them. It's not that there were more clothes than usual, though there should have been considering there were more youngins around. By this time, two of his daughters had babies. They were still almost babies themselves. One was just twelve and the other fourteen. There were no husbands living in that house, only Rosen and his sons. No one knew who the fathers of those babies were, though I had my suspicions.

When it came to the Rosens' clothes it was as if the dirt, which I scrubbed out of them each time, went right back into the fabric. Layers and layers of dirt and filth and God knows what else stained those clothes. I was getting ready to rinse the soggy pile, which had been put through one washing, hoping another wouldn't be needed. I was filling the washtub with fresh water when Sam arrived.

Well, that pile of laundry never got rinsed until late that night. Sam came in and started talking. His voice was friendly and nice, and things he said made me laugh. Before long I told him he could stay and I asked him to supper. I wasn't fixing much, just some dumplings with a special sauce I made from vegetables and pieces of pork fat for flavor. As we sat at the table, surrounded by heaps of laundry, he told me he was known for growing the largest and tastiest heads of cauliflower one would ever run across. "In fact," he added, "you wouldn't be able to run across them 'cause they're so big they would trip you." Then he laughed. And then I laughed. I laughed until I cried. And then we both laughed some more.

Laughing may not seem like such an unusual thing to someone whose mouth readily goes from a smile to opening wide and letting out excitement or joy or whatever it is that makes people laugh. I couldn't remember the last time I had laughed. Not that there weren't occasions. Like when the men in town would huddle together out on the street, saying who knows what. Suddenly, out of the middle of the group, laughter would erupt in a roar. It would draw those passing by into it. Sometimes, as I walked by in my hurried fashion—"Why do you walk so fast?" was a usual question from anyone who might try to walk with me—I would hear the laughter or see something that was downright funny. But I wouldn't laugh. And you know what? I was glad that I walked quickly past. Maybe if I had walked a bit slower I would have been hooked into it and joined in. The truth was, I had no desire to laugh and so I didn't.

That night, after Sam and I had each settled in from the evening—I had never felt so wonderfully tired—I lay in my bed and listened through the wall to his snoring. When my boys had slept across that wall and cried out in the night, waking me up, I sometimes wished that the wall was thicker. Thick enough to deafen their noises. This night, lying there, feeling so comfortable with this man who had come into my home, I wished that wall was thinner. I got some unexplained pleasure from listening to his breathing and snoring and occasional rustling.

Not being able to sleep, I got up and walked over to the window. Looking out, I gazed up into the sky. The stars, scattered in clusters, made me think of street lamps glowing bright on a dark night. It was as if they were showing me the road to heaven. A road that was as wide as it was deep. In one of those silly thoughts I get in my head, I heard a voice say, "Hattie, you could pick and follow any one of these stars and eventually get to where you are aiming to go."

Something in that night changed something in me. The next morning when I woke, I was a bit startled by the smile that spread across my face. I hadn't smiled in the morning for a very long time. Well, as life would have it, I continued waking with a smile for the whole six weeks that Sam shared my home and even after he left. No man had ever been kinder to me than him. There were plenty of men in our town and most tended to be civil. Some occasionally would even be pleasant. But none were kind in the way Sam was. And no man had ever made me feel the way Sam did.

One day when we were talking about husbands and wives, he said to me, "Hattie, for whatever reason a man takes a wife, he had better learn to feel kindness towards her. In return, a kindhearted woman will give back to that man a life that will warm his heart." I just sat there and listened. This was not something I had ever heard a man say. Then he added, "And a man without a warm heart is no man at all." I understood what he meant.

There were times, though, when his talk was like riddles and it confused me. Sam told me a story about a sheriff he heard about who had to decide between arresting one of two brothers who were blaming each other for damage caused during a drunken brawl. In the end, the sheriff decided not only to arrest both brothers, but also to arrest the pa. He said that the brothers' deeds and lack of concern for each other meant that they were raised wrong, and he blamed their pa for that. By the way, there was no ma. She had died in childbirth when the youngest brother was born. If there had been a ma, I wondered if she would have gotten blamed, too. I could not understand the sheriff's reasoning. This made me feel all mixed up. I believed that sometimes, no matter how hard a ma and pa might try to bring up their youngins to be good, they still might go wrong. So I tried asking Sam some questions. But it didn't help how I was feeling. Then I just got real quiet. I knew of no other way to hold mixed-up feelings.

When Sam saw that I was sad and troubled over what he said, he suddenly jumped up from the table, knocking over his chair, and he pulled me to my feet. "Hattie," he said, "there are times when dancing not only brings our bodies to life, but also airs out the mind." Humming a tune, he half pulled and half danced me across the kitchen and by the washtub, which sat empty. Its roundness, sticking out of the corner of the room, was like the belly of a fat man sitting back in a chair. A belly that sticks out no matter how he tries to suck in his gut.

When I was a young girl, there was a man with a belly like that. He used to stand around in my uncle's store. I remember giggling with my sister Annie about how fat he was. We would come in the door and, if he was standing there leaning up against the counter, we'd have to politely maneuver ourselves around his belly while trying not to knock the cans off the shelves. We'd go over to where the sacks of grain were piled and sit on them and quietly giggle until our pa would come over and tell us to hush.

Anyhow, Sam managed to waltz me, if that's what you could call it, out of the kitchen and into the front room. He would have taken me out into the street if I hadn't stopped his waltzing feet. I was surprised that he got me as far as he did because I had stiffened up like a plank of wood. He must have felt like he was dragging me 'cause I sure wasn't waltzing.

At that moment I was angry. I was so angry at him. I was angry at his grabbing me. Angry at his thinking that he could behave that way with me. Angry that he thought interrupting my silence with humor and dance was what I needed. How dare he do that! On top of all that, he frightened me. His sudden embrace terrified me. I didn't know how to respond to what he was doing. I didn't like surprises and Sam had taken me by surprise. Having him touch me caused strange feelings and I was confused enough. It had been a long time since this body had been touched by anyone. Let alone held.

His right arm, wrapped around me, reminded me that I had a waist. It rested just above the curve of my hips. Damn! Without even trying, he had found a comfortable spot on me that his arm fit into. But his left hand, though gently, had grasped not my hand but my wrist. It felt like he was not giving me any choice in the matter. This I didn't like at all. Not one bit!

Somehow, even though I felt like a massive fist was lodged in my throat, I managed to find my voice. My angry words, echoing as if coming from the inside of the empty washtub, stumbled out at him. The sound of my voice reminded me of those rare days, long ago, when Zak and Jeremy would put their heads into the empty washtub and holler, "Hello in there." They liked listening to the way it changed the sounds of their voices. This day, the sound of my voice changed. It startled me and it scared me. It also caused Sam's face to redden as I said, "How dare you think that you can waltz through my home as if you belong here. And waltz into my thoughts as well."

To me, my words sounded dramatic, like a person speaking lines in a play. I don't know how they sounded to Sam, but his arms let go of me then and dropped down to his sides. He looked at me and backed away. Just then his trick knee gave out. Moving backwards, he did not have the balance he needed to prevent the fall. Down he went.

He hit hard against the edge of the wooden bench before landing on the floor. The thud of his body against the floor was so loud. Louder than any of the thoughts and feelings I was having. I glanced down at Sam. I could see his pain. I could see his embarrassment. My heart jumped then. Its movement somehow untangled the anger and mixed-up feelings that had me all twisted up. It was like when I would take a washed, wrung-tight sheet outside and flap smoothness into it.

Though my anger was gone, the thud Sam's body made kept coming. I kept hearing it in my head. Over and over again. And for a slip of time, it brought me back to a place where thud after thud echoed as my body fell stair over stair. During that fall there had been no pain, just the sound of thuds and the shadow of Harry.

Before I could extend my arm out to help Sam, and, to tell you the truth, I don't know if he would have reached for my hand anyway, he lifted himself off the floor. I stood there and watched his body slowly unfold, giving him his tallness back. He waited for a moment, then came over to me. He came close, but not so close that his breath was on my cheek.

"Hattie," he said as he let out a deep sigh while his hand rubbed the small of his back.

"I am not a fool and neither are you. I did not waltz into your home. You let me in. And so far as dancing goes, it wouldn't hurt anyone to dance more."

Once again I found myself listening. He let out another sigh as he said, "There is much too little music and dancing in this world." Then he became very quiet. I could see my words had injured him more than the fall. His eyes showed me that. They were wells of sadness. I was surprised that they didn't show anger. They weren't fiery.

He finished by saying, "I apologize for offending you."

That could have been the end of Sam the Cauliflower Man and Hattie the Washtub Woman, but it wasn't. I hadn't really been all that angry at Sam, had I? No. I had been angry at myself. I had forgotten, or maybe didn't ever know, what a man's touch could be like. I could only remember Harry's slaps, Harry's pawing, and Harry's suffocating stench. I asked myself then if I was only going to remember the past, or was I willing to see to what the stars had shown me?

Sam and I did finish our waltz. After more talking, as we sat side by side on the porch steps, my bare feet nervously rubbing away the few remaining paint chips that had until now held tight to the step, I told him that I wanted to try dancing again. This time though, I wanted him to take my hand in his and not grasp my wrist. Slowly his arm once again circled around my waist. My body relaxed in his gentle hold and I felt my curves fit into him. As we danced across the porch, spinning around, I caught a glimpse of tiny chips of white paint whirling off my feet into the air.

For a very short time, Sam and I were as man and wife should be. Then, six weeks to the day that he arrived at my door, Sam left. He left saying how much he hated to go, yet had to go. I believed him. I hated to see him go, too. But I knew from the start that he was only passing through on his way further east, and I would not stop any man from aiming toward his dreams. When Sam left, he took a part of me with him. A part I had never shared with anyone. With him I spoke of the miracle of Ellie and the vision of peaceful flight that she and I had shared. It was my gift to him.

He insisted on paying his boarding fee and left me with some extra money, too. Sam hated seeing me use the wash-tub. "If you give those arms a rest Hattie, you may be surprised at what else they can do," he said. I believed him. As much as I wanted to stand out in the street and watch him leave, watch the Cauliflower Man tripping away alongside his mule, I couldn't do it. My heart ached so badly and the tears were bursting out of my eyes. So I raised my crooked arm in one last wave, then I ran into the kitchen and bent over the washtub. Quickly, the tears filled it to the brim and overflowed it. Never before had that washtub not been able to hold what I put into it.

Neither of us knew then, and I myself didn't know until Sam had been gone for a few weeks, that he had left me with a greater gift than he could imagine. I was carrying his child. Lord, after all these years, I was going to have another child.

Waiting to Be Born

Adelphia was good to me. She was the midwife to some of us women in town. She herself wasn't from the town. She lived in a small hut up in the hills and would travel down on her horse Mingo to visit with me. Childbirthing for me wasn't difficult, at least not at first. My twins were born with ease. Quicker than I ever expected. She said that they waited, curled up just so, and when the time was right found their way from my warm insides to my waiting arms. My second son was more stubborn. It was as if he didn't want to be born. I vaguely remember Adelphia's strong palms pushing on my heaving belly to quicken his pace into this world. I bled buckets after he was born. I didn't know then that he would take more out of me after his birth than the birth itself took. I was young in those days and my mind had no expectations. I thought I could handle anything, or at least I tried to. With this third pregnancy I was older. I had almost forgot what it was like to birth babies. It was close to two decades since my last one had come into this world.

At first, Adelphia reacted as many of the women in the town had when they noticed my belly swelling under my cotton dresses. She at least had the courage to say what the other women only said with their stares. "Good Lord, Hattie," she said. "What were you thinking of?"

By then, Adelphia was old. I remember her once telling me how old she thought she was. Some believed she was even older than that. In a town like ours, especially for the folks living in the hills, age loses itself in the growth of the land. After a while, people start judging their passage in years by the size of the trees growing around them. For me, Adelphia's age didn't matter. She knew what she was doing and I had faith in her ability. She paid me extra attention during my time. She did not ignore my condition as many of the others did. She would ride up on her horse, slide off his bare back with the ease of a young woman, tie him up to the front porch railing, which was in dire need of a painting, and clop up the porch stairs in her oversized boots, the leather tongues flapping out of them nearly as much as her own tongue would flap when we started our talk.

Once, thinking she might appreciate a better fitting pair of shoes, I offered her a pair of my shoes. But she shook her head. "These here belonged to my husband," she said. "He used to say to me, 'Deli,' that's what he called me, 'Deli, if you only knew what it was like to be in my shoes.' So when he died, I took them boots right off his feet and put them on. I wanted them to show me what it was that made a man's life so much harder than a woman's."

Then she sighed. It was a deep sigh, as if letting out

air that hasn't been let out for a long time. Air that would smell stale if it had a smell. "They haven't shown me anything yet, but they sure keep my feet warm," she said. Then she smiled and her eyes twinkled.

She always had something to share with me, be it a bit of something she had grown in her garden, or cooked up over the fire—smoke was always streaming out of her chimney—or just a snip of knowledge. Not gossip, mind you. Adelphia never gossiped. Gossip, she once told me, was for those people who had nothing inside their heads and were looking for anything to fill the hole. She said that gossip never fed a person. It just took up space like if someone had swallowed a rock. And, like a rock, it sat there until you got tired of it and spit it out at someone. Knowledge on the other hand, the kind that Adelphia shared with me, filled her being through and through. It gave her strength as much if not more than the strength one got from eating. And in bits and pieces she fed her knowledge to me. Craving to let it out to make room in her head for more knowledge. She also said that certain knowledge was just "waiting to be born." Waiting to be born. I held onto those words.

From the moment I found myself with child, I never once thought that I shouldn't be having a baby. I never thought that I was too old or in the phase of life when a woman begins losing her womanly nature. Without a doubt, even before that youngin started moving in my womb, I knew he was there and he was there because that's where he was supposed to be. I never worried about it none either. I never wondered about what would happen after he was born. I just enjoyed every minute of his life in me. It was the first time in my own life that I had the peace and the uninterrupted time to feel my child's gentle moves, to listen to the gurgling sounds coming from my belly as a tiny part of him nudged up against my skin, little bumps poking out of me, to imagine what he was thinking, to wonder how he felt being inside of me.

Thank God I didn't have Harry in my life to destroy my feelings. He had always had a way of killing any hopes I harbored in my heart. Without Harry interrupting my stream of life, without the bodies of other youngins hanging around my legs begging for attention that was sparse and thinly spread, I eased myself into a motherly state. Even the washing that kept me busy took on a different meaning. Day after day, pleasant thoughts held me as I scrubbed all those clothes. I even began to hum and then sing out loud songs that had been hiding in my voice box since I was a little girl. Loving this baby inside me reminded me of Ellie. Of the joy she had brought me. But even though I remembered all the joy I had felt from her, in a way I wished that she could have stayed inside my womb and rested there instead of coming into a world that was not suited to her.

When I was about seven months along, Adelphia came

by on one of her visits and we sat sipping some of her herb tea. My eyes were looking at my cup when I felt her gaze. It's not enough to say she looked straight into my eyes, which by then had met hers. Her look went deeper than that. It reached parts of me that I wasn't even sure existed. As she looked at me with dark, worry-filled eyes, eyes I hadn't seen before, she asked, "Hattie, how attached are you to this child?"

My eyes strayed away from hers, back to the cup I was holding. I didn't try to ask what she meant, or why she was asking such a thing. I knew there would be no point in it. It wouldn't change that look in her eyes or whatever caused it to be there.

"I love him," I said. "I love him for what he is. For what we are sharing together."

"Good," was all she said. Then we went on to talk of other things.

That night, long after Adelphia left, I walked through the house. The sound her boots had made, as they clapped against the floor, still echoed in my head. I found my own footsteps trailing in that rhythm. As I walked about, I looked closely at everything the house held. There was the kitchen scrubbed clean, the water pump too old to stop drops of water from escaping it even though no one was pumping its handle, the white table slowly splitting up the center seam, paint chipping off it, and the three chairs, seats bowled and rubbed thin from years of use.

It used to be four chairs, but I never did fix the one that broke when Sam knocked it over in his hurry to dance with me. I looked into the sitting room. I saw Sam and me sitting together, talking to each other, like it was real, right then and there. I could almost smell him next to me. I walked up the stairs to the rooms above. So dark. So empty. The slanted ceilings suddenly made me dizzy. I put my arm up against a wall to steady myself and stood there until the spinning stopped. In the dark I could hardly see my bed. The bed Sam and I had laid in. Our bodies fitting into each other in a way that told me God had created us out of the same form. I stood there feeling the darkness. Feeling the emptiness. Then I cried. Oh God how I cried! I knew what Adelphia could already see as I hugged my round belly and patted the little foot that kicked at my embrace.

The following morning I walked up to the meadow. It was a glorious day. The birds were chirping and the winds, traveling between the trees, hummed along to their tune. I sat with Ellie and Steven, which is the name I decided to give this baby. I sat with them and the three of us enjoyed a moment of togetherness. We were a family.

A family should be a loving group. Extending tender touches, caring about each other, laughing over spilt milk. My mother used to say, "Better to laugh than cry over spilt milk. Save your tears for worse things." She said this, but never did it. She always said things one way, but acted another. And she never really laughed. But this day I wasn't thinking about my mother. I sat there with Ellie and Steven. Thinking about them. Thinking about myself. The three of us embraced in a moment that lasted until twilight and gave me the strength to go back to the empty house. That house was nothing to me. I had lived in it for years and it meant nothing.

When the baby finally came, I was ready to receive him into my arms. Three days before, we had already said our goodbyes. I was lying in my bed and could feel him struggling. It wasn't like he was trying to come out. He was just struggling with himself, I guess. And then, after a while, he just stopped. In her wise way, knowing that his time had come, Adelphia arrived the next morning. She stayed with me for three days. The horse was unhappy about being tied up to the porch for that long. But she said that he didn't matter, I did. Soon after, my belly started tightening up. Oh, how nature has its way of taking from a mother what does not belong to her anymore! My labor lasted only three hours and was not difficult. When Steven emerged from between my legs, except for being blue, he looked perfect. His skin was silky and covered with white frosting. His tiny fingers were not clenched in little fists, they were loose and spread apart. I lifted his hand to my face. I put his palm against my cheek and held it there. Then I gently moved it back and forth. Back and forth.

Not once did Adelphia try to take him from me,

or soothe me with talk of how God works in mysterious ways. Not once did she try to come between the touch of his skin against mine. She stayed around and took care of those parts of me that needed taking care of. And I held my Steven. I knew he was gone from me, yet a part of me wished my own warmth would penetrate his cool skin. That he would open his eyes and look at me with a longing for nurturing. I wanted him to open his tiny mouth and take my breast and suck. Bringing me the feelings I had when I nursed my other babies.

It's hard for me to remember when it was that I carried him up to the meadow. All I remember is that I held him as long as my heart could bear, and then I walked through torrents of rain clutching him to my chest. It hadn't been raining when I left the house, but somewhere along the way, the massive gray clouds that had for days hung in the sky hiding everything beyond them cracked open and spilled out their heaviness. By the time we got to the meadow, the rain had stopped and the clouds moved aside, freeing the April sun's light. I dug his grave next to Ellie's and very gently, so as not to awaken him, I laid him in it. I thought his spirit might still be traveling up to his home in heaven and I didn't want to keep him from his journey. I didn't want him to turn back. I didn't want him to see the sorrow painted over his mother's face. All my youngins had left me. His leaving just came before I could get to know him. And that was my grief to deal with, not his.

The next day I knew what I had been thinking for a long while. I knew that Chapel Ridge, which was the name of this town, so full of the misery I had lived for so long, was not my home. I was ready to leave it.

The Blue Agate

It's time to talk about Harry, Jeremy, and Zak. Life wasn't easy for me and the boys, but we managed and made do with what we had. Jerry and Zak were at opposite ends of the rainbow, but because they were brothers and had little choice of playmates, they learned to be together. In time they even shared secrets. They accepted the fact that they had a pa who was rarely home. Yet when he came home they would cling to him, ask him questions, and act like he was their hero. When he wasn't around they would once again move closer to me, though with a caution I could not understand.

Jerry was the quieter of my two boys. Though he didn't say much, I know he held thoughts in his head. When he was out of Zak's earshot he would occasionally talk with me. He never asked me about the butterflies again, but he would ask me about Harry and why he was always going away from us. It was hard for me to answer because I knew he wanted an answer he could understand. One that would not hurt him. One that would somehow glorify his pa's actions. It is hard for a youngin to admit his pa is a stinking drunk who doesn't care about anyone but himself.

I would make up excuses and tell him his pa was looking for better things so that one day we could all be together always. Afterwards, I felt like spitting at these words. I shuddered at the thought of being with Harry forever. For always.

Sometimes, in the middle of the night, Jeremy—he tended to have waking dreams—would come into my room and lie down beside me. Those were the only times he would openly embrace me and tell me he loved me. His love frightened me, for it brought back all the guilt that I had from neglecting him when he was so little because I had Ellie to be responsible for. Oh God, I don't think I could have done things any differently and I hope Jerry understood that.

He would say, "Mommy"—he called me that when we were alone—"I know you love me."

One day he asked me if I wished that he had died, too. I said, "Child, what in the world would make you ask such a thing?"

He got very quiet then. So quiet I thought I heard the stars in the sky whisper to each other. I looked into his young face lying next to me. He was thinking so hard that his little face was puckered from a deep frown. Then he told me he had a dream that he and Ellie were playing in the field together. She was running around with him but she couldn't run as fast as he could. Then I appeared in the field and I whisked Ellie up in my arms. Holding her high I said, "Fly, Ellie, fly." When I let her go, Ellie grew wings and flew away into the clouds. Once Ellie was out of sight, I turned to him and asked him if he wanted to follow her. If he wanted to fly up into the sky, too. I told him he could watch over her. He said that he got scared then because he knew that if he flew away he wouldn't come back. Yet I looked happy, as if I wanted him to go up there. That was when he woke up.

I was surprised that he had such a dream. Though I never kept it a secret that he had a twin sister who died, for one reason or another, as time passed, we had stopped talking about her. I didn't think he remembered her much. He was so young when she died.

"Jeremy," I said—I called him both Jeremy and Jerry depending on my mood at the time—"I don't want you to die. Only God knows when our time is right. But I do know that when our time comes, heaven is a wonderful place to fly away to."

I hugged him then, hard enough to squeeze his breath from him. I felt his ribs, I felt his heart beating fast, and I smelled him. That faint sweet smell of a child. A smell that becomes more and more distant as it is overcome by the smells of perspiration that come upon us as we leave our mothers' arms and start moving on our own.

Zak never came to me at night. Zak kept his distance and kept his meanness. He wasn't mean in the sense of hurting a bird that is unable to get away because of a broken wing. There were youngins who would prey on a creature that had no ability to escape their grasp. Standing over a lame bird and throwing stones at it. Zak wasn't mean like that. His meanness was more because of his lack of knowing what tenderness was. He did not think about another person's feelings. He would want things done his way, at his demand. Sometimes his words were as cold and cutting as a knife. I remember when he was not even four years old, I had asked him to move out of my way because I was carrying the washtub full of dirty water. My arms were stinging from pain. My hands were cracked and raw from the constant exposure to soap and water.

"Zak, help your ma out and move out of the way," I said.

He looked at me as if I had asked him an impossible task. His blue eyes were empty. His face not caring. He did not move. He behaved as if I wasn't even there. I hate to admit this, but Zak scared me. His lack of concern reminded me of his pa. I could have put the washtub down and smacked him, but I didn't have the strength for it. I stepped around him, and part of me wished the washtub would slip out of my aching arms and land right on his legs. But it didn't. Afterwards, as I was coming back up the steps into the house, I heard him laughing and repeating my words. Mocking me. This was my child. This boy was of my blood. At that moment, I hated him.

God forgive me, but there were times when I

wished Zak was never born. He manipulated things around him and he hadn't even learned to wipe his own snot yet. Can a child be born evil? I prayed for his soul more than I prayed for anything else. Maybe he would throw stones at a bird with a broken wing if no one was around to see him do it. That was the horror I held. Not knowing what he was capable of doing. I would feel his lies growing in him. His deception waiting for innocent victims. It pains me to share these thoughts. How could a mother think such things? But as God is my witness, I could see no good coming from this child. Sometimes I feared that he would erase the good in Jerry. That somehow the darkness, the coldness that grew in Zak, would come out and embrace my other son and make him stop loving me. Times like this I was glad to be struggling to keep us fed and clothed. The struggles kept me so busy that I did not have much time for this kind of thinking.

Harry had a fondness for Zak that was quite obvious. When he came home, he would whisper things in Zak's ear that would make him laugh. Jerry would sit aside Harry pleading for some attention, but he never got what Zak got. Jerry might get a hot cinnamon candy that would burn his mouth, while Zak got a sweet licorice stick. Always that little bit of difference that to a child was like a slap that left the skin stinging and red. Harry was tougher on Jeremy. Quick to punish him. Quick to put him down while in the same breath praising Zak. Harry was mean.

Intentionally so. And then, when Jeremy was already hurting, he would trample upon him even more with cruel words or worse. Harry was a violent man. How violent depended on his mood or his level of drunkenness.

It is so difficult for me to recall those things that broke my heart. That broke me. To have life drain out of your soul, to have everything destroyed. How is a woman supposed to survive? My guilt is that I did not die, that I lived through it all. My guilt is that I did not stop it. My guilt is that my arms were not strong enough, my voice not loud enough, my courage not there to stop the man who destroyed what little I had. Maybe if I just tell the story and not feel it while I tell it, maybe then I can go on.

Another month or two or three went by, and Harry again came home. Jeremy was seven then, almost eight. His birthday was coming up in a couple of weeks. We did not have money to buy nice presents. Even so, I always tried to do something special when one of my boys had a birthday. That year I was thinking of getting Jeremy some paper and new pencils so he could draw. He liked pictures. Using a stick, he would often draw lines in the patch of sand in the yard that refused to grow any grass. He would draw something and come yelling for me to see it before Zak stomped the picture away. I had saved some pennies here and there from my washing and was going to buy him these things. I was a good ma. I tried to be a good ma. I really did. Even with Zak, I tried not to let my feelings and fears keep me from being good to him. And I did love him. I loved him the most when he was sound asleep. His eyes closed tight. I would pull the covers up to his chin and, looking at his face, I would love him because he was my blood. He was my child. Without those cold blue eyes staring at me, I was able to find my love for him.

Well anyway, Harry came home this time acting kind of crazy. I could see he had been drinking and was in a foul mood. I warned the boys to let their pa be and not to upset him with their questions and bothering attempts for attention. That night Harry slept. He slept soundly, while his snoring like the gale winds of a storm shook me through the night. I lay there and hoped that in the morning he would be better. He woke up late as usual on these home visits, and he woke up evil. Cussing at me. Cussing at the boys. Cussing his life.

What happened? Everything is like a moving picture to me, not within my grasp. It's like I couldn't move into the picture. It was Harry, Zak, and Jeremy.

The boys were out back of the house playing with some marbles. Marbles that belonged to their pa. They were his from his boyhood. I wasn't paying much attention because I was in the kitchen cooking. It was a hot day and the boys were using my washtub. They had filled it with water to splash around in and cool off between their spurts of playing or doing whatever they were doing.

At one point I glanced out the window. They were putting the marbles in their mouths and seeing if they could spit them into the tub of water. A silly game. A game that I should have stopped because I know it's not safe for youngins to be putting things in their mouths. But it was such a hot day and it kept them from getting into other mischief, so I paid them no mind.

My hair was tied up on my head with a rag. The kitchen was unbearably hot. I was wearing a loose sleeveless dress that let the small breezes caused by my movements to float in and out around my skin. Not being form fitting it also didn't soak up the beads of perspiration seeping out of me. I could feel them joining together, swelling into streams, and running down the length of me. I'm surprised I didn't have a puddle at my feet. At first Harry had been sitting by himself out on the front porch, but then he came into the kitchen. He was sitting there at the kitchen table, smoking his cigarette, when suddenly he got up and went out to where the boys were. I hadn't heard anything because my mind had been thinking. Thinking about other things.

I had been daydreaming. Remembering being little and lying in bed between two of my sisters. Remembering the cool breeze as it came in through the window. Remembering how it was gently lifting the fabric of my nightgown. Remembering how, while the both of them slept, I lay there quietly watching my dress flutter, as if it was trying to lift off me and fly into the darkness. I laid there for a long time. Awake. Watching the cool breeze on a quiet night. Suddenly, I stopped remembering. Suddenly, I heard the laughter. Zak's laughter. Then I heard Harry's thundering voice and Jeremy's cry. Or was it a scream? I don't know. Odd how laughter doesn't always mean something good is happening.

I went to the door to see what was going on. Harry was standing over Jeremy. Screaming at him to give him the marble. Jerry had a look of terror on his face. His mouth was open but no words were coming from it.

Zak was taunting his brother, saying over and over again, "Jerry's not minding Pa. He won't spit out the marble."

Harry's voice kept thundering, "Give me the marble, boy. Give me the marble."

He's choking on it, I thought. Yet I couldn't move. The cool breeze I had been dreaming about had turned into a chilling wind. Freezing me in place.

"Turn him upside down. He's choking on it. He's not disobeying you, man. He's choking on it. Your son is choking!" The sound in my head was loud enough that my words were like thunder, yet nothing, not a whisper, was rising from my throat. The words wouldn't come out.

Harry. Stupid Harry was blind to what was happening. All he knew was that his son was disobeying his command.

"The blue agate," he roared, "give it to me, boy. Right now! I said give it to me!"

As Jerry's eyes began bulging from the pressure of his breath trapped in his lungs, Harry grabbed him and slapped him across his face.

"Mock me with your look, will you," he screamed as he slapped him again and again.

Finally, something happened. Something inside me shifted and I screamed and ran into the yard.

"He's choking," I cried. "He's choking. And you're killing him. You're killing him."

By now Harry was totally consumed by his fit of rage. Whether he heard me or not, I don't know. All he saw was Hattie running at him holding a kitchen knife. I honestly don't remember grabbing a knife. I just remember the look on my son's face. The look of total helplessness. Of total defeat. Of death. Harry let go of Jeremy then. As his small frail body slumped to the ground, his head hit the side of the washtub. He lay there, eyes open, his skin no longer pink, his lips blue. Slowly the large blue agate rolled out of his open mouth and into the dirt. Spittle on the marble caused it to pick up grains of sand. Its dark blue swirls disappeared behind a coating of brown dirt as it rolled away from Jerry towards Zak's feet.

Harry had let go of Jerry to deal with me. His hand grabbed my arm and twisted it, forcing the knife to fall to the ground. Then he grabbed me by both shoulders and flung me up against the side of the house.

I kept screaming, "Jeremy! Oh God, he's dying. Please help him!"

I tried crawling over to where he lay, but Harry kicked me in the gut. My insides exploded in pain. I lay doubled over, choking on my tears and vomit.

"You're a crazy woman," he screamed. "This boy is not dead. He was disobeying me. Look here. He's just passed out."

He went over and grabbed Jerry. Pulling his limp body up, he shook him as if to wake him from sleep. Jeremy's thin legs and arms dangled in the air. They reminded me of how the sleeves on shirts, hung out to dry, randomly twist in a whipping wind. Then Harry, who must have totally lost his mind, started dunking him in the washtub water. In and out he flung Jeremy's lifeless head. In and out of the water. In horror I watched Jerry's face disappear and appear. Disappear and appear. I thank God that Jerry had already escaped into a faraway place. For if he had any breath left in his small body, he had none left when Harry finally stopped. The stupid, heartless man either got tired or finally realized that his son was not going to open his eyes and obey him. Jeremy was dead. As dead as the ants that had been squashed under Harry's boots during this rampage. Harry shook him one final time. Then he let him go, dropping him on the grass. He looked over at Zak who had since stopped laughing and had backed away from this hideous scene, and then he looked over at me.

"Woman," he said, as if he was telling me something I didn't know, "our son is dead."

He licked his lips. His tongue and mouth seemed enormous. His hand wiped the sweat from his forehead. Then his thick fingers smoothed back his hair, which made him even more frightening because now I could see his full evil face glaring at me.

Words hissed out of his mouth. "If I ever hear you saying that I killed him, I swear I'll kill you. Just like this." Then he picked up the knife I had let go of and stabbed the earth with it.

I crawled toward my baby then. Pulling myself over the dirt. I almost couldn't see him past the pools of tears my eyes were sunk in. My arm reached out to Jeremy's face. I just wanted to touch him. To say, "Mommy's here." Instead I heard myself whisper, "They fly to where they want to go." Then Harry's boot stepped into the space between us, and Jeremy's face disappeared.

"Enough of this," he said.

He wouldn't let me touch him. He picked him up and began walking away. I grabbed at Harry's trousers.

"My baby, my baby," I pleaded.

But he kicked my fingers' grip off his leg and carried Jeremy away, leaving me lying in the dirt.

I closed my eyes. I could see Jeremy flying up to the clouds, following his sister. I wanted to fly with him. I wanted to feel my arms turn into wings and glide me up into that sky. I searched to find the courage to pull that knife out of the ground and pierce my heart with it. But I couldn't do it. Instead, I lay there tasting the dirt that had found its way into my mouth.

When I finally moved, I turned my head to see if Zak was still huddled up against the tall oak tree that stood in the yard. He was not there. I didn't know where he had run to and I didn't care. All I saw was Jeremy's sweet face, distorted from terror and anguish, pleading for understanding. All I knew was that I had not saved my child. I had killed him just as Harry had killed him. My hesitation, my lack of courage, my inability to stop Harry's actions had killed my son. My baby. Oh God. Forgive me. I did not know what I was doing.

Later that day, Harry came back. He was dripping wet. I wonder if he had dunked himself in the river trying to cleanse himself of his sins. Zak was with him. He came out from behind Harry and started walking into the kitchen. He hesitated when he saw me. I was sitting at the table, unable to move from the pain in my belly and side. My insides were all strangled together. I looked miserable. So dirty and bruised. As his eyes caught mine, I thought that maybe he was going to run up to me, into my arms— as my soul at that moment wished—and remind me that I still had one youngin left. He glanced from me to his pa, back and forth a couple of times, and stayed put. His little feet never ran to me.

Still grasping at any hope that would make my heart feel alive, I whispered, "Zak, come to your ma."

Zak looked to Harry for permission to move. Harry did nothing. So Zak did nothing. They just stood at the doorway. The two of them together.

Finally Harry spoke. "Woman," he said, uttering the words with hate and disgust, "pack up Zak's clothes. We'll be leaving in the morning."

I opened my mouth to protest, but Harry silenced me with his look.

"Zak, go to the yard. I wanna talk to your ma," he said. Zak obeyed without question. By now he knew better than to cross his pa.

"I buried him," Harry said. "No need for anyone to know what happened. I'm going to take Zak away from here. If anyone asks, you tell them that I took the boys to visit my sister."

He came close to me then. His eyes, burning with hate, reflected his true nature, his evil. And even though a flame burned in them, his eyes were lifeless. They were the eyes of a dead man. He held no love, no longing for anything. He held so little and yet controlled so much. I felt myself shudder. I never said a word. Not one word. My throat tried to speak. I could feel the gurgling moving around. I could feel the saliva collecting in my mouth. But the voice wouldn't, couldn't, release itself.

That night, while Harry and Zak slept, I packed Zak's clothes. Far into the night, I crept into the boys' room and gazed at this child of mine. Was he ever really mine, or was he just a pawn in this man's world? As I looked at him, I wasn't feeling anything for him. I didn't even think about missing him. I was still seeing Jeremy. The agony in his young body. His bulging eyes pleading for help. Then, for a brief moment, I was seized by an urge to wake Zak up and run away with him. But I knew he wouldn't have gone with me. He would've wanted his pa's permission. He was under his spell. Then I thought about killing Harry. I truly did. I went into the kitchen and found the biggest knife I had. I thought about going up to our room, standing over the sleeping man, and stabbing into his heart. My mind wanted to. Oh, how it wanted to make my hands grip that handle and bring the knife down into his chest. Make his eyes bulge open. First he would feel pain, then the surprise that I, his wife, had the guts to do this, and finally the realization that he was dying. But I couldn't do it. My soul said "no" and I had no strength left to argue with myself. I fell asleep at the kitchen table.

Zak woke me up. The sun, just rising, was bringing a soft glow in through the kitchen windows when I felt a pulling at my dress. With my head still slumped sideways over my arms, I opened my eyes. They looked directly into Zak's blue ones. They weren't just cold eyes anymore.

They had seen too much. Now they were searching for something.

Oh, I get so tired of talking about this, because the pain starts so deep inside that I can't pull it out and toss it aside.

"Ma, Ma," Zak whispered, "Pa and I are going on a trip, Ma. Pa said that he wants me to see new things."

He looked at me for encouragement. He wanted me to say something.

Why?

I'm not sure. It never seemed like he really needed me. But maybe in thinking that, maybe I was wrong. Too late though. Too late for me to change what Harry had started. What Harry had done to my Jeremy. I couldn't stop his heart during the night and I couldn't stop him now.

"Zak," I said quietly, "your pa wants to take you out there to see the world. You go with him son. Ma will be all right. I'll take care of the house and I'll be here if you ever want to come back."

Then I had to say it so he would have something else to remember. I wasn't sure if it was love I was feeling or just the knowing that my last youngin was being snatched away from me.

"Zak, I love you."

I took him in my arms and he pulled himself close to me without hesitation. He was finally willing to feel my arms. Feel the warmth of my body. As I held him, my nose searched for even the smallest hint of a child scent. I wanted something to hold on to. Something to remember. But I couldn't find it. All I could smell was death.

"You'll be all right, Zak," I whispered in his ear, trying to convince him as well as myself. Then I held his face up to mine and looked him square in his eyes.

"Forget what you saw yesterday," I commanded. "Forget what happened to your brother. He had a bad accident. He choked on a marble. That's all. Your pa didn't know what was happening. He got angry, but that's done with. Let your little head just forget what happened."

I kissed him then. Hard and long I pressed my mouth against his forehead, hoping to push what he knew deep inside him. Someplace where it could get lost. He stood there quietly. But I could see that, even though his voice was silent, his eyes were questioning me. He was still looking to me for something more. I had nothing else to give him.

He's like a puppet, I thought, A puppet doing whatever he's made to do.

A huge sob nearly escaped me then. It came suddenly, without warning. It burned against the walls of my throat as I fought to keep it in. I was helpless to do anything. I was as much a puppet dangling from Harry's arms as Zak was.

Soon after that, Harry came downstairs. I fixed them some food. They ate like they were real hungry. As they were going out the door, I grabbed Harry by his arm. I caught his shirt sleeve and my fingers held tight, pulling it away from his skin. I didn't care if he killed me. He turned his face to me. I had to ask. I had to know.

"Where did you bury him?" I pleaded.

"Don't matter none," he answered. "I don't want you to go and do something stupid like digging him up."

I wanted to run after Zak and look to him for the answer that Harry refused to give me. But I couldn't. I had told him to forget what happened. I didn't want to make him start remembering again. Did Harry tug his sleeve out from between my fingers or did I let go of it? I don't know. The next thing I knew, Harry and Zak—Zak no longer visible, his little body blocked from my sight by Harry, who sat behind him on the horse—were riding the road out of town. I knew Harry wouldn't go through town. He was afraid of questions. He was leaving me to do the answering when people started asking where my boys were.
I don't remember when I began to forget. As neighbors asked about my boys, I would say that Harry took the youngins to visit his sister. Each time someone asked, the lie became more real. After a while, it was easier to believe that Jeremy was off traveling with his pa rather than lying in a grave dug by the hands that killed him. After a while, it was easier to forget the truth altogether than to remember the lie.

I'm so tired now after talking like this. I know it does a

soul good to let its innards flow out. But only to a point. After a while, truth starts doing just the opposite. The pain starts up again. Starts killing you. I can't go on. I have to stop now. I want to talk about happiness.

I remember a time when a woman friend of mine, her name was Maggie, came to visit one day. We were both feeling a little low and lonely, too. Her husband was gone, working on some farm, and her youngins were straining her. So, one afternoon, she left them with her eldest daughter and came to visit me. We started talking like we were schoolgirls and laughing about the silliest things. I laughed so hard I nearly wet my underpants.

Maggie was the kind of woman who collects moments in her head and saves them for conversation. Of course, by the time they are talked about she has added her own flavoring to them. Maggie could make one laugh at a funeral if she wanted to. Many of the womenfolk in the town didn't talk to Maggie. They thought she was a bit odd and much too boisterous. When she moved away, they continued to use her as an example of how not to be.

But I'll tell you something. The day I finally lifted myself out of the house and went into the backyard to pick up the marbles, I wished that I had Maggie next to me, laughing about one thing or another. Nothing I tried to do stopped the ravaging pain that tore me to bits and dropped me over the parched soil. Scattering me like the marbles that had rolled into the footprints Harry's boots left in the earth.

Snippet

The birds fly south. I watch them as they go by. They are sure of their direction. I am not sure of mine. I go around in circles. Stuck in this place. How can I leave my babies? How can I go away from this earth that holds them? I walk over to where Ellie rests. I sit there and talk to her about leaving. I don't think she is holding me here. Or Jeremy, wherever he is buried. I think it's me. I can't seem to move my feet out of the footprints of this place. I even thought of taking Ellie with me. Digging her up, but what would I do with her? I thought of burning her body, whatever is left of it, and taking the ashes wherever I went, but I couldn't. I didn't want to disturb the safety I had laid her in.

The Sound of Silent Screams

I don't know when I stopped screaming. First, the loud screaming that everybody can hear, then the inside-screaming that tears into you and kills off feelings. I remember the first time it started to happen. My daddy was working out in the barn. I was young then, real little. One of the horses went wild and kicked him in the head and then stomped on him. I was playing near the barn and saw him lying on the ground. He was not moving and there was blood all over his face. I opened my mouth to scream. I heard the sound forming in my throat and rushing toward my open mouth, but then nothing happened. No sound came out of my mouth. Instead, I felt the scream change direction. It reached deep inside me. It mixed up my insides.

I remember being so afraid of all the blood that I couldn't touch him. My mother came looking for me and she found me and him. She grabbed me and shook me until I threw up. Throwing up must have unplugged my voice, but not the scream. My father didn't die then, but he was never quite the same after that kick to the head. I was never the same either. After that day, my screams would often go inside me instead of out of me. And the only one who heard them was me.

One time though, I remember it real clear, someone must have heard my inside scream. We all, meaning my ma and pa and sisters and me, had traveled up to Vermont to visit my Uncle Jake and his family. He was my father's youngest brother. He was an inventor. People laughed about him. They said things like, "He has a loose screw." But what I heard my mother whisper to herself the day we pulled up to his house was, "What a mighty fine place he has."

I don't think she intended to have anyone hear what she was saying. She was not one to offer anyone praise. But I had this knack of being able to catch my mother's words. If my ears didn't hear them, then my eyes must have learned to read her lips because not much my mother did escaped me. But I'm getting off the subject of screaming. Anyway, it was winter and it was cold. A cold that none of us were used to. Even though Ma had packed our warmest, thickest clothes, we had to borrow our cousins' clothes to wear over our own. Ours just weren't enough to keep us from freezing.

In some places the snow was up to my waist and all the ponds were frozen over. Even though I wasn't used to the cold, it didn't stop me from going exploring. Usually a group of us would be outside playing together. One day though, the others were busy doing one thing or another. I went out by myself to the edge of a pond that was just down the road from my uncle's house. All bundled up in my cousin's winter coat, I was sitting on its bank. Little pieces of snow were falling out of the sky. I thought they were too small to be called snowflakes and was trying to think of what to call them. I thought of some pretty names like starflakes, snowdust, and snowlight. I sat there for a long time. My behind was getting numb from sitting on the snow. As I tried to get up, I slipped down the steep bank and my feet hit the ice at the edge of the pond. The ice must have been thin because I broke through it. I couldn't think fast enough as I slipped into the water. Before I could reach out and grab a branch, I was pulled down into the pond. The water reached up to my chin. It was so very cold as it seeped through my coat. My small hands grasped the edge of the ice, but it just kept breaking off. I tried to keep myself from going under, but I was getting so cold and so heavy and my hands were numb. And I couldn't yell for help. Even though I opened my mouth, my screams went right inside me again.

Just as my hands let go and I felt the water coming over my face, someone grabbed hold of my collar and pulled me out of the water. I felt myself being lifted up until the ground became flat and I could stand up. I stood there shivering, my teeth chattering like they never had before. I had never been this cold or this scared or this surprised as I stood there looking at this person who had saved me. It was a lady. She had on a white fur hat and a long gray wool coat. She looked like she belonged in one of those magazine books I liked to look at. She took me by the hand. Her hand was so warm and soft. She never said a word as she led me up to the road. She just kept smiling this small, gentle smile. Her whole face was like a light. It made those tiny pieces of snow, which had continued to fall even though I had almost drowned, glisten as they drifted past her.

The next thing I remember was standing at the door to my uncle's house, and my mother hollering at me.

"Where the devil have you been, Hattie?" she yelled.

Then, realizing my nearly frozen condition, she pulled me into the house and started yanking my clothes off. It all happened so fast. I heard her calling out commands to others in the house as she was pulling off my clothes and rubbing my skin. Then she had me all bundled up in blankets and was giving me hot tea to drink. When I told her about the lady, she said that I must have imagined it.

"You must have been delirious," she said.

"What would someone like that be doing out this way in the hills?" she questioned. Then added with scorn, "Just waiting to save you?"

I didn't even try to answer her. I didn't know what the lady was doing out there. What I did know was that she had saved me. Secretly I believed it was a miracle. The lady had heard my inside scream and saved me from drowning. I never forgot that lady. I never stopped wondering about her. I still remember the feel of her hand holding mine. My own mother's hand never felt like that.

Snippet

As a little girl, I used to sing songs to myself. Make them up in my head as I went along. There was a swing in the back of our house. I would sit and swing and sing. Sometimes my sisters and other youngins would tease me, but then they would get tired of watching me keep swinging and they'd leave me alone. I think they hoped their teasing and meanness would make me get off the swing. It never did. I just swung even more and sang even harder.

"Hattie you're a sweet girl
So pretty and fine.
You swing on a swing like it was a vine.
No matter that they tease you so
Cause you understand
There's always one youngin
That gets picked on like hell."

Then I would giggle to myself for saying the "hell" word and just keep swinging until Ma or Pa called me home.

One Clear Summer Night

Even though I grew up seeing bottles of alcohol run dry, having a drink myself was not anything I was interested in doing. At the least, I saw alcohol make fools of men. At the worst, it turned them into violent beings. Not that I ever swore not to drink, I just never did. Never until that one summer night. A night I chose to swig down some whiskey. A night I never intended on getting drunk.

Old Man Mills from over the hill had his special brew all ready. This pretty much determined when the town's summer dance would be held. All the townsfolk were planning on going. I wasn't so much in the mood for a get-together as I was for just being in different surroundings for a change. Harry was looking forward to seeing all his men friends, and I'm sure he was looking forward to seeing all the women gussied up.

I put on a dress that usually stayed tucked away. It was white with small blue flowers sprinkled over it. Its neckline, cut deeper than the everyday dresses I owned, scooped low enough to show some of the freckles that rose up from the space between my breasts. Being fitted at the waist, it squeezed me a little too tight that year. I hadn't worn it in a few years and had grown stouter in that time. Still, not meaning to brag, I had a pretty good figure and could manage to draw my share of glances. Rarely did any of them come from Harry. Harry didn't pay me much attention. All he said, when we were leaving and I was putting my shawl over my shoulders, was that my hair looked like the wind had blown through it one too many times. He didn't want anyone saying that his wife looked like a wild woman. It almost made me laugh hearing him say that. I thought it funny because I had no idea what it would take to make me a wild woman, or even what being a wild woman meant.

Most often my hair was pulled back off my face. But for the dance, I had let it down. After washing it and combing it through, I let it dry in the afternoon sun where it got lifted a bit by an occasional passing breeze. I even tossed my head a couple of times and ran my fingers through my hair feeling pleasure as it passed over the skin of my hands. That day my reddish brown hair, "like the color of horse chestnuts" my pa used to say, made its own set of waves, some going in different directions, all flowing down past my shoulders.

Anyhow, we finally got to the dance. It was being held in one of the big barns. All the women brought food. That was expected but also agreeable to us because it gave us a chance to show off some of our finest recipes. I made some blueberry pies and bread. It was a dark brown bread with a hint of banana flavor. I brought along a big jar of honey and a crock of butter for those who liked it that way. The fiddle player was already making music when we got there. Everybody looked cheered up and ready to enjoy the evening. Myrtle Hooper, a tall, heavyset woman whose husband was just the opposite, thin and small, was directing all the activities. Telling the women where to put their dishes. Telling the men where to put the chairs. She even brought some sheet music for the fiddler. Before too long, a couple of the men start arguing over one of the single women. Sure enough, one pushes the other and, before you know it, Myrtle is standing between them. Cussing at them like she was a man. She grabs one by the shoulder and pushes him into a chair, and then tells the other one to leave unless he behaves himself. I don't know what it was about Myrtle Hooper, but she was the only woman in town who could get away with behaving like a man.

I rather enjoyed watching this whole scene until I realized that Harry was gone. I had no thought as to where he went. I walked around the dance floor, zigzagging through small groups of people, trying to spot him, but I couldn't find him anywhere. So I stepped outside. The summer night air was taking on a coolness that was much welcomed. There were quite a few couples outside the front of the barn. Some looked like they had danced right through those wide-open barn doors without realizing they were outdoors. Young couples gazing into each other's eyes, forgetting the world around them. I strolled around the side of the barn thinking that maybe Harry was out back. It was quite dark in this direction. There was no glow of light at the back of the barn as there was out in front of those open doors.

Harry had already been drinking quite a bit. He had started before we left home. So I thought maybe he was feeling sick or something. As I turned the corner, I heard his voice. He wasn't alone. He was talking with someone. He was keeping his voice real low, like he didn't want it to travel beyond where he was. I should've just gone back inside. But I'm a curious sort. Staying near to the barn wall, I edged closer to a spot where I could make out what he was saying over the sound of the fiddle and banjos and the stomping of dancing feet. I hadn't heard anyone else's voice yet, so I was wondering who he was talking with. Then I heard another man's voice and I got sick in my stomach at what they were saying. The other man was talking like he had drool stuck in his mouth. He was gurgling the words. And then I heard a soft moan and whimper that came from their feet. I wasn't seeing anything, but I knew that some poor young girl was lying there with them standing over her.

"Tell anyone about this and we'll kill you," Hank, whose voice I now recognized, was snarling.

"Yeah," Harry agreed. "You're a bitch if I ever saw one." Then he added, "Who'd believe her anyway?"

They started to move then, and I pulled deep into the shadows so they wouldn't see me. Once they were gone, I ran to the spot where they had been standing. As dark as it was, I had no trouble seeing. There, lying on the ground was a young girl, one of the children from the hills. She couldn't have been more than fourteen. She must have snuck down to watch the goings on. The poor thing was shaking so bad I couldn't help her up at first. Her dress was torn and muddied. Her large brown eyes looked like pieces of black coal, dull and lifeless. She pushed me away from her, straightened up, and ran back into the woods.

I stood there fighting the urge to heave up the food I had eaten, while trying to clear my head about what had happened. But how does one make anything that is already so clear any clearer? I was attempting to clear my head because what I had heard and seen, what I knew to be real, was already getting muddled by my not wanting it to be real, by the fear trapped in my gut that was tearing at it like a wild animal devouring its prey, and by what I knew others would say.

"Oh no, that's not possible."

"Harry and Hank are such good, hardworking men. Why Hattie, you must be mistaken!"

Or, worst of all, I'd hear, "If anything did happen to that girl it was because those women from the hills are all tramps anyway. Don't you know they come down here looking for our men?"

I knew how the townsfolk handled these types of things. All this thinking just made me feel more confused. I stayed put long enough that the moisture from the rain the night before started seeping in through my shoes. When I realized my feet were soaked was when I walked back inside the barn.

I walked past people, not seeing anyone. I went to where the jugs of brew were and poured myself a cup of whiskey. I didn't care what anybody said. I swallowed it like it was water. Then I poured another and swallowed that one, too. A couple of men looked at me, elbowed each other, and laughed. One of them hollered something out to Harry, who didn't hear him. He was busy dancing with Mary, one of the better-looking women there. Dancing! After what he had done! I went over to Harry and told him I was leaving. Going home. He made no effort to go, which I was glad of. I thought if he had left with me he would have seen a wild woman. He would have seen her say or do something I would regret later on.

I walked home by myself in the dark. All I heard was a night owl hooting, and in the distance the slowly fading music. I went home and went to bed. I lay there with the room spinning and kept thinking about that poor girl out there. Carrying forever the hurt from those two men. I knew she would never be the same. As drunken waves came over my thoughts, blurring everything into itself, still in my dress I rolled to the very edge of my side of the bed.

My last thought filled me with disgust. When Harry got home, he would be lying down next to me and I would let him. My head rolled off the edge of the bed and I threw up.

Snippet

Life is hard. At times I felt like my life was spent in hell. Each smile had little time to evolve, for grayness would pass over and erase any trace of it. It's a wonder I continued to have faith in God, but I did.

I remember my mama telling me never to blame God for evil things in man. I didn't blame God. But I wondered about the evil in man, even though I saw good in him, too.

"Hattiedear"

My grandmother Ida lived with us when I was a little girl. Ma called her Ida. Pa called her Mother. I called her Grammie. She was a silent woman who didn't have to say much to get her ideas across. If she didn't approve of something, you'd know it as soon as her eyes touched upon you. But she was always fair and she was never mean. I loved my grandmother more than even my own mother. In the early part of the day she would sit me next to her. She had a small box in which she kept her hairbrush and things like hairpins and an occasional ribbon. She would unbraid my hair. Her fingers would float through the strands. I could feel her round, firm fingertips rubbing against my scalp. Then, after a few minutes of this, she would take her ivory-handled brush out of the box and slowly start pulling it through my hair.

"Hattiedear," she would say, putting "Hattie" and "dear" together in such a way that they became one, "you have such beautiful hair."

Not once, not ever, do I remember her hurting me. Even the most stubborn tangles somehow melted away under her touch.

Bits and Pieces

My pa was a man of stature. He was tall and strong and sturdy and reminded me of the oak tree in front of the house I grew up in. This oak was so old and big that it would take five of us youngins, our hands joined, to encircle it. There was a story told about that tree. That tree had once been used for the lynching of a colored man who was accused of assaulting a white woman. Sometimes, looking out at that tree, I thought I could see the rope swaying to and fro from the weight below it. I could even hear the creaking of the branch. I never told anyone this. I never told that I also saw the form of a man hanging from that rope. Hanging like a rag doll and swaying. Swaying with the wind. Once he lifted his head and looked up into the window right at me. Oh, the look on his face scared me so. His eyes were filled with horror, and his mouth open in a scream. I didn't hear no scream though, except for the one that rose in my own throat and that I muffled with my fist, for I did not want to have to explain my fear to anyone. I squeezed my eyes shut, and when I opened them again there was nothing there but the old oak tree.

A half-heart was carved into that tree. Danny, a

boy who had his eyes on me for a while, came by one day. He told me that from all of us girls—I had four sisters—he liked me the most. He said he would prove it to me. He did not know that this tree was something special to Pa. It was like Pa compared himself to that tree. Pa came up on Danny as he was carving the heart into the tree. Quickly, and with a bit of fury, Pa put a stop to the carving. Danny only had half a heart finished. It must have been a sign or something, because nothing ever came of me and Danny. Not that Pa's anger was enough to stop Danny from coming around again, but he lost interest in me. I was twelve years old and he was sixteen.

My older sister Lydia was fifteen. She had a real pretty face and big eyes, and she would flirt with those green eyes at Danny. One day Danny just decided he liked her better than me. That didn't bother me none 'cause I never really liked him much. Oh, I liked the attention he gave me, but I didn't like the way he looked. His teeth were crooked, he was tall and skinny, and he was clumsy. He never seemed to move well. And he never felt good to me. I remember when he took my hand. His hand was cold and sweaty. As his fingers curled around mine, it didn't make me feel nice. It made me feel like I had a spider wrapped around my fingers. Whenever I thought of him after that, I thought of spiders. Nothing came of him and my sister, neither. Some other girl in town claimed he fathered her child, so he ended up with her. I imagined all their youngins would have a mark of a spider on them somewhere.

The house Harry and I lived in, in Chapel Ridge, was not really ours. It belonged to the Clemens family. The Clemens family name was my father's mother's side of the family. His maiden aunt, Aunt Mae, had lived in that house. Well, when she died of pneumonia, my father got notice that the house was left to him. At that time, me and Harry were wondering where we were going to put ourselves. We lived near my family but Harry was not happy with farming. He was looking to make "big money" he would say. So when Pa mentioned this house, Harry started thinking. He figured, being a strapping young man, he could get just about any job needing physical labor. He had heard about mining operations and lumbering mills in other places, so he figured we should move.

I hated the thought of leaving my family. I didn't know any other life. But at the same time, I also hated the thought of staying around my family. By that time most of us girls were married. Between family and farmhands there would always be a group of people wanting to gather together. Sometimes they would settle like flies around a spot and just buzz around not doing anything purposeful. Going around and around. Sitting, talking, drinking, and sometimes gambling, though the gambling only happened when Ma was busy in the kitchen, where she was always complaining about something.

I didn't like complaining. It served no purpose. I

remember once, when I was bleeding real heavy during my time of month and feeling real poorly, I mentioned to my ma how it was. She looked at me like I was crazy for feeling bad.

In a scornful way she said, "Hattie dear, we women don't complain about those things because there's nothing at all you can do about it. You just keep washing those rags as quick as you use them and keep your mouth shut so no one knows what's going on."

Maybe that's when I got really good at getting stains out. After that, whenever I had something on my mind, I would just start scrubbing as hard as I could. I would scrub and scrub, and the harder I scrubbed, the tighter my lips sealed. I don't know what I was looking for by telling my mama that I was feeling poorly, but I was hoping she might at least smile when she told me not to complain. What I saw in her face was that she didn't want to be bothered by such nonsense, or by me. So I never said anything to her again.

Apron Strings

Harry and me started off getting along pretty well at first. We shared the same bed and, even though I never liked him touching me, all else seemed to go as I was told a marriage should be like. He worked and I tended to a wife's duties. I didn't get pregnant right off as so many of the women do, but maybe that's how it was intended to be. While waiting to have babies of my own, I got a lot of experience seeing my sisters having youngins. I would help in their birthing. Cradling those little babies as they were born while listening to their mothers' screaming. My sisters knew how to scream. I remember how Lilly, my oldest sister, would take to howling like a coyote when the pains started coming. Even when the menfolk would leave the house and go down to the barn, they could still hear her howl. I always thought she screamed more than was necessary. Afterwards, though, she always seemed more relaxed than the others, so I figured those yells did her some good.

Lilly's husband was a decent and patient man. James was his name. I always liked James. A widower, he was a mite older than Lilly. And he was as quiet a man as she was a loud woman. I remember one time when Harry got angry at me for something, James came over and led him off toward the woodpile he had been chopping. Even though he was talking to Harry, his eyes looked at me with a certain understanding that told me he didn't think I deserved to be hurt. James had no children from his first wife and was thrilled by having children with Lilly. Last I knew they had nine children, four boys and five girls. Two sets of twins in there somewhere.

After Harry and I moved away, I lost touch with most of my family. Not at first, but gradual like. And it wasn't only the passage of time that killed our seeing each other. It was something that Harry did one time when we went home for a visit. He hurt my pa's feelings real bad and we never went back there again. To this day I don't know what it was exactly that happened. But it had something to do with some money Pa had loaned Harry. Pa was not one to hold grudges, especially over things that didn't matter so much, but Pa was a proud man. Whatever it was that Harry had done, Pa could not forgive it or forget, especially after this day.

I had been in the kitchen with Ma, washing dishes, when suddenly the men's voices turned to yelling. Well, actually, Harry was yelling. Pa's voice was loud. Harry was banging his fist against something. Pa was sitting in his chair. As I went to see what was going on, Ma grabbed my arm to keep me in the kitchen. She didn't believe that women should interfere in these things. I didn't even think about what I was doing when I pulled my arm out of her grasp and walked out of the kitchen. As I entered the room where my pa and Harry were, I saw Harry grab my pa by the neck and pull him out of his chair. Harry's face was twisted up into a sneer. He said something to Pa and then shoved him back down. Pa slowly stood back up and straightened himself out. By then I had moved closer to the two of them and clearly heard Pa's words.

"Get out of my house. You are no longer welcome here."

I knew Pa was talking to Harry, but I also knew the duties of a wife. At that moment, it was as if half of me fell away. Crumbling into pieces at my feet. I was like one of those rockslides. One minute you're looking at a huge rocky ledge, thinking how solid and rooted it is, and then, just like that, large chunks of the rock break away. Smashing to the ground below. I stood there, in the same spot on the rug, for as long as it took for the pieces to fall. Even though he looked right at me, I don't think Harry noticed me before he walked out the door. My pa had lowered himself back into his chair. His head slumped into his hands. I don't know if he saw me or not. I stood there wanting nothing more than to have a choice. I had none.

The next thing I remember was Harry coming back into the house and grabbing my arm. "We're leaving," he commanded.

I startled out of the place of no choice. As I shrugged his arm off mine I said, "I want to say goodbye."

My feet moved awkwardly as I stepped over pieces of me. I went over to my pa and scooted down. Leaning up against his legs like I used to so long ago, I said, "Pa?"

He lifted his face out of his hands.

"Hattie, I'm sorry," he whispered "You, my daughter, are always welcome here."

But we both knew that I would not be back. My duty was to be with my husband. I said goodbye to Pa and then looked toward the kitchen door. The door was open and Ma was standing in it. As I walked over to her, her arm went up telling me not to come any closer. She had no expression on her face. It was stone cold. Funny how my ma could be. She was not caring about what just happened. She was not caring about my never being able to come back. She was still holding the anger from my breaking out of her grasp and disobeying her command to stay put in the kitchen.

"Ma?" I kind of stammered because I couldn't believe she was doing this.

But her arm stayed up. Finally, without saying a word, she turned around and walked back into her kitchen. I watched her move away. Watched her hands move to the back of her gingham apron and smooth out its strings, which were as always tied into a perfectly shaped bow. I watched my ma shrink away to a sliver and then disappear as the door slowly swung closed. I stood there waiting for another rockslide to occur. But nothing else moved.

Watching My Ma

Far off I could hear a steady hum, and I knew I was nearing Mr. Haskin's bees. He had a bee farm. Thousands of bees. Everyone had many times over heard the story about how one of the local boys went up to Haskin's farm intending to pull a prank. He unlatched the doors and set the bees free. When he did this, the bees went for him. The poor boy was covered with hundreds of welts. At first, those that found him didn't know who he was. "Unrecognizable" was what they said. He ended up dying. We all knew that to fool with bees was not something anyone did, unless they knew about bees. I just liked to sit in the woods, near to where the bees were kept, and listen to the hum of their steady buzzing. I'd find a spot next to a tree and lean up against its trunk. I felt that the sun's light, falling through the tops of the trees, was washing me with its glow. It was like being touched by heaven itself. As the birds were chirping, and the leaves rustling, and the bees humming, I would close my eyes and drift away into their music.

A circus bandwagon came through our town once and we all hopped around the wagon clapping our hands and wanting to hear the music. At first it was fun. But after a while, I found myself pulling away and clapping my hands over my ears. It was too loud. It was noisy. And it was not music to me. Over the years, I found the music I liked best was soft and gentle. The kind of sound that reminds me of Christmas bells tinkling in the distance. A music that would make me sway my body in a gentle motion. A music that made me feel peaceful.

I sat in the woods for what seemed like just a few minutes when I heard someone, far off from the direction of our land, calling my name.

"Have I lost track of the time again?" I asked myself, preparing for another scolding.

I got up quickly and ran out into the clearing. Well, I realized it hadn't really been long at all. I could see that the sun hadn't moved much from its place in the sky. But there was such an urgency in that call of my name that I knew something was happening, if it hadn't already happened. I ran as fast as my legs could run, though I was never really good at running like the other youngins. I was always the last one to reach any place we would run off to.

"Hattie, Hattie, come quick, come qui...ck."

My sister Lilly was standing in the field, jumping up and down and waving her arms. She was more excited than I had ever seen her. As I reached her, she grabbed me by the hand and started pulling me along as she ran. I was already out of breath and just about ready to fall into the grass, but I had no choice in this matter.

"Move your legs," she yelled. "You won't believe the news Pa's brought home!"

"Lilly. Wait. Stop," I gasped. "I can't run anymore."

She just kept on pulling me. It felt like I got lifted in the trail of wind she was creating. Lilly was a fast and strong runner, and her trail of wind carried me along. I hardly felt my feet touch the ground.

I had no idea what it was that Pa did that made her so excited, but I figured it must be something wonderful. Something that had never happened before. We got to the house. Up the porch steps we flew, at which point Lilly let go of my hand. I had stumbled on the steps, but nothing was going to slow her down. I watched Lilly leap through the door into the house. By now she had me so excited that I ignored the bump to my knee, which later turned a purple red color, and in her tracks I followed. I just about flew through the door myself even though I was no longer being swept up by Lilly.

Everyone was in the sitting room crowded around Pa, who was at that moment sitting tall and proud. Sometimes he was just my pa. Other times he was an important man. Looking at him from across the room, it seemed that to-day he was both. I noticed his hair was neatly combed. Pa had a full head of silver hair. He always said the gray came early because he had so many women to deal with. Pa had wanted a son but was "blessed," as he put it, always adding a wink, with five daughters. He never made us feel that he was sorry to have any of us. He taught us what he would have taught a son and we helped him on the farm without ever complaining that he expected too much from us.

Being the youngest moving daughter—I had a younger sister but she was in her cradle at the time so I figured until she moved on her own I was the youngest—I ran right over to my father and sat at his feet. Something really important was happening. Even the farmhands were there.

I wonder now why I didn't sit so I could see his face. Instead, I sat so I could hear his words and watch my mother's face. The room was buzzing with something that I could feel but wasn't able to understand. I so wanted to be a part of what was happening. I so wanted that feeling of excitement that had started rising in my stomach to keep growing, to keep rushing through me. Some people call it "butterflies," but to me it was like a whole flock of birds suddenly lifting out of the trees that hid them so well.

I glanced over at Annie, my quiet sister, who always had a stitch going on some piece of fabric. I saw her hands furiously moving back and forth, pulling a deep blue thread in and out of a piece of muslin. I was amazed how she could do that without having to keep her eyes on her work. She would have been a good blind person because she lived by touch more than by sight. Even though her eyes were set on my father's face, I wasn't sure what it was that she was seeing. Before too long my eyes once again found their way to my mother's face. To all of her. She was sitting in her chair directly opposite to where I sat nudged up against my pa's legs. Everyone in the room was moving, responding to the excitement that was holding them, except for my mother, who just sat. There was no look on her face to express what she was feeling or to show that she was interested in what was happening. She sat perfectly still. Her hands clenched together in her lap. If anything, she had the look she always had when pulled away from whatever she was busy with. An expression that said she was wanting this to be over so she could remove herself and go back to doing what she was always doing—cooking, cleaning, directing activities. She didn't like it when someone else took over the director's role in the house. The house was her place to be in charge.

I wished that she would smile or lean over a bit as one does when they want to be sure to catch every word that is being said. As I sat with my ears listening for my pa's voice and my eyes on my ma, I felt his hand brush the top of my head. His fingers gently moved down my hair from the top to the back and then lifted off at the spot where the strands of hair joined into a tight braid. This little gesture was something he did whenever I sat down at his feet. A quick slight touch that I thought no one ever really noticed. But at that moment, I saw a look flash through my mother's eyes. A look so swift, like the motion of my father's hand, which I thought no one would notice. Except she did. My ma saw.

My mother and I were alike in that way. We saw things. She saw my father's hands touch me. I saw her react. If someone else had been watching her maybe they might have noticed her eyes narrowing, or the way her hands gripped together more fiercely, causing the veins running through them to pop out a bit more. But everyone's attention was directed at Pa. I though, was not spared her look. I caught it smack in my chest. A look of distaste and displeasure. A look of disgust. It hit me hard right where my heart was lodged. Suddenly my heart fell into my stomach and was quickly carried off somewhere by the flock of birds. Where my heart should have been, a huge empty space appeared.

The excitement, the sense of adventure that had been stirring me, moving about, getting ready to rise through me and burst into some kind of joy, got lost somewhere. I know that Pa started talking. I could hear the sound of his voice through the fog I suddenly found myself in. I could see faces, eyes getting bigger, smiles appearing, bodies moving. Annie even dropped her piece of fabric. But everything was so far away from me. I wanted to be there with them. But I wasn't there any longer. I was back in the woods. Listening to the hum of bees and seeing patches of sunlight coming through the leaves of the trees. I don't remember crawling between the legs of everyone as they came up to where I had sat leaning against my father's legs, but I must have done that. When the fog lifted, I found myself sitting up against the far wall, one of our cats curled up in my lap. I had lost that special moment. I didn't hear what my father said. I didn't share in the excitement with the others. I just went somewhere. I didn't do anything but crawl away. Just one glance shared between my mother and me had the power to erase everything else.

Later on that day I watched Ma move through the kitchen in her usual busy way doing what she always did—stirring the food cooking on the stove, peeling vegetables, wiping up after herself as she went along, calling out to her daughters to set the table for dinner. I watched her burn her hand on the handle of a hot pot and just keep moving. Her burnt hand stirred the soup in the pot, then over to the sink she went and pumped cold water over the hand. On the way back to the stove she slipped a smudge of butter out of the butter dish and smeared it over the burn, and then she started mashing the potatoes. Not once did a glimpse of pain pass over her face. Not once did she falter in her steady steps from one duty to the next. The burnt hand could just as well have not been hers.

At some point that day I remember Lilly coming over to me and saying something about how she was going to buy the dress she had been admiring in the fancy dress shop. Up to now she had only dreamt of owning it. Now it was going to be hers. She asked me what I was going to ask for. From what she said, I guessed the piece of paper Pa had earlier held in his hands meant that he had made some kind of deal. That we were going to have more money and be able to have special things. Things we had in the past wished for without ever really believing they could happen. But what Lilly said wasn't enough to make me feel excited again. Nothing seemed to matter. I still had bits of that awful empty feeling in my chest. Once again I had missed a moment of feeling joy. Missed it because my eyes had been trained to the spot where Ma sat. Trained to watch her. She had broken the spell of glee I was briefly under. Broken it. Pieces flying away. Unsalvageable. Her loathing sent me away into a place that saved me from feeling the darkness of that empty hole in my chest, but also kept me from feeling everything else.

The next morning, as my ma put a hard-boiled egg in front of me, I couldn't help but look at the huge blister, nearly the size of the egg I was about to eat, that had appeared overnight on the top of her hand. I suddenly felt sorry for her and noticed that my heart was back in its rightful place. Funny how my ma could make my heart both disappear and come back. I turned to her and asked her if her hand hurt.

She answered, "It's nothing, but this blister's in the way. I need to burst it."

Between giving me my egg and a piece of bread, she

picked up a needle—there was always a needle within arms' reach—put it over the flame on the stove, and stuck it into the yellow, fluid-filled bubble. Pulling a clean handkerchief out of her apron pocket, she wrapped the seeping swell of skin. There was always a clean handkerchief tucked somewhere in or beneath her clothes. "One never knows when they are going to need a clean piece of cloth for something," she would say. As she handed me the piece of bread, I couldn't help but steal one more look at her hand. My gaze was interrupted as I was told to eat. I turned my eyes to my plate and bit into the buttered bread, which she had sprinkled with tiny pieces of chopped garlic. I wondered if any of the others at the table noticed the circle of yellow seeping through the white cloth.

Snippet

These are moments of my life, moments in my life, moments of me. Wisps of me that stayed with me. Tucked tight in my head just like my hair that turned gray but held fast. I now share them with you. Do with them as you wish but allow yourself to do. Only you can know if you are feeling the right spot in your life. My gray hairs have long since with me been buried. Disappeared into time. But the moments last for all eternity.

Weeping Willow

The willow stands tall outside the door. I rarely step into the shade of its shadows. I refused to allow its leaves to drop over me, surround me, and hide me from the world. It never offered me safety. It made me believe that it could hide me from the outside world. It fooled me. One time when I was little—I had on a blue print dress—I ran into the arms of the willow. I was so sad and afraid. I ran into it thinking I could hide there. Thinking it would hide me. But it didn't. Soon the loud voice found me. Angry eyes found me. There was no safety. I was found. Never again would I trust the willow tree. I don't care how strong or deep its roots run.

Had my mother been alive at the time Ellie died, she would have said to bury Ellie under the branches of a willow tree. "It will protect her," she would have said. But I knew better. My child would be safer under the sun. In an open place. The sun would send down its rays and show her the way to heaven. Would having willow trees around my house have helped save me or my children? Nothing could have kept Harry's evil away from us, except his death. I remember wishing for his death. Where is he these days? Maybe he is dead. But I worry that he is alive somewhere. Spreading his evil. Killing others. Destroying lives.

In the past, I got myself in trouble. I didn't know enough, see enough, reach enough. There came a time when I refused to be inadequate. I decided to learn more. I read as much as I could. One reason for this could have been that I had little else to do. I had no youngins to take care of. No husband to act for. I even stopped using the washtub. I didn't need it anymore. I didn't want it anymore. As much as it had helped, it had damaged me enough.

I began cleaning houses for families that had money to pay. But it wasn't their money I was after. It was the books they usually had in their libraries. Most were willing to let me borrow a book or two. I read books. I read newspapers. I read all I could and slowly noticed that the words that came from inside my head were changing. Not being totally different but becoming stronger, clearer, and more painful. You may wonder why I say more painful. You see, the more I read, the more I found words to describe the things that had happened in my life. Sometimes there are no words for those things that happen, but sometimes there are words just not yet discovered. I would think about my life, my time with Ellie, Jeremy, and Zak, and find words that helped me understand. The words were like keys unlocking memories, unlocking pain, unlocking the chains that had held me in place.

Part 2

By the Stream

Snippet

My voice has been quiet, dormant, for a long time. It is time to again begin speaking. I hold off for long periods of time because sometimes the world revolves so fast that I have to hold my thoughts so they don't get lost in the confusion of everything.

It is hard at times to hold myself safe when everything around me speaks against it. Harry wasn't safe. Harry was anger and hate and evil. I managed to talk about him, but even then with a sense of fear. He was a mean man. He was an evil man. Many a day I wished that he would die in the mines he worked. God forgive me for those thoughts, but with all the evil he held he should have been buried deep within the earth.

I sometimes wonder where he is. What happened to him after he left?

A Dream

Regrets. I got so many regrets that I couldn't begin to tell about all of them. Why think about regrets? "Why," I ask myself, "must I be so aware of all the things I should have done and didn't do?" Because it tore me up inside. Because I realized that my backbone was not strong. Because I began to understand that sometimes moments of life unfold according to what one does or doesn't do. Realizing these things made me look at myself. My ma and pa never taught me how to look at myself. They never said, "Hattie, you can do better." No one ever said that to me until the day I said it to myself. That was the day I was able to walk away from the meadow where two of my children lay buried, the day when I was able to walk through my house without wanting to pull the walls in around me, the day when I packed one big bag and closed the door behind me. That was the day I said, "Hattie, there is more to life than this."

I was almost out of the front yard when I realized that I had to find a way to say my goodbyes to Jeremy. Ellie and Steven, their goodbyes had been happening right along. A week didn't pass that I wasn't sitting in the meadow next to where they lay, talking to them. But Jeremy, where was Jeremy? I put my bag down and slowly walked around to the backyard. I stood there in the spot where he died. Dry dirt whipped about my shoes from a sudden wind. I called out to him.

"Jeremy," I cried. "Jeremy. Forgive your ma."

I stood there, vividly remembering the horror of that day so long ago, and I wept. The tears ran in rivers down my face. Soon my feet were standing in puddles. If I had stood there much longer I would have seen the creation of a pond. So as not to drown, I gathered myself up and spoke a few final words.

"Jeremy, if you and your sister haven't already found each other, find her and fly together."

I walked out of the patch of dirt over to where the earth allowed seeds to sprout. Over to where I last saw Jeremy, lying so still, before Harry took him away. I pulled up a dandelion and blew at it. Its round white puff disappeared as it split into bits, into tiny white things that got swept up into the air. They reminded me of the fine goose feathers that once streamed out of a pillow whose seam failed to hold when I was squeezing it really hard. You know what I did then? Such a silly thing. I threw my hands up into the air and tried catching some of those wispy seeds. I found myself running after them. I couldn't keep up with the different directions they floated away in. I knew better than to try. But I tried anyway. I didn't get even a one. "Once you release them you can't get them back." I knew that but I tried anyway.

In the center of town, it really was in the exact center—once, someone using a map had taken much time to figure out that this was the middle of the town and had put a sign up stating that fact—I caught a wagon to the train station a couple of towns over. There I bought a ticket to Philadelphia. That's where Lady Isabelle lived. I had not heard from her since the letter she had sent me after Miss Jean's death. At this point in my life, I had no other place in mind to go to. So I decided to head towards a place from which someone had shown me respect and kindness simply because they thought I deserved it. Maybe heading in that direction was not right, as some of the neighbors had said to me when I told them I was leaving. All I knew was that every time I said "Philadelphia" I thought of Lady Isabelle. Thinking of her brought lightness to my heart. And even though I was afraid of what I was doing, I was more afraid of doing something else, or not doing anything at all.

Sitting in that train station and holding my bag, I wondered what my arms would do without the washtub. I had left that old tub sitting in the middle of my kitchen floor. I had stared into it for the longest time before leaving. It was as if I thought it would say something to me. As if a voice might rise out of it and echo its disapproval. I even nudged it a couple of times with my foot. Kind of like I used to nudge Harry when he would fall down drunk on the floor. A nudge that was firm enough to rouse him if he was rousable, yet gentle enough that it would not startle him into an explosive rage. But the washtub remained silent as any old washtub would. "It's just a big hunk of metal," I told myself convincingly.

Now, sitting in that train station, I had no desire to ever see that washtub again. It was strange to be in the station alone, and in the company of people I didn't know. One woman holding a child smiled at me shyly, then turned her eyes to where her husband stood talking to another man. I must have looked out of place. I wore an old coat that had once belonged to my ma. It was a dark green color that had since faded to a color of leaves. Not the beautiful, bright color of leaves in the fall, but the drab, greenish brown color of dying leaves. I didn't need to wear a coat, but there was no room for it in my bag. I decided it would be easier to carry it on my shoulders than to have to use my arms. On the top of my head I put a hat that looked more like a cover to a pot than a hat. I didn't particularly like hats, but on the advice of something I read in a magazine, "A woman should not be without a hat when traveling," I picked this one. I only had two hats. The other one, a deep red color, had a very large brim that nearly hid my face completely. Harry had brought it home for me once. Even though I didn't care for it, I was touched by the idea that he had brought me a gift. So I held on to it though I only wore it once or twice. One day I mentioned to Harry how nice it had been to have him give me a present. You see, Harry was not one for doing nice things.

"Oh, that hat," he said after I had reminded him of it. "I didn't buy that for you," he said with a grinning satisfaction in setting me straight. "Some woman got mad at me after, well, that part don't matter, and she threw it at me. So I picked it up and took it."

So even though I had two hats to pick from, there really was only one choice.

The shoes I wore gripped my feet tightly. I didn't like shoes and didn't often wear them. I liked feeling what I was walking on and my feet supported me just fine on their own. The soles of my feet were leathery like the soles on shoes, and my feet were big.

"One swift kick from those feet," Sam once said jokingly, "and they'll know better the next time."

So anyway, put together as I was, even though things didn't quite fit right or feel right, I got on the train. After I settled into my seat, I took my hat off and gave my head a little shake. You can imagine my joy when I saw floating there in front of me, a part of the dandelion puff. I watched it as it slowly drifted down to my lap and gently landed. Its seed end planted itself into the buttonhole of my coat.

I hadn't been on a train since I was a little girl and my pa took us up north to visit his brother. I had forgotten how it felt to sit in the moving car and hear the steady sound of metal against metal. It was like a loud rushing stream of water over a huge fall, with the occasional sound of screeching birds mixed in. The noise of the train entered my head and wove its way into my thoughts as I felt myself falling into sleep. Not a deep sleep, but one of those sleeps when everything around you turns into something else, and you forget where you are even though all the sounds are still there.

I had a dream riding that train. A dream that I remember even now. Outside, the rain was coming down in torrents. Jeremy, Ellie, and Zak were all babies and they were lying on the wooden floor of the house. I was sitting down next to them. The sound of the rain and thunder was not bothering any of us. Each one of the babies was holding something. Even Ellie, with her frail little hand, was able to grasp. Jeremy had a cup of water and, no matter how much of the water spilled out, the cup stayed full. Zak held a thermometer in his hand and it glowed red. And Ellie, Ellie held a pocket watch. It was a beautiful gold watch like none I had ever seen. She was dangling it by its chain. Swinging it back and forth and laughing at it. Suddenly, I heard Harry's booming voice come into the room followed by Harry himself. He came in and sneered at my babies.

"Give me those things," he said. But the babies held tight to their treasures.

"I said give me those things," he yelled, but his roar made no difference to the youngins. He bent down and tried pulling the cup away from Jeremy. He couldn't do it. As he attempted to take the other things away from Ellie and Zak, the same thing happened. Angrier than I had ever seen him, he screamed at me that he was going to step on them babies and squash them over the floor unless I got them to give up their treasures.

"You can't do that," I said. "They're stronger than you, Harry."

"Well then," he screeched, "I'll just squash you."

He raised his arms up high and gripped his fists together. It looked like he was holding a huge hammer over my head. With all his force he brought the hammer-like fists down, but he missed my head. Over and over he tried. Over and over he kept missing me. I just stood there. Not so much fearing him, but holding a curiosity to see what was going to happen next. He finally got so tired that he stopped. When he stopped he found he couldn't get his hands apart. They had cemented into each other. He stood there and then started crying and yelping like a wounded animal. Soon he stopped making sounds and the room fell silent. I lifted my eyes up to look at him, but he was no longer the Harry I knew. He had turned into stone. There he stood. His mouth open wide. His hands clasped together. His eyes bulging. A huge, unmoving mass. I picked up my babies, who still held their treasures, and ran past him out of the house. My first instinct was to scream for help. Then I thought, why? I left without looking back.

My eyes opened to darkness. I realized it was night. The train was still moving.

Faltering

The more I tell my stories, the more depressing my life appears. Happy times seemed to just be slight, passing glimmers between sad and hard moments. Was my life really that miserable? Was I really that pitiful? Was Harry right when he would call me those names that stung my heart? "You worthless piece of shit," he would say. "You're scum. I should just wash my hands of you." As his words came at me, I would fight with them. Tossing them every which way I could manage. Trying not to let them hit me. Especially, trying not to let them hit that spot in my chest, which could easily turn into that big black emptiness. Sometimes though, I thought maybe he was right.

I'm telling you now what I never let myself say out loud to anyone. I thought if I did speak, it would make it too real. You see, there were times when I believed Harry's hurtful words. I believed that I was scum. That I was no good. But I didn't want to be the one saying those things to myself even though I often heard them in my head. At those times I needed to hear Harry saying those terrible things. When I heard him calling me names, I would remind myself that Harry was a stupid man. Can you understand how much easier it was to fight off his words, get away from the sounds coming from his mouth, than it would have been had I said those mean things to myself? Harry's noise helped block out my own. Once Harry would get done with me, I would go off to the meadow and try to forget.

I've done wrong things. Bad things, too. Things I was ashamed of. I stole money a couple of times from people who trusted me. Did it matter that the youngins were hungry and I had nothing because Harry used up all we had? Maybe I should've begged for food from the neighbors, but I wouldn't or couldn't. I didn't want to admit I was faltering. I would watch my life going by me, slipping by me, and I couldn't grasp it.

The laundry kept me going but I hated it. The youngins kept me moving for which I was thankful. And Harry kept me alive. In a strange way I have him to thank for that. Because of him I refused to die. I wouldn't give him the satisfaction. Sometimes, late at night after Zak and Jeremy were asleep, I would sit and do mending. As I was sewing up holes that appeared in places where I had already mended over and over, as I picked up a sock that was supposed to warm Jeremy's foot and found it so thin from wear that my fingers showed through the threads, I would wonder, how can I possibly fix this?

When life felt out of hand, instead of mending I would start to pick at myself with the needle. I would watch the point go into my skin. I wouldn't even feel it. One day I took the needle and pushed it into my arm. It went in a good inch. I sat there and looked at it sticking out of my arm. My eyes fixed on the strand of black thread attached at the eye of the needle. It was like a tightrope. I followed it all the way down to where it held to the limp sock in my lap. I don't know how long I sat there just staring. Not feeling anything. Wondering if it was worth mending a thing that was so used up. I think it was Zak crying out in the night that startled me back. As I got up to tend to him, the needle pulled out of me releasing a trickle of blood.

Snippet

I always wanted to go to Colorado. Don't know why. I liked the sound of the word C-O-L-O-R-A-D-O. I liked the sound as it came out of my mouth. Jeremy liked it, too. Usually when we said Colorado to each other we were having a happy time together. We would be playing and laughing. I would tickle his behind and he would scoot away from me only to scoot right back. Jeremy had a silly laugh. He would let a burst of laughter out and then inhale it right back in. Funny how a little thing, saying one word, could make one feel joy.

The Agony

You may wonder about my beliefs in God. I believe in a heaven. And, having experienced Harry and the brutality of Miss Jean's death, among other things, I believe in hell. I believe in evil. Sometimes people do bad things. But other times something in one's eyes and in the way that person makes the air around you feel goes beyond being bad. It is evil in them. And it doesn't matter if they smile at you. It doesn't change the air.

In a way, I had no choice but to believe in a heaven. In a goodness somewhere in the universe. I was fortunate enough to have shared some of my life with people who held goodness. My children's goodness and radiance, at least Ellie's and Jeremy's, was angel-like. Their innocence was untarnished. Untouched by badness. Zak, though, was different. I don't know about him. Was he ever angelic? I would say no. But I was so distraught by Ellie's death, the loss of her, that maybe I didn't see what otherwise could have been seen in Zak when he was born.

One day I asked Adelphia, "my birthing woman" as I sometimes called her, about Zak's birth.

She said to me. "Oh, the agony? You want me to tell

you about that?"

At first I was afraid to have her continue. That time in my life was all such a blur to me. Yet I needed to know. I needed to know because I was trying to find a way to hold Zak in my thoughts without feeling only badness about him and about me.

"Yes, I want you to tell me," I said in barely a whisper.

"You waited too long to summon me," was the first thing Adelphia said. Then she told me the rest of the story.

"It was the neighbors who got concerned when you didn't come by for their dirty laundry. They went to your house and found you laying in the bed, soaked in perspiration and blood, grimacing in agony. It was they who came and told me to come quick. When I got to you and touched your face, you looked at me with eyes that told me you were in a faraway place. All you said was, 'Please.'

Jeremy was sitting, huddled in a wooden box in the corner of your room. He just sat there and asked me if I was going to help his sick mama. I asked the Rosen girl to take him over to their house.

Hattie, I don't know, because you couldn't tell me, how long you had laid there like that. Judging by how hungry Jeremy was when he went to the Rosen's—they told me later it took a long time to fill his belly—I thought you had been there, in that way, a full day if not more. The baby was stuck in you. Your body struggled to push him out and he was not willing to come out. We worked hard to get him born. I usually don't need help in birthing, but I remember needing it that day. I was fearing that we were going to lose both of you.

Oh, your poor belly. So hard. So full. Heaving until it could heave no more, yet heaving still. And you, you wouldn't scream. I kept saying, 'Hattie. Hattie, yell out the pain. Let it out.' You would slowly turn your face to mine and whisper through clenched teeth, 'No. Never.'

I couldn't understand why you wouldn't. I think screaming can do a woman good. But you wouldn't scream, at least not through your mouth. Instead your body screamed.

I never felt such resistance as my hands, arms, and whole body pushed, rolled, and moved your belly and the baby in it. At one point I said that Harry should be here. I don't know what saying his name did, but your eyelids flung open and the weakness and faraway look you held was for a moment gone. A mix of terror and anger rose with those lids. Where you got the strength for your voice I don't know. Loudly you said, 'No, no, no!'

'Please,' 'never,' and 'no' were the only words you spoke that whole day and night as we worked to turn that baby. When it finally happened, it happened quickly. It didn't even feel like it was due to my pushing on your heaving belly. It was as if he finally decided to move, or your body decided to set him free. And when he moved, he came out—screaming, mind you. I'd never seen a baby's head come out screaming. Then, finally, you let out a cry. Not a scream. Not a cry of relief. But an agonizing wail I will always remember. Your sound nearly made me forget the baby that I was holding. Then you must have fainted, because as I was announcing that this one was a boy, I looked over at you and knew you hadn't heard me.

I stayed with you for days. You didn't wake up for a long time. I'll tell you, it was the strangest thing to be trying to fit this baby up against your breast so he could suckle, and have you be laying there as if sleeping soundly. The odd thing was, when I would bring a glass up to your mouth, you would swallow what I offered though your eyes stayed closed. You didn't speak. You didn't move. You just laid there in your own strange sleep.

A couple of days later, when I was in the kitchen fixing myself something to eat, I heard you moving about. I turned around and there you stood. You said to me, 'Adie, the baby's out of me?' You were rubbing your hands over your shrunken empty belly as if you weren't really sure. 'Yes,' I said. 'He's over there.'

I had laid him in the box that Jeremy had been crouched in when I arrived. At that moment he was sound asleep. I thought he was a beautiful baby and told you that. One would have thought, after such a difficult birth, that he would have been swollen and bruised. He wasn't. He came out looking perfect.

You walked over to me and looked at him from a distance. 'Beautiful?' you asked, as if wondering what baby I was talking about. Then you walked over and knelt by the box. I watched your hand reaching out and was glad you were finally going to touch him. But you didn't. Instead your hand touched the wooden box. Gently, lovingly, you caressed the side of the crate but you didn't touch him. Then you stood up and slowly walked up the stairs to your room."

As I listened to Adelphia telling me about that time in my life, I thought, how could I have been like that?

Maybe Zak was born beautiful. Maybe, somehow, I made him into something ugly. In my grief over Ellie, I shunned him. Not just after his birth but also during my pregnancy. Everything was confusing to me. He had made me suffer so. I didn't want another youngin hanging on to me then. I didn't. He must have felt that from me. I guess I'll never know for sure. But having heard that Adelphia saw him as beautiful gave me some hope. Maybe Zak was held by a goodness that I had not seen because my eyes couldn't bear to see anything back then.

Snippet

I sit alone, feeling separate from this world, ready to die. My children flutter in and about me, brushing me gently with their wings. Showing me how to fly easily and painlessly away with them. My twins play together, Sam's son looks older, and my boy Zak, though different than the others, less happy, is there too.

Stirring Together

Sometimes I would feel like all kinds of things were stirring inside of me, and then sometimes I would feel like I got stirred. There was a difference to these feelings I can't explain. Standing over the stove, stirring a pot of soup, I watched pieces of food moving around, floating, disappearing into the broth, and reappearing. Never in any predictable way. Pieces of beef, carrots, potatoes, onions, and celery floating around. And then there were the parsley leaves that would stubbornly latch onto the ladle and the sides of the pot, clinging until I stirred a bit more furiously.

I stood there staring into the soup. I don't have things inside me. I got me inside me, I thought, and kept stirring much longer than was really needed. I smelled the vapors rising up into my face. I occasionally sipped the broth, its flavor constantly changing as the hours went by. I would think about how all these foods tasted on their own, and how, when put together, they made a whole new flavor. Silly, but I felt amazement at such a simple thing.

The Sounds of Me

What happens when there is no one to talk to? I know what happens. You start talking to yourself. Then you start thinking that maybe you're crazy. Then you decide either you're crazy or you're not. I came close to believing I was crazy. Then something happened to make me see I wasn't. To make me understand I was just alone. Such a simple thing.

I had come across a letter I had written to Miss Jean's sister. It was after Miss Jean's awful death. It was after the letter I sent telling her sister about her death. It was after I had done more washing and cleaning and mending and cooking. It was after I was too tired to do much of anything else. I wrote this letter believing with all my heart that I would send it. But I didn't. Of all places, I found it tucked in my sewing basket. Deep down beneath all the thread and needles and pieces of fabric. I saved pieces of cloth thinking that I could make something of them someday. But I didn't. There was no one else living here. I didn't need to make a quilt for myself. I had enough blankets and quilts to keep me covered the rest of my life. Too many.

I was sitting on a stool in my bedroom, the big basket at

my feet. I had been doing some mending for the neighbors. Over the years all those things I washed for them started needing fixing. So, one thing led to another. I washed, I mended, and sometimes I ironed. I hated ironing more than anything. Getting wrinkles out was something I was not good at. If anyone complained about my work it was usually because of the wrinkles and creases that I missed.

"Oh Hattie," they would say. "Look at this here."

And I would look as they—usually it was women who complained about the wrinkles—held up a dress or shirt and pointed with their accusing fingers to a rough spot. To a place where smoothness, evenness, did not exist. It didn't matter to them if this was a wrinkle that wouldn't show once the shirt got tucked into their husband's trousers. Sometimes I thought they got pleasure out of pointing out my mistakes. When it came to my washing abilities rarely did one ever find anything to complain about. The ironing, though, gave these people a chance to complain. It seemed like I always had my hands full of someone else's clothes. Other people's stains and tears and wrinkles. Other's complaining.

Anyway, I was sitting there on the stool, my shoulders bent, and my hands weeding out the pieces of cloth. Pulling at each piece. Looking at it. Trying to remember where it came from. What had it been a part of? Then, for lack of knowing what to do with it, dropping it to the floor. Each piece fluttered down like a tired bird with no more energy left for flying.

All of a sudden I had the letter in my hand. Though I had totally forgotten about it, I knew what it was the minute the paper touched my fingers. At that moment I remembered it clear as day. The pieces of cloth had kept the letter well hidden. It wasn't even yellowed. The paper was still as white as freshly washed sheets. I undid the folds. I looked at the words and decided to read them aloud.

"Why not?" I said to myself.

More and more over the years, I found myself talking aloud, even though there was no one else there with me. I would talk to things in the house. Sometimes, when heaving my washtub, I would say, "I just don't have the strength to carry you like I used to." Or, when walking through the meadow, I would stop and touch a flower and say, "What a pretty color you are." Sometimes when I stepped out onto the porch and saw dark clouds hanging in the sky, I would question them, "So, are you going to be sending us some rain or not?" As time wore on I began to talk to myself. I'd look in the mirror and wonder out loud, "So Hattie, what's today going to be like?" Or, as my hands were immersed in the washtub, scrubbing some piece of clothing they had scrubbed hundreds of times, I'd say, "I'm so tired of all this."

You see, the sound of my voice was better than no sound at all.

So there I sat reading the letter. As my eyes read each word, my mouth gave them sound and my ears heard.

Dear Isabelle,

I miss your sister. I miss writing the letters for her and reading yours back to her. It was good for me to have her as a friend. Even though we never said much to each other, the letters were enough of a bond to keep us connected. And it was through knowing her that I got to know you. I've been thinking about leaving Chapel Ridge. Maybe even seeing what Philadelphia is like. I was hoping that if I came to Philadelphia, I could stop by and visit you. I feel I got to know you some through all the letters you and your sister exchanged and thought how nice it would be to meet you in person.

With deep regards,
Hattie

When I finished reading, when the last echo of "Hattie" faded into the air, I remembered why I had put the letter away and never sent it. I remembered saying "wishful thinking" as I pushed the letter down to the bottom of the basket. The thought of leaving this place had been real enough. I wanted to do it. But wanting to do something and doing it are two different things. On top of that, being ready to do something is a whole other story. That letter, laying there in that basket, was like all those ragged pieces of cloth I had put away. Put away hoping to one day do something with them. Yet they were still there. Pieces amounting to nothing. There I sat realizing that Hattie is a woman whose life was full of remnants like the pieces of cloth that got tucked away. That now lay scattered over the floor.

"Why?" I screamed at myself, throwing the letter down. It didn't even flutter. It fell like a bird shot out of the sky and lay there staring at me with a blank look.

It's hard to explain what happened next. As if some tightly sealed door flung open releasing a room full of voices, I was being ravaged by so many feelings and thoughts I could hardly understand what they were. Everything was screaming at once. Torrents of words gushed from my mouth. I couldn't keep up with myself.

At one point I remember saying, "So this is it. I must be crazy."

But then, little by little, the chaos I was hearing started to make sense. It's as if my mind and my heart started to work together instead of against each other. Looking back, I know I had a darned good talk with myself. Some of my words sounded stupid to my ears. Some sounded sad. Many sounded angry. But at least I had words. At least I spoke out loud, even if only to myself. When I finished, I knew I wasn't crazy. I was alone. I was trapped. Trapped by my past. Held in place like all those idle pieces of fabric.

Trapped because I was scared. Scared of not being alone. Scared of not being crazy. Scared of doing anything but what I'd done my whole life. Scared of being.

You must understand, though the aloneness at times was unbearable, it was more bearable than trying not to be alone. It was more bearable than reaching out to someone and then losing them. Oh God, how the pain grabbed me then, twisting my insides, as I thought of Ellie, Jeremy, Zak, Steven, Sam, and Miss Jean. I saw each of them, there in the room with me, as clearly as the pieces of fabric strewn all over the floor. My arms tore away from my sides as I reached out to them only to see each one fade away. In desperation I grabbed at the pieces of cloth that had not disappeared.

"Sew. Sew. Sew." A voice was yelling at me.

"Piece them all together."

But I couldn't even thread a needle, my hands were shaking so bad. There on the floor I knelt, slumped over. My shadow falling over the pieces of fabric I clutched, which were soaking up my sobs. How I wished someone would take me and sew me into the quilt that I could not make.

It was dark out when I finally rose off the floor. I couldn't see the colors anymore, but I could feel the different pieces of fabric slipping off of me as I stood up. I was alone. All I had was myself. My hand reached up to my face. My fingers slowly brushed over my forehead, my eyes, my nose, my mouth. They slipped down my chin to my neck. Then my hand moved down over my breast. There it stopped and waited. The strong beat was there. My chest rose and fell. I was alive.

That night, before I drifted off to sleep, as the night air was flowing in and out of the open window, I heard my voice whisper, "I'm alive. I'm not crazy."

And then it said, "The reason I didn't sew those pieces of cloth together is because I didn't want to do it."

Lacking Friendship

Though people talk about friendship, I believe many of them don't really understand what the word means. I had some friends, but few real friends. The people in our town liked to get together and have fun. They would sit and joke and laugh and pick on others and eat and drink for hours at a time. I would be there with Harry. Yet over hours of this type of getting together, nothing touched the heart or anything inside me. I got tired of this socializing real fast. But I kept doing it because that's what everybody expected.

Harry used to be good at socializing. He was one of those men that everyone thought was real entertaining. When the conversation began to dwindle, Harry would say something or do something to get it going again. He always had some story to tell about the places he worked and the people he met. Sometimes I knew he was lying, but what did it matter? The others would listen. If it was something exciting he was telling, I could see the blood starting to rush. The men would start moving around more, voices would get louder, and one by one the women would slip away. It didn't matter what the men were talking about. It wasn't so much the topic of conversation that would send the women in different directions, it was the rising excitement that never failed to lead to some kind of trouble. Eventually that rushing blood would just make someone fly off the handle.

In our town there was a fine line between men having fun and getting excited, and men acting like wild animals. The women knew this. You would think that all of us women, knowing this and seeking an escape, would gather together and talk about things. That rarely happened. Silence was an unspoken rule. And so, as the women left the group of men and came upon each other—each one of them holding a dreaded anticipation or outright fear—they would say things like, "So, how are the children?" or "It's so unbearably hot today!" or "Have you seen the Sears Roebuck catalog?"

No one wanted to talk about anything that stirred the soul. That's why I had few real friends. Early on, Adelphia had taught me about what real friendship could be like. She and I would talk not only with our mouths, but with our hearts and our minds. I liked feeling like I was sharing myself when I was with a woman friend. But for that to happen I had to trust her. The way gossip flew in our town, trust was a flimsy thing. It seemed to wear quicker than the clothes people wore out. It's not that I wasn't interested in having friends, it's just that there were few, if any, women in our town that knew what real friendship was about. People here saw things as they needed to have them be. Like Harry, for example. The townsfolk all saw him as a hardworking man who came home just as often as he could. They saw him as a helpful man who was willing to lend a hand to his neighbors when they put up barns or went looking for livestock that got through a broken fence. They saw him as a husband and father who provided for his wife and youngins. They saw him as a man who liked to have fun at the gatherings. None of them ever said anything to me that would tell me they knew what Harry was really like.

There were times when I so wished I could talk to another woman about what was happening. Like that one time Harry held my hand over the fire because he didn't like the type of food I had fixed. He held my hand there until I felt pain and smelt burning flesh. I refused to let out a scream. He just laughed. As he pushed me away he twisted my arm even more. That night, after he had gone to bed, I took care of my hand. I put salve on it and wrapped it in a cloth. It pained me so but the pain in my heart was worse. The pain of my choosing him as a husband was worse. He was an awful man. I was glad he was gone away a lot because those times gave me a chance to gather my strength. During those days I would just keep saying, "Hattie, you gotta keep going."

A man can do anything he wants to his wife. There are no laws about that. I knew of a woman whose husband maimed her, and no one said anything except, "Poor thing. She should not have aggravated him so. She should've known better." He axed off her hand above the wrist. It was a punishment because she had lost her temper and snapped at him. This poor woman had eight little ones to take care of and he took away one of her hands. Men can be so cruel.

Harry was often cruel, but sometimes even Harry could be what I'd call nice. One day I remember he came home with flowers for me. It surprised me, it made me happy, and it made me start thinking that maybe he was changing. But before the day was done, he ended up stomping the flowers into the ground and calling me awful names because the sheets on the bed hadn't been freshly washed for his arrival. He was really mean. But at least I didn't get my hand cut off. At least that didn't happen to me.

Gathering and Holding

I went to a soothsayer once. It happened at a time when I didn't even see my life as a life. It was somewhere in between Jeremy's death and Sam's arrival. "Somewhere in between," though, means little to me because years drifted by in that space of time. In a way I thought it was a silly idea to seek out a fortune-teller, but Adelphia encouraged me to go.

"This isn't about fortune," she said. "This is about life." I thought Adelphia could have done the same for me. She insisted that she could not. Though she herself had a gift for knowing things, she said that she was too attached to me. Some things were not meant to pass between us. She said that she was my midwife and she was my friend, and that certain "knowings," as she called them, I was meant to get from others. So I went.

It was a cold, cold day. I bundled myself up from head to foot and wrapped a cloth like a scarf around my face. It wasn't a scarf. It was meant to be something larger. It was something I had started piecing together from bits of fabric a long time before. I had pulled it out of the trunk where I stored things that weren't used much, or things that were not yet what they were supposed to be. I couldn't remember what my intentions were for this piece of work, but on this day I needed to keep warm and so a scarf it became.

This type of cold weather was unusual in these parts. But unusual things did happen. Like my not being able to get a stain out, now that was unusual. Or a married woman taking a lover, now that was unusual and in the town I lived in it was near impossible. Anyway, I believed that if we paid more attention to all that goes on around us we would find many unusual things happening. We might also find that some things that we thought were unusual really were not, or that sometimes usual things changed their pattern—didn't happen as often—so then they became unusual. But here I go again, rambling on and getting off the track.

That cold day I walked five miles to Ada's house. I was told it was set way up in the woods. Woods that I hardly ever walked in. One might think, considering there was not too much up in those woods, that they were hardly ever walked by anyone. Yet the surprisingly well-worn path I followed told me that many a woman, at some point in her life, had journeyed to Ada the Soothsayer's house. Had at some time been driven by a desperate need to be given a sign or bit of hope. Something, anything, that could be placed in the palm of the hand and remind that hand it still knew how to gather and hold things.

When I got to where I was supposed to be, I found myself looking at a small hut standing between two huge trees. The sides of the shack were sunk in by the tree trunks pressing against them. It seemed like the trees and the shack were part of each other. Adelphia had told me to just walk into the place upon my arrival, as Ada was quite deaf and would not hear my knock.

"She'll know you're on your way," Adelphia had said, "so just go on in."

As I went up the stairs that hardly resembled stairs at all—there were more holes than planks, holes big enough for my feet to get stuck in if they made a wrong step—I wondered if this was worth doing. What if she couldn't hear what I said to her or asked of her? And I wasn't even sure I would ask her anything. I creaked through the door, or maybe the door creaked through me. I wasn't sure of anything except that something creaked loudly as I pushed the door open and closed it behind me. On my walk to this place, stones kept getting stuck in a couple holes in the soles of my shoes. I had to keep stopping to pull them out. As I stepped into the shack, I realized I still held one stone in my hand and was clutching it tightly.

Before I was able to look around the dimly lit room, I heard Ada say, "Come in closer. Show me what you hold." I followed the voice. She was sitting across the room in a chair that was more like a stool with one wooden plank running up the back. Behind her was a stove that shed the only light in the room. She was very small. Her frail, shrunken form was like that of a child. Long, gray-black hair came down from the sides of her head. Yet the top of her head seemed nearly free of hair except for a few short, black as black could be, strands that had a curl to them. A curl that the rest of her hair did not have. Her voice did not match the small body it came out of. Her voice was deep, though not with the hoarseness that sometimes comes with age. Her sound stayed in the room even after her words had been spoken. It was like an echo traveling through an endless cave.

As I went up to her, she pointed at my fisted hand. I put it out to her. She gently rolled open my fingers, unlocking the fist. My hand released the stone and she took it. The stone was gray, somewhat squared, flat on one side while rounded on the other, and had speckles of black in it. She took it from me, gazed at it, and laid it on the little wooden crate that sat on the floor between us. Pointing to a chair, which I could see had once been a very fancy chair, she motioned for me to sit. Remains of maroon velvet covered the seat. The frame looked to be mahogany wood with fancy carvings throughout it. In the time it took me to lower myself into the chair, I thought about how someone had decided to carve this piece of wood, putting his effort into making it into a chair. Had it been another day, he may have decided to make the wood into a table or a desk or one of many other things. Had that happened, then what would I be sitting on instead?

"Why do I think such silly thoughts?" sounded in my head and reminded me to stop thinking. What did it matter anyway? The mahogany had been turned into this chair and nothing else. A chair in which I was now sitting.

"The midwife told me you'd come," Ada said.

I could see spaces in her mouth between pebbles of what remained of her teeth. I found it unusual that she made none of the whistling sounds that others make when teeth are missing. Her words came out of her mouth solidly and fluidly. Even somewhat sweetly, I thought, though I didn't know why.

I reached into my pocket to retrieve the coins I had brought to give her in exchange for whatever she could tell me. The coins were mixed with a few hard candies I had also for some unknown reason stuck in my pocket. Before I could pull them out, she briskly waved her right hand back and forth, stopping me. That's when I noticed the half finger on her right hand. I would have started thinking about why half of it was missing, except her voice interrupted my wondering.

"Only after we speak will you know what to leave with me," she said.

Motioning to the hat and coat that had bundled me against the cold, and to the scarf-like cloth that now shrouded my neck, she added, "Unveil yourself."

"Ahhh," she drooled caringly as my thick hair was let

loose from beneath the hat and the cloth. She reached over and touched my hair. Her bony fingers slipped down a ways between the strands then floated away from me and settled in her lap.

"You have been looking for someone long gone," she said to me.

Then she lifted a glass jar from the top of the crate and told me to cup my hands. It was filled with many small, different-colored pebbles. She shook the jar, rattling the contents around, then spilled some of the pebbles into my hands. How many? I don't know. All I know is they held heat. As they warmed me, remains of the outside chill disappeared. Indeed, I was so quickly warmed up that I began to feel hot. I could have stripped off all my clothes. That silly thought actually slipped through my mind.

"Hold them," Ada said to me.

"Roll them in your hands. Feel them. Let them feel you."

Her voice was encouraging, instructing, and calming. It also seemed endless. Even when the words stopped coming out of her mouth, I kept hearing them. I felt that I could have sat there for days holding those pebbles and she would have sat there with me. She made me feel like nothing else mattered. She seemed to have no concern for time. I, though, was not willing to get lost in time. Getting lost in time was too close to being a madwoman, to being crazy. You see, for many months I felt I had been mad. I had been what others called crazy. Then, when I finally stopped being mad, I stopped being altogether. My body continued to breathe, my heart must have continued to beat, but little else would have indicated I was alive. When I finally started to move again, I felt it was just my body that stirred. It did what it needed to do and I just went along with it. During this madness I lost all track of time. All this had happened after Jeremy died.

As unforgettable as the events of that terrible day were, I had made myself forget. The more I lied to the people of the town about where Jeremy was and the more I began to believe that he really was off traveling with his pa, the more something inside of me grew wild. I would get up in the morning with every intention of using the washboard and washtub, but would instead find myself wandering into the woods. The woods into which Harry had carried Jeremy's body. But by this time I had already forgotten that.

In the woods I became like something wild that lived amongst the trees. Every sense I had—my eyes, my ears, my taste, my touch, and my smell—was at attention as I prowled. I was aware that I searched for something, but couldn't grasp what it was. I would reach a certain spot and smell the air, and then crawl over the ground. My eyes examined every twig, every stone, every leaf. Then I would begin to furiously dig at the earth. I would dig until my hands bled. I would dig until I couldn't dig any longer. Then I'd still continue to dig. I would dig until from somewhere a voice would say, "Enough." Only then would I stop.

This happened over and over again. My hands became the color of soil. My body took on the scent of damp leaves. The blue eyes I was born with turned brown like the bark of the trees. My knees became hard as stone. They became like the rocks that made deep indentations in them as I knelt, clawing at the dirt. As time wore on, I could not tell the difference between where the rocks ended and where my knees began. My voice took on the grunts and groans of branches that a fierce wind threatens to snap away from the trunks that hold them. And over the skin of my body, patches of moss appeared. Growing. Spreading over me.

I can't tell you how long I was like this. I can't tell you how many holes my hands dug. I can't tell you what season it was. All I know is that one day things changed. As I dug another hole, I again heard the voice. Instead of its usual "Enough," it said "Jeremy's not here." Suddenly, as if a curtain had been lifted, I saw the lie disappearing. Being told who it was that I was searching for made me remember who it was that I was searching for. Made me remember that awful day. Made me remember at least some of the truth I knew. The frantic desperation eased and the madwoman was stilled.

I stopped wandering through the woods. I stopped digging the earth. Everything just stopped. Knowing it was Jeremy who I was searching for meant knowing what an impossible search it was. Hopelessness requires no effort. For days I did nothing except breathe. I did not hear. I did not see. I did not touch. I did not smell. I did not taste. The only person who had the courage to come near me, to come near this woman who was acting very unusual, was Adelphia. She took care of me. She didn't know what was ravaging my soul. Still she took care of me. She didn't ask for explanation and I could not explain. Even so, she took care of me. She took care of me until I was able to do more than just breathe. She took care of me until I started to move.

The whole time I sat holding the small stones, they continued to warm me. Finally, Ada put out her hands for the pebbles, wanting them back. I brought my cupped hands over hers and let the pebbles slip carefully into her palms.

"Ahhh," once again sounded from somewhere deep inside her. She closed her eyes and held the stones. Then she spoke.

"You could forever search the ground, digging and clawing through the earth, and not find where your son lays. Hattie, you know he is dead. You saw him die. Trust that if you ever step on the spot of earth he is beneath you will know it. But don't look aimlessly, for you will not find what you seek in desperation."

Many seasons had passed since that awful day. No one knew about Harry killing Jeremy. No one. I had held that secret and it had held me. It was wrapped around my heart tightly like a vine that nearly strangles in its need to cling to something.

Ada continued, "The truth is in what you know. In what you have known since that dreadful day. The madness came not from knowing the truth, but from the lie. From keeping the secret."

A gurgle rose from somewhere in my throat then. I gagged and began to retch as the vine unleashed its grip and climbed up my windpipe, sprouting its tentacles out of my mouth. As it emptied out of me, the heap of vine grew larger and larger, nearly overflowing the small crate. When the roots finally emerged, Ada's small arms quickly scooped up the pile of twisted shoots and stuffed them into the belly of the stove. Loud crackles filled the room as the erupting flames raised shadows from their hiding places.

I don't know how long the crackles and the shadows roamed the room. I don't know how long Ada and I sat there. I don't know if my body moved. All I know was that I kept making sounds, though no words came. Then the tears, like a hail of pebbles, spilled out of my eyes. As they fell, they rolled over my arms, over my lap, and onto the wooden floor. The more I cried, the faster Ada reached after each one, gathering them into her jar.

She spoke of many things to me that afternoon. Even though I don't remember all of what she said, I know that somewhere inside of me I remember everything. I remember bits and pieces of her words and the pictures they brought to my mind. I remember the movements of her body. I remember the way she cocked her head to the side as she listened to something coming from beyond. Something only she heard. I remember how she knew things about me that I didn't know, at least not with my everyday mind. I remember how she took my hand in hers and looked down at my palm, and how her fingers moved over all those lines. I remember feeling the jagged edges of her nails scrape against my palm. Old skin slipping off revealing the lines hidden beneath.

I sat. I listened. I watched. When she was finished, she gently laid her palm against mine. When she removed it, I felt as if she had left something there in my hand. Yet it was nothing my eyes could see. That day she told me that I would never see Zak again. She also told me that I would carry another youngin. I didn't believe her. It took all I had to just hold and believe in the past she reminded me of. I was not willing yet to believe in a future. I was more concerned with trying to understand how I was to hold that invisible something Ada's old wrinkled fingers had placed in my hand. Something gathered and given to me that I gripped between tightly held fingers, not wanting to let it go. And yet I knew that for one reason or another something would require the use of the hand, and then, when the hand could no longer hold, where would that invisible thing go?

As if reading my mind, Ada said, "There are many ways

to hold what one gathers. As long as you're willing to gather and to hold what you gather, you will find a place for it." I still didn't understand. But I believed her.

When it was time to leave—nothing had been said to indicate that our meeting was over, yet each of us knew it was—I looked at the old, wise woman and I thanked her. Once again she brought up her right hand and waved it back and forth. Not dismissing me, but telling me there was no need for thanking. It was what it was. We were who we were. What happened, happened. What was spoke, was spoke. I reached into my pocket and pulled out the candy. I picked up the pieced-together cloth that I had worn as a scarf. I reached for the squared speckled rock. I handed them all to Ada. She took them from me without question. The whole time I had been there, though her eyes had sometimes shown a twinkle, she had not smiled. But as she held my gifts, her lips parted just a bit and a couple extra creases appeared at the edges of her mouth.

"Oh, how I love candy," she exclaimed in a voice more suited to her child-sized body.

Then, in the more familiar deep voice, she added, "Sweetness. Such a simple pleasure. Once you've known what bitter tastes like, then you know what sweet means. You've known both. Don't ever forget that. Don't let bitterness erase sweetness out of your life."

As I headed home, the cold didn't matter. The woods didn't matter. The long walk didn't matter. I felt wrapped in Ada's voice and in the warmth those little stones had sent through all of me. I knew I had learned something. Something great about life, about the unknown, and about the unusual. Something I had no words for. I looked down at my hand. It was open, the fingers unclenched. Yet I knew I had not lost what it held.

A Not So Silly Fairy Tale

One night, a time when Jeremy and Ellie were still alive, I had put them to bed and gone to my room. Harry wasn't home. I pulled on my yellowed-white nightgown. I brushed my hair, which I didn't usually do at night, and I got into bed. I found myself propping my pillow up against the headboard and just sitting there. I began remembering how as a little girl I often wished to be tucked in and read to. That night, silly as it seemed, I decided to tell myself a bedtime story. Maybe I was practicing storytelling for when Jeremy and Ellie would be old enough to tell stories to. I didn't know what I was doing or why. I didn't have a story in mind, but the words just came out of me.

Once upon a time, Hattie, there was a dog and a cockroach and they both lived in different spaces in the same house. The master of the house treated the dog well most of the time, but hated the cockroach. The dog could see this whenever the roach showed itself, which wasn't very often. The cockroach knew it risked its life every time it came out of hiding. But sometimes it just had to come out. It got tired and bored of crawling in the cupboard or below the floorboards where it lived. The dog, on the other hand, liked living in the house. Even though, every once in a while, he also got tired of the same surroundings, the dog never thought of going elsewhere.

The dog saw the cockroach a lot more than the master did. Sometimes he would see the roach scurrying across the floor only to disappear into a tiny space. At first, as a pup, the dog would jump and run to the spot the roach suddenly entered. Even though the roach was gone from view, he would sniff and paw at the spot. But as time went by, the dog stopped doing this and would just watch. He watched the master try to stomp on the roach when he spotted him. The dog didn't understand why the master found the roach bothersome. He wasn't very big, maybe an inch or two in size.

One day, having decided to put all of his effort into once and for all getting rid of the roach, the master threw one of his fits. The dog lay on the floor and cautiously watched the goings on. He knew that the master could be very mean. Once in a while he himself felt a swift kick or whack. Most of the time though, the master was decent to the dog. He fed him. He took him with him when he went into town. And he trusted the dog to guard the house when he was not around. As the master threw pots and pans about the room in his search for the roach, the dog knew that this time the master was angrier than he'd ever seen him. The dog slowly retreated to a corner of the room and sat quietly. All the while the master ranted and raved like a lunatic. When he grabbed an ax and started hacking away at the floorboards, the dog knew something was very wrong. The master had reached a point he had not seen him at before.

Suddenly the dog felt something move near his tail, which was tucked into the furthest spot in the corner. The roach was coming out of one of those nearly invisible openings he often disappeared into. The roach stayed there, safely tucked beneath the dog's tail, as the master fell deeper and deeper into his crazy fit of rage.

By the end of the night the master lay dead on the floor. His fit had killed him. This whole time the dog had still not moved from the corner of the room, and the roach was still under his tail. In the center of the floor was a gaping hole big enough for a man to crawl into. The dog finally went over and sniffed the dead master. The roach scurried across the floor and disappeared into the huge hole. For once, the dog wanted to see where the roach had escaped to all these years. He looked down into the hole. All he saw was earth, bits of stone, and pieces of wood. This was the roach's world.

The dog realized that the master had his world as did the roach. "What do I have?" the dog wondered. He couldn't go where the roach went, and he no longer had the master.

I didn't know how to end this tale. I also knew it was not a bedtime story I would ever tell Ellie and Jeremy. I scooted down under the quilt and tried to sleep, but it took a while for sleep to come. Even though I had stopped telling the story to myself, I couldn't stop thinking about the dog and his wondering, "What do I have?"

Keeping Things Separate

I should be the last one talking about love. Not that I haven't felt love, for I did. Many times. But the love I have known has always been so closely connected with loss that it's hard to separate the two. It's hard to enjoy one without feeling the pain of the other. I loved Ellie and I lost her. She left me. I loved Jeremy and he was taken from me. I loved Sam and I let him go without me. I loved Steven without a chance of sharing that love with him.

I loved my ma and my pa and my sisters, but that love seems lifetimes ago. And after I moved away with Harry, I began to question that love. That attachment that is born with family. I sometimes wonder how one knows what love is if it involves an attachment to responsibility. At one time I actually believed that I loved Harry. Now I know I didn't love him. I wanted to love him. I thought I should love him. In time I understood the difference between love and commitment, love and responsibility, genuine love and expected love.

The love I felt deep in my heart came to me, through me, and from me. Weaving in and out in moments of time. Yet always somehow interrupted by my having to do other things. So here I sit, wondering how is it that I am able to hold the love that was given to me through my youngins, through Sam, through those people—people like Adelphia—who happened into my life and loved me too. Why do some feelings stay with us and others disappear?

I'm folding things. Sitting in front of open drawers. Pulling out whatever is there, whatever is waiting for me. In my hands I hold a little white frock I would dress Ellie in. I sewed it myself. Fixing it up in such a way that I could slip it over Ellie's twisted little body without untwisting her too much. I remember struggling not to cause her pain as I would reach into that space between her arms and her bony chest that was hardly a space at all. Her arms were like tiny, featherless wings snuggled up against the rest of her. So frail that I was afraid they would snap if I moved them too much. But Adelphia encouraged me to get into that space. She told me to put cornstarch there.

"Rub her skin good with it," she would say. She scared me some because she said that I needed to keep the skin on Ellie's arms from growing into the skin of her chest.

"When two things are held so close, without any room to breathe, well, one day they may just cling together for good and you may not be able to find that space any more," Adelphia said.

I didn't really believe this would happen, but I wasn't going to have it happen in case there was some truth to what she was telling me. So I remained faithful in using that cornstarch while trying not to cause Ellie pain. Hoping that she would keep loving me even though I sometimes did things that made her cry out.

One Little Hairpin

It's odd how one little thing, one tiny object, can make my mind wander into places long forgot. I was putting my hair up one day in my usual quick fashion. A few fast brush strokes, which never quite got out all the tangles, and then twisting it around my fingers and securing it in the back of my head with hairpins. Hairpins that were held in a small wooden box that used to hold my pa's cigars. I'd had that box since I was nine years old. That was before I ever used hairpins. I can't remember what I used to store in that box, but I know it was something special. Anyway, back then before I used hairpins, first my ma and then my sisters, who took over the chore, would do my hair into braids. Always finishing up by using strands they had plucked from my head to twist around the end of the braids to keep them from unraveling. They must have pulled out hundreds of strands of hair doing that. I used to say "Ow" when Ma first started plucking out the hairs. And sometimes when the tangles wouldn't budge, I'd even cry a bit, but I quickly stopped. It did no good. They just kept doing what they were doing. When Ellie was first born I swore that if I ever put her hair into braids I would use ribbon or even pieces of string to tie off the ends. I would never pluck her hair from her head and cause her to cry out in pain.

But let me get back to the hairpin. I had picked up the last hairpin I needed to put my hair up. Before my hand could bring it up to my head, I found myself looking at it closely. I looked at its two ends and at the little wiggles in the thin strands of metal.

"Ma used hairpins for all kinds of things and was always running out of them," I found myself saying. Then I went from looking at the hairpin to staring at it. As it became blurred I felt myself shudder.

Why would a hairpin make me shudder? I wondered while still able to think clearly. Then I stopped thinking clearly. It was as if the hairpin was hypnotizing me. I remember once playing with my sisters and one of them started swinging a necklace in front of my eyes saying, "You will go to sleep." She didn't put me to sleep even though I tried really hard to do what she wanted. But now it was happening and I didn't want it to happen. Even though I wasn't going to sleep, I knew I was going into one of those places in my mind that made me feel foggy.

I could hear a man's voice saying, "Hold still." It was Mr. Beasley. The man who owned the store in town. I could feel him grabbing me. I could hear his breathing, quick and loud and wet-sounding. I felt my heart beating really fast as I got more and more scared. I didn't know what I had done wrong. All I did was go to the store to buy my ma the hairpins she needed.

Now that I wasn't "just a little thing," Ma let me take the long walk into town by myself. I liked going into town not so much because of where I was heading but because of all the things I might see on the way there. I would pick up pretty rocks or flowers that overnight seemed to pop up along the road. Once in a while a chipmunk would scurry by and hide under a large root or a rock and I'd try to coax it out of its hiding place. There were always plenty of squirrels and dogs roaming around and I'd talk to them as we passed each other. Though the squirrels kept their distance, the dogs would come up to me, sniff my hand, and sometimes walk along with me for a while.

When I got to the store, Mr. Beasley said he had the hairpins out in the back room. He told me to come with him. I remember thinking he was wrong because I could see a few boxes of hairpins sitting on the shelf where I knew they would be. But I listened to him and followed him down the aisle to the back of the store.

"Come in here, Hattie," he said. "You'll be surprised at all the things I have back here."

So I went through the door.

"I have some special candy," he said as he closed the door behind me.

It was dark in there and I waited for him to turn on the light. But before I knew what was happening he grabbed me and started putting his hands under my dress and into my underpants. I didn't know what to do.

All I remember saying was "I just want the hairpins. Please, sir. That's all I'm supposed to get."

Next thing I knew, the bell above his door that jingled every time someone came in or out started jingling. That's when he let go of me.

"Go out the back door," he ordered as he went into the store.

I got up really quick and very quietly, so that no one would hear, and ran out the back door. My bare feet hardly made any sound. I smoothed my dress down. I was glad that my hair was in braids and not all messed up. You would think that I ran all the way home. I didn't. I stood outside worrying about going home without the hairpins. I knew Ma would be mighty mad 'cause she really needed them. I thought of walking back into the store and buying them, except the coin that I had held on to so tightly through my whole walk was no longer in my hand. I must have let go of it in that dark room. So, without the coin and without the hairpins, I went home and took a licking when I told Ma that I had lost the money while walking to the store. As she strapped me, she said I was good for nothing. While the strap whipped over me, slapping at my behind and my legs, I tried to keep my dress from flying up, and so my arms caught quite a few hits. It didn't so much matter that Ma was hitting me 'cause I didn't even feel it.

Two times that day I fought to keep my dress down. First with Mr. Beasley, to keep him from tugging at my underpants, and then with my ma, so that she wouldn't see I wasn't wearing underpants. I guess she was right. I was good for nothing. I lost her coin and I lost my underpants. I don't remember that man ever pulling them off. I can't imagine what happened to them. I'll tell you, I had a way of getting into trouble.

Funny how one little hairpin held in my hand made me remember such a thing. I put the hairpin back into the cigar box. Then I started taking out the hairpins that were already in place holding up my hair, and throwing them into the box. My fingers searched for every last one of them knowing that those hairpins had a way of hiding. When I could feel no more of them and my hair flowed loosely over my shoulders, I grabbed the bunch of it and braided it into the tightest braid I could. Then I plucked a strand of hair from my head and twisted it, over and over again, around the end of the braid. When I was done I went downstairs and didn't give any of it another thought.

Young and Naive

I get to rambling on with my words. I forget when things happened. I even forget how old I am sometimes. I met Harry when I was fifteen. I was a real young thing then. Young and naive. Not that I hadn't already seen what people do to each other. I had. But it didn't make much sense to me.

My mama, soon after my real daddy died, married his first cousin. His name was Oscar. He was the only daddy I clearly remember. Back then Elizabeth was the youngest of us sisters. She was almost two. When she was four she died of something that Mama said attacked her lungs and strangled the breath out of her. That's all I remember her saying. Oscar stepped right in and became a husband and father. My mama said she was so happy to have a man who seemed to love us like we were his own and who took us in. I thought I was kind of lucky to have had two daddies instead of just one. Sometimes I got my two daddies mixed up into one. Sometimes I forgot that the daddy I grew up with wasn't my real father. That kick to the head didn't kill my real father right away, but he died soon after. I just forgot about it. I was still so little and I just forgot. I probably just didn't want to remember.

My second daddy never scolded us. The only thing he'd do if we were misbehaving was talk in a real low voice and let us know we were a disappointment to him. I thought my mama was mean to him sometimes. Sometimes I wondered why he married her.

I didn't understand my mama. She was odd sometimes. When she had bad days people would call her "the crazy woman" instead of "Oscar's wife." Sometimes she would sit all day in a chair not saying anything to anyone. At the end of the day my daddy would help her up to bed. The floor where she sat was scuffed from her shoes moving back and forth, over and over, hours at a time.

One time my mama told us she was making soup. She went out into the garden and scooped a bunch of dirt and grass into a pot, and mixed it up with water and put spices into it. You should have seen our faces watching what she was doing. When Daddy saw what she had fixed for supper, he didn't lose his temper. He just told her we weren't hungry. That night, after he put her to bed, he gave us all pieces of bread with honey to eat and some milk to drink. We didn't understand why Mama did this kind of stuff. We just knew she had bad days.

Another time I remember was when we went shopping with her. She had put on layers of clothes, insisting it was real cold outside. She made us put on heavy shoes and sweaters and scarves. It was a hot summer day and the group of us, Mama and her stupid daughters, walked to the store like that. People kept looking at us and shaking their heads, and then looking away. Mama just kept walking as if this was the most normal thing to do. Like it really was cold outside. We were all so hot and sweating. But Mama was moving her legs fast like she was trying to keep warm. Like all those clothes she was bundled up in weren't enough to make the cold go away. In the store she told us we could each have a piece of candy. But when it was time to pay, she had no money with her. The man in the store looked at her in a mean way and told her to tell her husband to do the shopping next time. I could tell he was thinking that she was really crazy. It was awful embarrassing to have a sometimes crazy mama.

Most of the time though, she was like everybody else. Except Mama didn't have many women friends. I think the women in the town were afraid of her. The menfolk, who would come by and visit with Pa, would sometimes bring their wives with them. Even though Mama was usually kind and mannerly, it still wasn't enough to make the women feel at home. They would sit rigid in their chairs while making small talk and glancing over to where their husbands were.

I felt sorry for my mama.

It Took Time

I often wondered if there was a time I could have changed my life. I'm talking about a change that would have taken me away from all that I lived here. All that I hurt here. All that I endured here. When I was younger, was there ever a moment that would have changed my life, a time when I could have left or run away? Looking back, I guess there were many moments when that could have happened. But I didn't leave and I didn't run away. I had nothing to run away to. Everything I had, everything I knew, was here. And I was always afraid.

My mama never encouraged any thinking that went past family and home. Never. Actually, no one I knew growing up did. No one, that is, except for my friend Jake, and that's another story. We were all somehow rooted to the ground we were born on. I was born in the summer. One of the hottest summers people recalled. My mama said that the water that gushed from her insides before I came out was nothing compared to the sweat gushing from her face that summer. She often told me how people dropped like flies in the heat. Everything slowed down that year. Crops withered under the hot sun. Stories have it that when the rain finally fell it was hot and the drops would evaporate before hitting the ground. The only place one might find a cool spot was in the woods where the trees were so thick they stopped the sun from coming in.

Mama said that I was a crying baby. She said I cried most of the time. She blamed my crying on the heat. Because of how red I got from screaming and from the rash that broke out over my whole body because of the heat, and from who knows what else, she said I looked like a "flaming tomato." Mama had an odd way of putting words together. I get the feeling she was at a loss as to what to do with me when I was a baby.

She said the only way I could be soothed was by her taking me into the woods. This, of course, she had little time for. But some days, even though to walk was a chore, she would take me and walk to the woods. She would spread a blanket down on the ground under the trees and lay me on it. She said that she would sit there and watch me become quiet and ease into sleep. She would sit there and be glad that, in this terrible summer heat, I was an excuse for her to feel some rest and comfort. It made me sad to think that Mama would not have done that for herself if I hadn't been there as an excuse for her to escape the awful heat. That's one of the lessons she taught me. Doing for others always came first. It was more important than doing for yourself. Yourself was not worth much attention. Was not worth caring about if you weren't doing something for others. Mama's days were filled with taking care of others. Whatever little time she had left to take her own breaths was spent wondering how tomorrow she would take care of others. It was no wonder that I could not imagine life away from family. Away from all I knew. Away from all I had been taught.

I don't often remember Mama as seeming happy. I rarely remember her being joyful. I mostly remember Mama always doing something while talking about what she would be doing next. There was something in me, though, that told me not to stop feeling joy. Not to get so lost in doing that I would forget what joy was. So even when I found myself doing chores that were hard or that I didn't like doing, I would enter into places in my mind that were happy. I would think of the simplest, silliest things and laugh to myself. On hot summer days as I worked in the garden—I didn't enjoy gardening much—I would sometimes watch a bead of sweat start at my armpit and slip down my arm. I would follow its path wondering which way it would slip over my skin. Where would it take me? As often as I did this, I could never predict the exact path my sweat would flow. Sometimes two or three beads would come together. This silly watching game was especially interesting if my arms were covered with the dust of the earth. Then the paths the beads traveled remained etched in my arms until I rubbed them away.

My mama noticed how I lingered at doing chores. She

would start hollering if it took me longer than she thought it should take. She would lean out the window and yell at me to hurry up. She saw my lingering as laziness. She never understood that to keep holding on to joy I had to linger. This took time 'cause to be able to hold on to joy I first had to find it. That wasn't always easy.

I'm not going to lie to you and say I often knew joy. For a long time I didn't feel any. Especially after Ellie died and then when I lost my boys. But even at the worst times, I kept reminding myself that just because I wasn't feeling any joy didn't mean I didn't know how to. Though at times I may have appeared deadened to those who knew me, and even to myself when I happened to look in the mirror, I wasn't dead. I was just wrapped in a cocoon. My heart was deep inside in a place where it would not be hurt. In a place that allowed it to not be destroyed altogether.

Just Gray

I'm sitting right now in a little room. It's my room. I've paid for it. My bag is here. I've been here for a few weeks. My feet hurt. They swell during the day. Here in Philadelphia I have to wear shoes. When I come home after working I take them off. I walk barefoot in my room, but the soles of my feet crave the touch of the earth. The other day I stopped at a place where there was grass and I pulled off my shoes. My feet were so happy to be against the grass. But then, when I had to put my shoes back on, I could hardly do it. Those poor feet screamed as I stuffed them into the stiff leather. I limped all the way to this room.

When I got to Philadelphia, I found work quickly. I got a newspaper and went to every house that was listed, inquiring about work. I'm no longer a washwoman. I'm a cleaning woman now. I work for several different families. Cleaning their homes. Putting their things in order. I even got myself a cleaning woman's dress. It's gray. Just gray. And it fits. I try to spend the most time cleaning the rooms that have books. I've been reading little bits of a lot of books. I can't tell you the names because what I do is I grab a book, whatever catches my eye, for reasons I can't say. Then I just open it and read a page or look at pictures. The other day I was reading something about an Inquisitor. It's a long word. There were many long words in that page of reading. I understood some. I didn't understand some. But I read anyway.

Part 3

Through the Woods

Little by Little

There were more fancy clothes in Philadelphia than I would have ever imagined existed. I couldn't help but stare at the fancy suits on men and glorious dresses on women. In my first couple of months in this city I worked hard, many hours each day, and I saved my money. I saved nearly all that I made. I spent little on food. I would always try to eat my meal at one of the homes I worked in. Have something there to replenish me. In exchange for the rent I would have paid, I made an arrangement with the landlord to keep the hallways of the tenement clean and to sweep the front steps. A couple of times the landlord asked if I would be willing to include other duties into our arrangement like washing his clothes. "I am not a washwoman," I said to him. I saved my money so I could buy myself a decent dress for when I went to pay a visit to Lady Isabelle. Asking around I found out where she lived and was waiting for the right moment to make my way to her doorstep. As it happened, I didn't have to buy a dress.

One day, Mrs. Clark, the mistress of one of the families I worked for, was emptying her closet of garments she had tired of. "These are no longer fashionable," was the way she put it. As she was getting ready to drop one more dress onto the mountain of colors and fabrics that was nearly taking my breath away, she noticed me looking at the pile on the floor and at the dress she held. It was a very pretty navy blue dress. Its long sleeves puffed at the shoulder. There was a delicate white lace around the neckline and a sash at the waist. It wasn't as fancy a dress as some of the others that were heaped on the floor, but I liked it more.

She waved me closer to her and said kindly, "Hattie, we're about the same size. Might you like to have one of these dresses?"

Well, I have to tell you, I was quite surprised by her offer. Back home I wouldn't have considered accepting. Actually, back home people usually wore clothes until there was nothing left worth giving away.

I stood there and answered, "Yes. As a matter of fact, I would very much like to have one of those dresses. Thank you kindly."

"Which one would you like?" she asked, which surprised me a bit because I assumed she would pick one out herself and just hand it to me.

"That one, ma'am," I said pointing to the one she still held, the satiny deep blue fabric draped over her arm.

"Take it then," she said holding it out to me, "I hope it fits. But if not I'm sure you can alter it."

I walked over and took hold of the dress as it slipped

out of her arms. What a beautiful dress it was. Though I thought I should say more to her, the mistress seemed anxious to get on with her sorting. As soon as she had let go of this dress she turned back to the many dresses that still hung in her closet.

With her back to me she said, "You're welcome to try it on to see how it fits."

I looked at the tall oval mirror that stood in her room. I imagined putting the dress on, feeling its smooth fabric glide over my skin, then opening my eyes and seeing the dress over me. I knew that as I slipped the dress on I would have my eyes closed. I imagined standing there and seeing myself looking different. But I was embarrassed to get undressed in front of the mistress. I didn't want her to see my tattered undergarments. And I didn't want her to see me wearing the dress before I had time to see myself. Before I had time to get used to seeing myself. Also, I have to admit that I feared that if the dress didn't fit she might insist I take another instead. I wanted this one. And I knew that if it didn't fit right I would be able to make it fit.

"Thank you, ma'am, but I'll just get on with my cleaning," I said as I hurried out of her room. Holding cleaning supplies in one arm and the dress in the other, I headed to the library, which I had saved for last.

It's funny how little cleaning I really had to do. How much dust can gather in a few short days, especially when there isn't much to cause dust to gather? In this house it was just Mr. and Mrs. Clark. Their children were grown and living in their own homes. The hired help did not cause much dust to cling to things. Mrs. Clark usually kept all the windows closed. She hated the noise and the dirt coming in from the streets. Since there really was very little of anything to clean in this house, I sometimes felt like I should put things out of order. Anything to bring a bit of a change into Mrs. Clark's life. Though she was a nice and polite woman, she always had the same look on her face. It never changed. She never smiled. She never frowned. Her voice stayed the same. I could understand why she wanted to have so many pretty dresses and things in her house, but I also believed that she could have used more dust.

Anyway, I went into the library and quickly polished the furniture and then reached up to pick a red, leather-bound book off the fifth shelf. It was a fine-looking book. For a few minutes I just held it and looked at the cover that had swirly carvings around the edges with thin lines of gold running through them like little streams. I held it. I looked at it. I flipped it open, ready to read whatever passage was there. But when I looked at the words, they made no sense. Without warning I began to feel stupid and confused. My lack of understanding such fancy words reminded me how little I really knew. Reminded me that I could never fit into the world of fancy suits and fancy words. A world that often, like now, confused me. I'm not sure how many minutes I stood there feeling out of place before I began to laugh. You see, I wasn't stupid after all. This book was written in a different language. No wonder it made no sense to me. I closed it and gently stroked the cover before putting it back into the open slot. Then I breathed a sigh of relief.

After I finished straightening up the library and put away my cleaning supplies, I scooped up my beautiful dress and headed back home. Back to the room I called home even though it didn't feel like home. It felt like the station I had waited in for the train. It felt like the seat I sat in and slept on in the train. It felt like the hotel room I slept in the first night I arrived in Philadelphia. It felt like the lobby of that hotel where, after checking out of the room, I sat for a very long time trying to decide what to do next. It felt like all those places that were meant to be for only a while. But since this room was all I had, I called it home.

I was glad it wasn't too far a walk because I was wanting to try on this dress. How can I describe what I felt putting it on? Having clothes slipped over my body was not anything that brought me pleasure. I wore clothes that had a purpose. I didn't often even think about what I was putting on or how I looked in it. But this piece of clothing was different than any other I had ever owned. To me it was about looking nice. It was about fitting well. It was about looking like a lady. It was about being different than I had ever been.

When it touched my skin, I felt like I was covered by the soft petals of a full-bloomed flower. This dress made me look taller and straighter. The long sleeves hid my crooked arms. The deep shade of blue made my eyes look bluer than I remembered them. It did need a few minor changes that I knew I could manage. All this I saw by holding my hand mirror at different angles and by propping it up on the cabinet that stood near the bed. Even though I was only seeing parts of the dress and me at any one time, like puzzle pieces I put them together and decided that the dress and I fit quite well. In a way I was glad that there wasn't a big mirror in my room. It might have been too much of a shock to see myself in that dress all at once.

"Little by little." That's what my grammie used to say to me whenever I was getting used to something new or struggling with something old.

"Little by little, Hattiedear," she would say. "Give it time. Things will work themselves out."

What If?

I loved my thick, chestnut-colored hair. My fingers would disappear into it as I lifted it away from my face.

Somehow I didn't notice the gray hairs happening. Did they come one by one, or did they just one day appear? All I know is that I suddenly noticed they were there. The chestnut-colored hair was no longer as I had known it. "Am I now an old woman?" I asked myself while examining what seemed an unfamiliar head of hair.

Yet my face showed few wrinkles. My hands were still strong. My body still stood tall, unlike many of the women in town whose dresses I hemmed shorter as their bodies shriveled. From the back they looked like children. It was when they turned to me that their wrinkled faces reminded me that they were closer to their graves than to birth. Sometimes I feared growing old. At those times I was glad that I lived alone so that there was no one to remind me that time was passing. Few things in my house changed over the years. Sometimes I would sit in the front room of the house and imagine no time had passed. It was when I happened to glance at a calendar that I would be reminded that my youngins had been here and gone. That had things been different, they would be older now, which of course meant I would be older, too. It was hard to imagine my youngins older than how I remembered them.

What would I have kept Ellie in had she not died so young? Would she have been comfortable in a bed, or would I have built a bigger box for her to lie in every year? Where would I have kept it? Or maybe she would not have grown bigger. Maybe, knowing that her ma would eventually not be able to lift her and hold her in those crooked arms had she grown into the size of a normal youngin, she would have stayed small.

Throughout my life I entertained silly thoughts like this, sometimes imagining a courage that maybe only existed because it would never be tested. Maybe I would not have had the courage and strength to continue taking care of Ellie had she lived. Maybe I would have tired of giving her goat's milk. Maybe I would have begun to see her toothless smile as ugly. Maybe God took her when he did because he knew that I would not have mothered her properly or as caringly, had she gotten bigger. Always looking to me for her every need while lying helplessly in her box.

I don't know why I am talking like this about things that did not happen, except that it forces me to think about how I may have been had things happened differently. And just as I suddenly discovered that my hair had turned mostly gray, I also suddenly began examining the "what ifs" of my life.

What if Harry had been a decent man, husband, and father? What if Steven had not died? What if I had not been a washwoman? What if Sam had not come into my life? What if Jeremy had not played with the marble? I could make myself crazy with all these thoughts. Yet it was like something was pulling at the hairs in my head and each one held a "What if?" This train of thought held me in my house for a couple of days as I went through all the "what ifs" I could come up with. It seemed there was no end to the "what ifs" of my past. And then this thing happened that made me believe in miracles. Not like a vision of something God sent that one reads about in the newspaper. Not an apparition that is deemed a miracle by the church. This was actually something quite simple and something I would have easily missed had I not been paying attention. To tell the truth, I don't know why, after being in such a state of aloneness, I even had the ability to notice.

You see, there was this little boy in our town who would go door to door asking people if they would like him to do a chore.

"A chore for a coin?" he would ask.

Or was it "A coin for a chore?"

I'm not sure which he said as he came knocking at my door during the "what if" time in my life. I must have not latched it properly because his knock caused the door to open. After having sat in a darkened house for a couple of days with the curtains pulled together, the light from the outside was blinding. He stood there as I looked at his shape in the doorway, not quite able to make him out because of the sun's brightness.

"Ma'am," he said, except to me it sounded like Mom, "it's so dark in there. What if you come out on the porch?"

Hearing him say "what if," after saying it to myself hundreds of times in the last couple of days, was a sign of something. Not only did this child's "what if" somehow quickly tie together all those loose strands in my head, it also called me back into the day we were in. His "what if" question was about that very day. It was not about the past or regrets. It was about choosing something in the here and now. Funny how sometimes simple things are the hardest to get to. It was suddenly clear to me that once something of the past becomes a "what if" there is nothing one can do to change it. In the past it leaves us no choice. No room for hopes or dreams of any kind. But a "what if" in the present or future, well, at least it allows for something different to happen.

I rose up from my chair and walked toward him. He backed up a little as if a bit afraid. Then I realized he was just making room for me.

As I got closer he said, "A chore for a coin?"

He must have thought me a mite odd 'cause I took him by the shoulders and said, "Child, you don't have to do any chores and I'll still give you some coins."

I reached into a purse and pulled out a few pennies and stuck them into his hand.

He looked at me as if wondering, "What did I do to deserve this?" Or maybe he was thinking, "That lady is a bit crazy."

It didn't matter. I would have paid ten times as much for what this boy's "what if" did for me.

I stroked his sandy-colored hair and for a moment imagined that Sam's son would have been near this age had he lived. He broke free then and hollered, "Thanks, ma'am. Gotta go. Time's a-wasting," as he bounded down the street toward the next house.

I stood there in the doorway, my eyes once again used to the noon sun, and just like that decided that I was going to stop tormenting myself with the "what ifs" of my past. And then I allowed myself to ask, "What if Sam still wants me?"

Snippet

Have you ever thought of what is held beyond? I did. Not often, but once in a while I would look up into the sky and wonder about the vastness. Vastness is a frightening thing when one is afraid of stepping outside of what is familiar. To me vastness was the biggest challenge.

A vastness roams the outskirts
of all that is familiar.
It reeks of fear and challenges
to the point of striking terror.
To enter into the vastness
I'd surely have to be
the bravest of all those surrounding me.

Only then would I venture into the vastness unknown.

There are stories in my life that are too far away from me. I don't know why I can't recall them, but it feels impossible. I like telling about my life. It frees my soul in a way I can't explain in words. Or maybe I could if I tried. Sound comes out of my mouth and is heard. But more than heard, it is felt. Felt by those, or at least some of those, who hear. Felt by me.

Food for Thought

Have you ever heard silent sound? I used to hear it. I won't say a lot, but enough that it made me question sounds. I would hear things even though there was nothing around me making noise. I would hear these things in my head, but they would sound like they were really happening.

One night it was so dark that when I woke up everything was black. There was no moon shining for the eyes to see. There were no stars lighting the way in the sky. It was so black that shadows couldn't be seen. Anyway, I woke up suddenly in the middle of this very dark night. Why? I didn't know at first. It was my body that woke me up with a jolt. I sat up in bed wondering why I felt strangeness. I was ice cold and I felt afraid. And then I heard it. It must have been one of those silent sounds. I heard my sister Annie's voice calling out. I don't remember thinking that she was calling out my name. What I know is that the sound was so clear it was as if she was right there in the room with me. Though I hadn't seen Annie in a few years, I recognized her voice 'cause when she got upset she stuttered, and the voice I heard was stuttering. Even though the sound was clear, I couldn't make out all that was being said, but it was something about her being scared and not wanting to go somewhere.

I may not have paid this much mind except for the way it made my body feel and the way my heart was racing. Then, as quick as it came, it was gone. The sound in my head that is, but the feeling in my body stayed with me the whole night. I laid awake thinking about Annie and being scared of something I didn't know. Didn't understand. Finally, at the crack of dawn, I got out of bed and I knew I had to go to her. It was more than a full day's ride in a buggy. I had no buggy. I had no horse. I had nothing to move me further than my own legs could take me. I kept telling myself that I was being silly for thinking I had to go see her. But this feeling of having to go wouldn't leave me. So I went down the street knocking on neighbors' doors, until one relented to my pleas and lent me the use of his horse. I thanked him kindly and promised to do a month's washing for no fee in exchange for this favor.

I wasted no time in leaving. As much as I could take, I galloped the horse as much as it could take. I slept one night off the side of the road in a patch of grass near a little stream. One of those streams that manages to make its way through dips and bends in the earth when rivers cannot hold all the water they're given. A stream that forges itself ahead even when someone says that it should not be there. A stream that may one year be full and flowing with small fish swimming about and dragonflies skimming the surface, and the next year be merely a trickle of water like those last few drops that settle at the bottom of a glass after one thinks all the liquid has been drunk. Then you look and see that there's a bit left at the bottom but when you raise the glass to your mouth it's just a trickle that only wets the tip of your tongue.

This stream that I lay near hardly made any sound. For a stream it was quite still. Hardly moving. It was somewhere in between being full and dry. I lay there under the stars and tried to hear Annie's silent sound again. I concentrated really hard, but I couldn't hear anything except for an owl that kept hooting through most of the night. My body continued to feel a coldness that would at times make it tremble. The only thing that calmed the shaking would be my pulling myself into a tight ball with my arms wrapped around my knees. Even then I could still feel an echo of the trembling. And the cold didn't stop.

I only slept about four hours and then set off again. I knew I risked tiring the horse, who was no longer a young animal, but as long as he was willing to keep going, we would go. It was near midday when I got to where Annie lived. I was amazed that I found my way there because I had only been to visit Annie a couple of times before. Once after Harry and I had gotten married but before Ellie and Jerry were born, and once after they were born, when they were just babies. The second time I visited I had heard that a farmer from our town was going to Trident, where my sister lived, to see his aging mother. Harry, as usual, wasn't home, so I packed myself and my babies up and hitched a ride with Edward the farmer.

It's funny how families either stick really close together or get spread out—going where they need to go or have to go. Annie had gone to live in this place because that's where her husband Thomas had his family ties. He was a farmer. They lived in a three-story house he and his brothers built for him and Annie. He had six brothers, all a year apart in their ages. Thomas's family owned all the land around. Miles of it between all of them. The twins and I stayed for a couple of weeks or so. I can't quite remember.

Annie seemed happy living out there, even though she had her hands full being a farmer's wife and mothering three youngins. And, though sometimes tired from carrying the one on the way, she rarely stopped to rest. At least not during the day. During the day she was always busy doing something, and it seemed like she enjoyed what she was doing. She and I had not been very close as youngins. Not so much because we didn't get along but because back then she was a quiet sort who didn't fancy doing much outside the house. In a way she was like our ma. Not in temperament, but in her attachment to her home, her household duties, and most of all her kitchen. She was a wonderful cook. There was always something baking in her oven or simmering on the stove. Usually it was both.

During that two-week visit we had little time to spend alone together because of the youngins needing us much of the day. But in the late evening, after the youngins were asleep, she and I would sit in the rockers on the front porch looking out over the flat sheets of land that lay like blankets around her house. We would sit there and talk, quietly as not to wake the youngins. We never talked directly about certain things. I never said much about Harry. She never said much about Thomas except what a hard-working, Christian, family man he was. She would talk about her cooking, baking, and her recipes. I would talk about my washing. But through those talks we somehow told each other about all those things we didn't talk about directly. I came to understand that in talking about her cooking, baking, and recipes, Annie was also talking about her life with Thomas.

One day she angrily—at least, for her—but still in her usual mild way said, "That darn bread didn't rise the way I thought it was going to yesterday. I hate when that happens. I put so much time into making it and it just flopped. I don't understand what I did wrong."

Sure enough, when Thomas came in from the fields, I sensed an angry distance between him and Annie, a tension that remained 'til the following day when she talked about the failed bread. In the evening hours of that day, as she and I gently rocked back and forth—Thomas, having offered to settle the youngins into bed, was upstairs singing them songs in a grand voice that belonged in a church choir—Annie started talking about food again.

"Wasn't that new beef and noodle recipe I tried for supper delicious?" she asked. Smiling she added, "It came out perfect."

"Did you notice how Thomas had three helpings of it?" I asked her, knowing that if she hadn't noticed it would surely add to the joy she was feeling.

That afternoon, just as she had started cooking this new recipe, Thomas happened to come in early from the fields. I could see the two of them whispering something to each other, after which Annie said that she wanted Thomas to try on a shirt she was sewing for him and together they snuck off for a while.

"Please stir the stew every few minutes, Hattie," she had called out as they went up the stairs.

So I kept an eye on the cooking and watched the youngins until Annie returned. Afterwards I could sense an easing of the tension that had held them apart for the last day or so. I saw her hand move slowly down the center of his back, gently smoothing his shirt, as he got ready to head back to work. I saw him turn around and kiss her forehead while his hand gave her behind a squeeze. I could have predicted that the new dish she was fixing for supper was going to come out perfect.

Annie's recipes and Annie's loving went hand in hand. If there was a problem with one, the other also suffered.

But now, as I neared her house, I noticed how quiet everything was. There was no farm equipment moving through the fields. Actually, there was no farm equipment in sight. There were no youngins running through the yard. There was no sound of youngins' voices coming from secret hiding places in the tall grass. I rode up to the porch and tied the horse to the railing near a bucket that was half full of water. The ground was wet from a recent rain, though it must have come and gone quickly for I had not felt a drop of rain during my ride. I noticed that the rocking chairs that she and I had night after night sat in were not on the porch. Then I noticed that the house looked different.

Annie always took special care of what was hers. When we were little it was her dolls that lived the longest. She always took such good care of them. Washing their little dresses. Keeping their faces clean. The rest of us would be carrying around dolls that were missing an arm or a leg, with hair that was matted into clumps and dresses that were torn and dirtied, while Annie's dolls looked brand new. That's why I was so taken back by the run-down condition of the house. I also realized that the fields, which by now should have been harvested, were overgrown. There was a paper stuck to the front door. I went closer.

"Eviction Due to Bankruptcy," was what it read.

"Oh no. Poor Annie. They've lost their home," I said aloud.

Knowing Annie as I did, I could only imagine what

this had done to her. Annie got her strength from the walls that stood around her and from all those things she did within those walls. From the recipes she fixed, from the hearty loaves of bread she baked, from everything that she created and did for others within these walls.

I looked through the windows. Most of the furniture was still in there. I could even see the stained glass lamp that had belonged to our mother. It was one of Annie's favorite pieces.

"They must have lost everything," I said aloud again as I tried the front door, which was locked.

I stepped off the porch and slowly walked around to the back of the house. There were no flowers growing in the spot where I remembered Annie having a flower garden. Instead, in that spot there lay a dead cat. Flies buzzing around it. It was so thin. "Must've starved to death," I said to myself.

But then I remembered there was usually a constant supply of field mice around. Something else must've killed it. I walked around the cat trying to avoid its dead gaze. The back door was also locked, but a window with a couple smashed-out panes of glass gave me a way in. I managed to get it open and crawl through it into Annie's kitchen. Inside everything was tidy. The kitchen table still stood in the center of the room. Dishes still in the cupboards. All her pots and pans crowded onto a couple of shelves. But there were no signs of any food. I walked over to Annie's oven and ran my fingers along it.

"Oh Annie, Annie." I whispered, remembering the way she had happily moved through her kitchen. My heart broke for her.

I opened the oven door. There sat a loaf of bread, burnt to nearly a black color. I pulled it out and put it on the table. It was as hard as stone. Not even fit for animals to eat. I rapped the top of it and got back a hard, hollow sound. "Oh Annie," I whispered again. "What a mess your life must be." I walked through the rest of the house. There was not much to see. Not a stitch of clothing needing to be washed. There was nothing for me to get my hands on. Nothing to do.

After giving the horse a bit longer to rest, I made my way to the nearest house. I couldn't remember which of Thomas's brothers lived there. Once again I came across an eviction notice and emptiness. I continued making my way over the land that Thomas's family owned. Going house to house. It was all the same. Houses, still full of furniture, locked up. No signs of life anywhere in them or around them. All with notices posted on the front doors. Still looking for something, needing some kind of answer, I headed into the town where all those eviction notices must have come from. A place I found myself feeling hate for.

Usually I'm good at keeping my feelings to myself, but by now I didn't care. My distress must have been as clearly written over me as those eviction notices posted on the doors. As I approached the man behind the desk at the town hall and asked about the Jenkinses, he quickly pushed his chair back and stepped away from me. His chair grated across the floor, making an irritating sound, as he said, "I don't want no trouble here."

Even though I must have looked like I could cause trouble, what trouble was I going to cause? I was just a tired, worried, and, I'll admit, a somewhat angry woman who wanted to know what happened to her sister, Annie Jenkins.

"They all moved on as best as they could," the man said rather sternly.

I asked what he meant by that, but he seemed tight-lipped. I finally burst into tears—which surprised me more than him—and pleaded with him to tell me what he knew about this whole situation. Once he realized I meant no harm, even though I may have seemed like I was ready to boil over when I first walked through the doors, he told me all he knew.

All the Jenkins property had been owned by the father. Though Old Man Jenkins had given land to all his sons, he had failed to deed it to them. Apparently Old Man Jenkins—who wasn't really so old, but being the head of such a large clan he was given that title—had incurred many gambling debts over the years. So many that in the end he lost everything. As much as his sons tried to cover their pa's losses, the debts were just too great.

"What about Thomas and Annie Jenkins? Where did they go?" I asked, not really caring about the others.

The man got up from his chair and walked over to a pile of papers. Searching through them, he pulled one out. I could see there wasn't much written on it. He read it and told me that the only information he had was that Thomas and Annie and their children had headed north. No specific destination was mentioned.

I thanked him and got ready to go. He must have felt sorry for me because he asked me to sit down and wait for a moment while he went and talked to his wife about this matter.

"Mabel always seems to know more about what goes on in town than I do," he said. "Sometimes I think she should be doing this job," he added, letting out a meager laugh.

I managed a little smile. After a few minutes, Mabel came out into the room where I sat. She was a big woman. Reminded me of Gertrude who was our town clerk and gossip. She came over and crowded herself into the chair next to mine and leaned right into me.

"He," she shrugged her head in her husband's direction, "tells me you're Annie's sister. If you had gotten here a day sooner you would have seen her. They left yesterday."

Then she stopped talking. I could tell she was trying to decide what else to tell me. Maybe she was hesitating 'cause I still looked like I could cause some trouble. I managed another smile.

"Is there anything else I should know?" I asked in a polite voice, trying to encourage her to talk.

"Well, I don't want to worry you, dear, I'm sure she'll be doing better once they've gone a distance. Your sister was not well when they drove out of town."

"What do you mean? Was she sick?" I asked, realizing I was now leaning into her as much as she was leaning into me.

"It was nothing physical that was ailing her. I think her heart was badly broken by losing most everything they had. I didn't see her myself, but I heard that when it was time to go she started crying uncontrollably. She became so hysterical that Thomas had to carry her away from the house."

Then, as if worried that she was telling too much, she leaned away from me saying, "I don't want to be upsetting you."

"Please. I need to know whatever you can tell me," I said quietly. Though I wanted to scream, "For God's sake. It's my sister you're talking about. Of course I'm upset!"

Finally, convinced that I would not cause trouble, Mabel continued. "As Thomas carried her away, she was screaming and kicking, reaching her arms in the direction of the house. As they drove away, her two older boys had to hold her down in the wagon to keep her from running back."

By the time Mabel finished talking, I was so tired from not showing my distress that I just sat there feeling empty. I knew there was really nothing else for me to do but head home and hope to hear from Annie once they got to wherever they got to. Mabel offered me lodging for the night but I politely refused. I couldn't manage another smile. I just wanted to get out of this place and find some spot for me and the horse to rest. I wanted once again to sleep under the stars. Be in a place where if I wanted to be upset it would not cause trouble.

I headed home, full of worry for Annie.

"There's nothing else you can do, Hattie," I told myself.

I was again passing by Annie's house, once cared for and full of the smells of cooking. There in the distance to the left of the road it stood. I imagined Annie being carried by Thomas away from all she had created in that home. All those things she had made. Suddenly I thought of something and turned the horse in the direction of the house. I galloped around to the back. Once again I climbed inside through the window. I knew just what I was looking for. I went to where I remembered Annie keeping them and opened the cupboard door. There they were. Her cookbooks. Pages and pages of recipes between which were tucked loose pieces of paper that held the ones Annie herself had created. I took those books off the shelf, determined, one way or another, to get them to Annie.

Maybe she left them behind because her mind wasn't

working clearly. Maybe she left them behind because she was feeling hopeless. Maybe she left them behind because she forgot. Maybe she remembered that she left them behind and that's why she was screaming and kicking so. Right now the reason didn't matter. What mattered to me was that my sister Annie needed those recipes as much as she needed her husband and youngins in order to go on living. I went out the door with the books in my arms. I'd had enough of climbing through broken windows. I packed those books into the bag that hung off the saddle and headed home.

Through a Pane of Glass

You know how sometimes one begins to feel regret right away? From the minute you utter the words or do something, regret starts to be felt.

Well, I began feeling regret the moment that I said "no" to Sam. But as I began feeling it, I also felt the fear. And the fear covered over the regret and made me pay more attention to it. I know I'm talking in circles, and that's just how I felt with this regret and this fear. I felt like I was just going around in circles.

A couple of days before Sam left to head toward his dream of settling down in the place he had heard of called Willow Grove, a place that he said called to him for a reason he couldn't name, he had asked me to go with him. He sat me down on the front porch steps. By now I was getting used to those times when he wanted and needed my attention. He told me how much he loved me and said that more than anything he wanted me to leave with him. He said he would fix up the broken-down wagon that stood idle in the backyard, and he would help me pack up everything I wanted to take.

He was real stubborn when it came to me. Stubborn

in a wonderful way. While I was used to shutting away things that were important to me—things that mattered but that I made seem like they didn't—he was stubborn in saying that I did matter. That what I needed and wanted was important. Yet it was this stubbornness that also kept me from going with him. Another man would have just thought that he knew what was best for me. Another man would not have taken "no" for an answer. But Sam remained stubborn. Not just about what he wanted, but about paying attention to what it was that I felt I needed and wanted. He realized that I still needed to stay put. And so he respected me and the choice I made, even though he wished to share his life with me and knew I wanted to share a life with him.

When he said we would pack up everything I wanted to take, I thought of Ellie. I knew that I couldn't take her with me, and I knew I couldn't leave her. The thought of going away, of leaving that spot in the meadow where Ellie was buried, was something I felt I couldn't do. Every time I thought of going with Sam, the idea of leaving her made me so afraid that I couldn't think of anything else. There was no way what that meadow held would fit in the wagon and go with us. And I didn't know of any way of taking it with us. I tried as best as I could to explain that to Sam.

He must have understood because eventually he just said, "All right, Hattie. Maybe now's not the time. Maybe some other day you'll be ready. When you are, I'll be waiting for you."

So you see, Sam didn't just leave. He left with hope. He left believing there was a chance for us.

When I was carrying Steven, I wanted to write to Sam and tell him about the baby. I really did want to. But I didn't. I didn't want to make Sam think he had to come back here. I know he loved me, but he didn't love this place. And I didn't want him doing something that would make him feel regrets. I felt enough of those for the two of us. Also, when I was holding Sam's baby inside of me, feeling him growing, feeling him filling me up, I didn't pay much attention to the regret of not going with Sam. I was thinking about the baby and me. Nothing else seemed to matter.

When I was about seven months along, I got a letter from Sam. He sounded happy. He had bought himself a piece of land. Not huge but big enough for what he wanted. About a hundred acres. He said that there was a shed on the land that had one side falling in, but he was fixing it up and one day it was going to be a nice little house. He also wrote how much he missed me. Once again he reminded me that he wanted me to join him. He said he didn't mind waiting because he truly believed that we would one day be together.

When I picked up his letter at the post office, Gertrude, the clerk, handed it to me with a snicker and said, "You got a letter from that fella."

She said this, but all the while her eyes were staring at my swelling belly. As much as I wanted to tear the envelope open right then and there, I just took the letter from her like it was any other piece of mail, and walked out of the post office. I wasn't going to satisfy her curiosity by showing her my excitement. The walk from the center of town to my house was a couple of miles. I didn't mind walking. It was a clear, windy day. No rain in sight. I held the letter up against my breast fearing the wind would rip it away from me. My hands trembled. I could feel them fingers moving, refusing to be still.

As I walked, I was telling myself, "Just a bit further, Hattie, and you can find a spot to sit and read the letter."

My thoughts were interrupted by Gertrude calling to me. "Hattie. Hattie. There's another letter for you. I just found it in the bag of mail that arrived this morning."

Now this was very unusual for me to get a couple of letters at one time. I turned around and walked back toward Gertrude. I walked slowly. I was actually enjoying watching her making an attempt to run towards me. Her very wide hips were swinging side to side. Her half run was more like a fast waddle. She was waving an envelope in the air. When we reached each other she was quite out of breath and patting her chest as if trying to calm her breathing or stop her breasts from heaving.

Gertrude had a huge bosom. She was the talk of the town on more than one occasion. No matter how long people knew Gertrude, they were always amazed by the size of her bosom as if seeing it for the first time. I wondered how she was able to carry such weight, but she did. It didn't seem to bother her.

Anyway, apparently she was even more curious about this mail than the letter from Sam. Rather hesitantly—as if not wanting to part with it—she held it out to me and stood there looking at me as if she thought I might actually open it in front of her. Gertrude was one of those people who make it their business to know everyone else's business and then spread it around. Well, this day she would be disappointed. I had no intention of adding to her fire of gossip.

"Thank you, Gertrude," I said politely as I reached out to take the letter from between her fingers. She must have hated letting go of something she was so curious about. I actually had to tug at it to pull it out of her grasp.

Now I walked home holding two letters. The one from Sam I was anxious to read. His letters put a smile on my face. This other envelope caused me concern. It felt heavy in my hand. I didn't recognize the handwriting and the postmark was smeared. As much as I was yearning to pause in some spot off the side of the road and read Sam's letter, I didn't want to open this other envelope until I got home. What I knew as I walked along was that I was going to open the unknown letter first and that I needed to be behind closed doors when I read it.

I used to do things kind of on the spur of the moment. But in recent years I had started learning to pay attention to what I was somehow knowing inside of me. On this day, I was knowing that I was supposed to wait. And I didn't run home, either. I walked along, my heart beating fast, different thoughts racing through my mind. I walked past the place that I would have stopped at and sat quietly to read Sam's letter. I walked past the grove of fruit trees on the Rosens' property. I walked past the Rosens' house, paint peeling off its boards. I was hoping no one would run out the door hollering that they had laundry for me. Then I remembered that the house was now empty. Mr. Rosen had died last year, and his remaining youngins had been taken away by someone who said they couldn't live there anymore. By then he had lost a second wife, who left him with another bunch of youngins. I walked past the path worn deep by my feet that led up to the meadow where Ellie lay. I walked and walked. All the while clutching the letters in my hands and going between breathing hard and hardly breathing.

There was the house. My house. My father's house. My father's aunt's house. My great-grandmother's house. Standing still. Waiting for me. I opened the door and stepped in, not knowing what I was feeling. The front room was dark. Some clouds had moved into the sky overhead, dropping a shadow over the house. Along with the porch roof hanging over the windows, there was not one glimmer of sunlight coming in. I walked into the house and for once wished I had shoes on my feet. I would have liked to kick them off and hear them thud against the floor. Any sound to break through the silence. I went straight for the kitchen table. Pulling the chair out, I listened for even the slightest squeak of a wooden leg scraping against the floor. But there was none. I began to wonder whether there was no sound or whether I was not hearing sound. I sat down into the chair. Its seat bowed from years of me sliding into it. I fit just so into this chair. "Fit just so." I remember saying those words before. But that story I've already told.

I tore open the envelope. I heard the sound of the paper being torn, so it wasn't me after all. The silence I had heard was real. It wasn't me. I felt a relief I couldn't understand. I wasn't to blame. I could hear. There just hadn't been anything to hear. Silence. What an odd thing. How does one meet silence? Silence is different than quiet. Silence makes one question their being. In quiet you can hear your heart beating. In silence one risks forgetting they have a heart that beats. Quiet is something one yearns for. Silence is something one fears. Quiet allows one to know stillness in being while still being. Silence is an introduction to death. To losing being. To going past stillness into nothingness. Yet for a moment it seemed I was with silence and I did not die. Oh, how my silly thoughts wander into places I have no business going. Into lives I have no business leading.

I pulled the letter out of the envelope. Something else, something smaller, slipped out from the letter's fold and fell to the floor. I didn't know what to look at first. The letter, already in my hands, made the choice for me. I unfolded it and looked at it. At first, all I saw was a bunch of words on paper with a very formal signature at the bottom. Then I began to read.

Dear Mrs. Paine,

It is our regret to inform you of the deaths of Harold and Zak Paine. The circumstances of this whole situation are quite unusual. Our services have been requested by Mrs. Paine who, after the death of her husband Harold, discovered papers indicating that you may still be alive. Upon their initial meeting, Harold had told her that you had died. Once your existence became evident, Mrs. Paine came to the conclusion that you were Harold's wife and Zak's mother.

Zak had for several years lived with Mr. and Mrs. Paine, but then had to be put away because of being insane. He was at Hollow Hill Insane Asylum. On Zak's fifteenth birthday, Mr. Paine paid him a visit. During that visit, Zak escaped. Mr. Paine went looking for him into the surrounding woods. All we know is that Mr. Paine's body was discovered the next day. He had been killed. His head crushed by a rock. A distance from Mr. Paine's body, your son's body was found. He had hanged himself.

Funerals were held for both of them, and they were buried in a Christian way. It was not until some time passed that Mrs. Paine discovered the note to you from Harold, which is enclosed, indicating that, contrary to what she had been told, you were not deceased. If you have any further questions, please refer them to my office. I'm very sorry to have to deliver this news to you. Please accept my sincere condolences.

Yours truly,
Matthew Grossman,
Attorney at law

I leaned over and picked up the paper that had fallen to the floor. I wish I could tell you that I was frantic or sobbing or angry or anything. But at that moment and through reading the whole letter, I was nothing. I felt nothing. I thought nothing. It was as if I was behind a pane of glass, looking at things I couldn't reach. Just looking. I opened up the yellowed scrap of paper. It had dirt streaks over it. It was dated about a year after Harry had taken Zak away. I don't know why Harry had written it because he hadn't mailed it. He hadn't even finished it. A few short sentences on a torn-off piece of paper. I don't know why he held on to it all those years. I looked at it. I didn't read it. I crumpled it into my hand and sat there. I sat there waiting for anything to happen. Nothing did. They were both dead. That I now knew. I tried to remember what Zak looked like. I couldn't remember. I opened up my hand and looked at the piece of paper. I uncrumpled it and smoothed it over my thigh. I read Harry's last words to me.

Hattie, we are going further west. Zak is fine. He doesn't even ask about you any more. I am fine. I wanted you to know that.

That was it. That was all. No ending. Nothing. I got up from the table and walked out the door with Sam's letter in my hand.

I thought I was done with the letter from the lawyer, but I found myself drawn back to it. I wanted more explanation. I needed to make it more real. To believe that Harry was really gone. That he would not be coming back this way ever again. And maybe even—if the feeling came—to allow myself to weep for Zak.

There was no one I could share this with. And though I read the letter over and over again, I wasn't reaching the place inside myself that I needed to reach to believe it all. To feel it. To make it real. So I reached for conversation with myself.

"Hattie," I said, talking a bit louder than usual to get my attention and maybe that of someone listening to the winds carrying my words. "Hattie, this is what happened. Harry traveled out west where he met and married a woman who believed him. He told her his wife had died. She believed him. He told her Zak's ma was dead.

She believed him. They lived together as a family. But Zak went crazy and was put in an insane asylum. One day Harry went to visit him. Somehow Zak escaped. Harry went into the woods after him. There Zak killed his pa. He picked up a big rock and smashed his head. Then he ran further into the woods. They found him later. They found Zak. They found your son. He had hung himself. He was fifteen years old."

I still didn't weep—not then anyway—but at least I knew it was real and it was over. At least on this earth, Harry as Harry could do no further harm. I went to stuff the letter back into the envelope and noticed another small piece of paper in it that I had missed. It must have also been found in Harry's belongings. I pulled out the slip of paper and opened it. On it, Harry had scratched another message to me. When? Who knows?

Hattie, I've made mistakes. I'm sor

At first this confused me, because it seemed that Harry may have had some regrets in his years away from me. Yet he could not finish a simple word that might have, if only for a moment, showed that maybe, just maybe, he had changed.

Endless Truth

I'm back to talking about Sam. There was much more to Sam and Hattie than I told before. Much more. And it had to do with truth. Sam loved me and I loved him. I remember when he first said those words "I love you, Hattie." It was a moment I will never forget.

I was standing at the sink where I was washing clothes, a mixture of some of Sam's things and some of mine. Washing clothes in the sink was not something I had done before. I had walked into the kitchen with the bundle of clothes in my arms. One of Sam's shirt sleeves, once a dark blue color, now quite faded, the color of the night sky when it has a film of clouds concealing its darkness, was sticking out over the top. It was close to my face. As I held these clothes, I could smell Sam's scent in that sleeve. The thought of immersing our clothes into the washtub became unbearable. I thought of all the laundry that washtub had held over the years. All the dirt and smells. I just couldn't put our clothes into that tub. I stood there feeling the truth. What I held in my arms was our clothes. Our smells. Our perspiration. Our stains. Our wrinkles. I held us. Sam and Hattie. And I didn't want to immerse us into something that had held everyone else's dirty laundry. So, I looked over at my sink. That's where I stood, rubbing Sam's shirt over the ripples of the washboard, humming to myself.

He had been out taking care of his mule. I didn't notice that he had come back into the house. He later told me he stood at the doorway for many minutes, just watching me. He even said, though I didn't quite believe him, that my hips were rocking back and forth in a dance to the music I was creating. I didn't believe him, because I never danced when I did washing. Suddenly he was there next to me. His hand reached out, across the front of me, and touched my arm. Gently guiding it to be still. Calming the scrubbing. I looked over at him then, and the look in his eyes frightened me. It wasn't a frightening look. It just frightened me because it was—what? I don't know if I can describe it. It was—endless. Yes, that's the word. It was endless. There was a longing for me in his eyes that immediately traveled into me and lodged itself in my heart. An openness into his being that made me feel like I was falling into a place of pure joy. I saw a strength that I knew could make me feel every bit of my heart. Could make me feel my whole being. I had to turn away. Not look any further. It frightened me to see and feel these things.

When I turned away from him, back to the familiar sight of the soapy water, the ripples of the washboard, and the shirt I was holding, his hand slowly reached up to my face. His palm rested on my cheek as he guided my face back to his.

"Hattie," he said softly.

I was amazed at how a deep, raspy voice like Sam's could sound so quiet. So soothing. You should hear how it sounded when he wanted his mule to start moving. But that was his mule and this was me.

"Hattie, I want you to look at me," he said.

With his hand guiding my face, I was willing to turn it to him. My eyes, though, had a difficult time meeting his. The fear had passed the moment I felt his gentle hand, but now, silly as it was, I felt embarrassed. He had already managed to guide the rest of me toward him. I was no longer leaning into the sink. My hands, puckered white from the water, were no longer immersed in the suds. My bare toes were wedged up against his boots. I don't know if this all happened quickly like a gush of water, or slowly like the flow of molasses. All I knew was that there we stood. Our fronts to each other. My eyes still unable to look up into his. While my gaze remained lowered, I found myself looking at the buttons on his shirt. I noticed that one button was broken in half. It was hardly able to hold itself in place in the buttonhole. My fingers reached up and, with the tip of one of them, I touched that button.

It was then that I looked up at Sam and said, "This one's broken. Did you know that?"

Before the words "I'll sew on a new one for you" had

225

reached my mouth, Sam's voice interrupted my mending urge.

"Hattie, I love you."

I believe I would have heard his words even if I had been scrubbing furiously at the washboard, because they filled the room. But I wasn't doing washing. I wasn't doing anything but listening and watching. I didn't turn away, which surprised me. I didn't get scared. I didn't get embarrassed. What I did do was hold my gaze to his eyes. I was searching for the truth. I was looking to see if what he was daring to say to me was the truth. For so many years I had not heard any man say those words to me. I had to know what they meant. And I had to know they were true.

The last time any man had said those words to me was when Harry had asked me to marry him.

His exact words were, "Hattie, I think we should get hitched. You're a good woman. Strong. Healthy. And good-looking too. You're just what I need."

Then he kind of stuck out his chest, rubbed it with both hands and said, "And I can give you what you need."

I remember standing there with him and silently talking to myself. Not about what I was feeling, but about what I was supposed to be thinking.

"Here's a man willing to be your husband. He'll provide for you. He'll take care of you."

"You don't want to be an old maid, do you?"

"You'll have babies before you know it."

No one needed to convince me of what I should do. I convinced myself.

"So Hattie, what do you say?" Harry asked.

I never did look into Harry's eyes as I said, "Yes, Harry. Let's get married."

I wasn't even looking at Harry's shirt. My eyes were staring at my feet and the new shoes I was trying to break in. They were so tight. I had gone from having a stinging, painful ache in my toes to my feet being numb. My ears heard Harry holler out a yelp of satisfaction as he turned away from me to run off and announce his success to his friends. Men who I'm sure were sitting around a table in the bar, by then half drunk.

As Harry ran, he managed to twist his neck and turn one side of his face in my direction. I heard him yell, "I love you."

That was the first and last time Harry ever said those words to me. I believed him. My ears had heard the words. Back then that's all I needed to tell me that what he said was the truth. And since he loved me, then I loved him. Clear and simple.

But since that day, so long ago, I had learned many times over that few things were clear and simple. I had learned that to find the truth, one sometimes needed to search deeply for it. So I stood there searching Sam's eyes for the truth. It was there. Everything about him and everything about me, from the way I felt in my chest, in my stomach, in my head, in my toes, which now comfortably rested over the brown leather of his boots, told me that Sam was telling the truth. And he was saying it not expecting anything in return except knowing that I heard him. He had wanted and needed to say, "I love you, Hattie." And he had wanted and needed me to hear him say it. To see his eyes. To see his lips moving as he shared those words with me. No man had ever made me feel as real as Sam did.

Meeting Isabelle

Sitting still, or sitting without doing much of anything, was something I had known in my life. But sitting in this way, in stillness and in silence, with another person was something I had never known until now. Let me tell you what happened.

When the time finally arrived and I made my way to Lady Isabelle's house, I was told she was very ill. For many years I had imagined we would spend hours talking. But when the time came for us to meet, she had little energy to listen and even less ability to talk. Her grief-stricken husband, himself looking worn and so very tired, explained that his wife had suffered a massive shock and was gravely ill.

"Near death," he said.

I was led into Lady Isabelle's bedroom by her nurse, who was kind enough, on this day and over the weeks that followed, to allow me time with Mrs. Sanders, as she referred to her, whenever I wanted it. I think it allowed her some reprieve from nursing a body that hung in a limbo of sorts. When I first heard about Isabelle's condition, I imagined that the nurse may have even been bored with her work. How much can one do for a body that shows little if no response to their presence? Monotony, day after day, has the ability to begin strangling the life out of those who are still very much alive. I, though, felt myself fortunate. I was not feeling boredom or monotony. I was finally meeting Lady Isabelle in person.

She was as beautiful as I had imagined. When I first laid eyes on her, I was standing just inside the door of her room. She was so still and quiet, with her eyes closed. She was like a painting. The white linens surrounding her made her dark brown hair look even darker. She was very pale and also seemed very small nestled into the huge four-poster canopy bed. The room itself was a sight for sore eyes. It was filled with greenery and flowers. I remembered how Isabelle loved gardening and cultivating flowers. She often would write about this in her letters to Miss Jean.

Isabelle's husband must truly love her to have brought her garden into her room, I thought to myself.

Vines of fresh flowers, which someone must have carefully entwined every couple of days, were hung around the canopy of the bed. On every table, and there were several, stood a vase nearly overflowing with flowers. Large, green plants as big as little trees stood in two corners of the room. There was no scent of death in this room. Or, if there was, it was covered over by the scent of flowers— a mixture of lilacs, daisies, roses, and some flowers I had never seen before that had petals the size of my hand.

Now you must understand, when I first arrived I was

already filled with all kinds of feelings. I was nervous and excited and a bit fearful that Lady Isabelle might not even remember me. So, on top of all that I already held inside of me, I was then given this news about her being gravely ill. Before I could get used to adding a feeling of deep sorrow and loss to all the other feelings, I was quickly whisked into a room that created even more feelings. To see this woman, who I had longed to meet for what seemed an eternity, in a room that was like none I had ever seen before, heaped emotions of surprise and wonder onto the existing mass of feelings that were swirling inside of me. It all left me momentarily dumbfounded. As the nurse spoke to me, I could barely utter a response. She pointed to a chair that sat empty near the edge of the bed, and left the room.

The nurse had not made any attempt to inform Isabelle that she had a visitor. At that moment, alone in the room with her, I felt like I had felt when I used to write the letters to her. It was a mixture of the known and unknown. And here I was, in her presence, and she had no idea that I was there. For several minutes I just stood in place. Then the silence in the room began to grow. As the silence intensified, I began to feel an immense sadness in the reality of this moment. Here I was, having waited so long, wearing my fancy blue dress, even having had my hair styled, and carrying what felt like a huge amount of wonder about Isabelle's reaction to my visit. And here was

Isabelle, so removed from living as she had known. I began to think how ironic it was that, as I had written letters for Miss Jean because she had not been able to do it, here I was with her sister, who I now could do the same for. Who now was no longer able to write letters. Except this was worse. Much worse. From what her husband said, she was no longer able to do anything but lay there. Lay there while looking somehow frail and strong at the same time. Or at least that's how my eyes saw her as I stood there less than a room's space away. I was so near to the bed. Just a very few steps. Yet the distance still felt great.

Without others in the room, I had time to ease myself into taking those few, though seeming huge, steps. I got my bearings and decided to approach the bed. I wasn't sure if Isabelle was asleep or if this was how she was whether asleep or not. I cleared my throat a bit. She didn't move. I searched for words to announce myself. I felt my mouth open.

"Isabelle, open your eyes and look at the wonderful garden in this room," I blurted out.

What a stupid thing to say, I thought. I could feel an embarrassing flush rise over my face and I immediately began to hear a rush of internal scolding. Before I could say anything else to her, Isabelle's eyelids fluttered open. I found myself looking into eyes that met me straight on. Eyes that told me this was a woman who was very much alive inside this "near death" body. She looked at me and she looked into me. I could see the questions rising in her head.

"Isabelle, I'm Hattie. Remember me? I used to write letters to you for your sister."

The introduction was as simple as that. There was no Mrs. Sanders or Lady Isabelle. There was no more searching for words. The words just came. As I spoke, I slowly lowered myself into the chair. Surprisingly, the feeling of being stupid was gone. I took her hand in mine and I touched her hair, brushing it off her face. I straightened the coverlet. I fixed her pillow. All the while I was quietly saying words to her. Short sentences that did not require an answer. It reminded me of the way I would coo words at Ellie when I held her in my arms and rocked her. I had no idea how much of what I was saying was understood, and I didn't want to say too much because I didn't want to tire Isabelle. After a few minutes, I just stopped talking. It was hard at first to sit there, because all we had was each other's eyes gazing deeply. Eyes that I knew were the doors to a vastness of words, sentences, and stories. Enough to fill volumes of books. We just kept looking at each other. I could have continued talking, but I chose not to. I didn't want to put her at any more of a disadvantage than she was at already. Her husband had explained to me that the shock left her unable to speak and with only the slightest movement in her right side.

"The left side," as he put it, "is totally gone."

When I first heard him say that, my imagination began

running away from me because I really didn't quite know what "totally gone" meant. I was relieved to see that Isabelle still had her left side. I know that, as a grown woman, I should have understood what he meant. But being swept up by the fear and disappointment of all this unexpected news, I just began imagining the worst. And the worst would be Lady Isabelle laying there "near death" and not even having her whole body to house her.

As I sat there, as she lay there, our eyes locked together, mine suddenly began to tear. I could feel the tears welling up inside of them. I struggled to stop them. She did not need to see me crying. The last thing she needed was to think I felt sorry for her. One thing I knew from all those letters she had written was that she was a proud woman. A woman who would not allow herself to succumb to weaknesses. But as much as I tried not to cry, the more the tears ran.

"Dammit, I don't want to cry," I said much louder than I thought. In fact, I thought I had just said it in my head, but I guess my head couldn't hold it, because the words escaped my lips. I felt embarrassed by this show of emotion and by my swearing. I didn't want her to see me as a woman who was weak and crass. And how would I even know what she saw me as since she couldn't talk? It appeared highly unlikely that she would do anything at all to indicate what she thought of me.

I should have known better than to give her so little

credit. As I wiped away the tears with the sleeve of my free arm, for the other hand still gently held hers, I felt the tiniest movement and most fragile squeeze of my hand by hers. It was a touch that reminded me of a time when, as a young girl, I became the savior of tiny baby birds. Birds that, for whatever reason, found themselves alone and totally depended on my care. I would find them, one here, one there, lying on the ground after having fallen out of a nest. I would pick them up and they would lie limply in the cup of my hands. Eventually, they would move their wings the tiniest bit. A gentle flutter against my hands. A slight quiver. A movement that, though hardly felt, told me there was strength left in each little bird. Those little birds were as near to life as they were to death. They could move either way at that moment of hovering between the two worlds. Near death. Those words hold such vagueness. It is part of that huge unknown of life that we live with. Always. Isn't being near death really something that begins the moment we are born? Never knowing just how near we are. Never knowing.

Yes. Isabelle's gentle squeeze reminded me of those baby birds. And something else happened along with the flutter of touch. She smiled. Not that it was a normal smile, for half of her face couldn't move and the other half could hardly move. But I saw one side of her lips rise just enough to deepen a wrinkle at the edge of her mouth. And what really gave her away were her eyes. While the hand

and mouth showed a glimmer of life, her eyes laughed this loud, funny laugh. How do eyes laugh? I don't know. But hers did.

They laughed and then said to me, "Oh Hattie, you silly thing. Get ahold of yourself. This is a moment of joy, not of sadness. We are finally meeting."

Then she added, "When you wrote all those letters and read mine, you never heard my voice. So, actually you should be used to this."

Then she laughed again.

I heard her words and the laughter clear as day, but I know that her mouth did not move. It did not utter any sounds. It did not speak the words. It was her thoughts that passed right into my head. It was the strangest thing, and yet to me it felt like the most normal thing in the world. Maybe I should have gotten scared, but I didn't. Now, there are those who would say it was all in my imagination. But I knew, beyond all doubt, what I heard in my head was what she was really wanting to say.

How is it that I can describe this day—considering the circumstances, strange as they were—as wonderful? Yet it was just that. Here we were. Two women who had never met. All we knew of each other was what we had shared through those letters so long ago. Letters that had only indirectly connected us. Even so, we knew each other. We understood each other.

Though I felt an incredible loss in not being able to be

with Isabelle as I had imagined—taking walks, talking, sipping tea, doing all those things that women do together—I felt I was being privileged to something even greater. It was a gift to me to be with someone who was in that place between life and death. A place of lingering that, though it disallowed many things, did allow for many unusual things. It was also a revelation. Being with Isabelle brought me stillness and silence. Forced me in a way to be with it as I had never been with it before. And there was no fear.

Not Meant to Be

My life held many moments. Some will never come forth. Others have come forth, been shared, flowed out, at times feverishly and in torrents, because that's how they happened. It's as simple as that. There is no explanation. There is no reason or rhyme to it. It all comes as it must. As it is meant to come. I never before had the time and also the strength, both things together, to allow for storytelling to be as it is now. Some things will remain unfinished. But isn't that how life is? So many things go unfinished. No ending. No resolution. No closure except that which death brings or imposes on us.

I never saw ocean waters. I never saw huge mountains. I only read about them. I never had a wedding band around my finger. Harry kept saying he would get me one, but he never did. Also my fingers had large knuckles. To get a wedding band over the knuckle would have meant a large band that then would have floated freely around the lower part of my finger. For a long time I wanted a wedding band. I even thought of having one specially made to fit around my finger like a bracelet and clasp in place. But who ever heard of that type of wedding band? Wedding bands are supposed to slip easily over the finger and rest right where they are meant to be. I finally accepted that I was not meant to wear a wedding band. It came down to that one simple answer. No ifs or buts. Just that I wasn't meant to wear one.

When I met Isabelle, I was taken with all the rings she wore on her fingers and the fact that her hands were so dainty. She had a very large diamond ring and a beautifully carved wedding band. She had an opal ring, a sapphire ring, and a black onyx ring. She told me that she had many other rings, including a little girl's ring with a pink heart-shaped stone in it that she had bought for her daughter. We discovered we had something else in common. She had also lost a daughter. She died at the age of three from tuberculosis. Isabelle told me that after her daughter Emily died, for a long time she wore that little ring around her neck on a gold chain. It hung there next to a cross she always wore. She never told me why she finally stopped wearing it. Isabelle also had a son, Martin, who had followed in his father's footsteps and become a very successful lawyer.

I wondered about that phrase "following in a father's footsteps." I wondered if it also meant a child could follow in a mother's footsteps. Except that usually one would say "She is like her mother." Why is that? Why the difference? Is it because mothers and daughters aren't meant to take steps anywhere?

Tommy Lee

Gales, gales, and more gales whipped me about the whole week that I sat in the house not doing any washing. The thought to step away from my washtub had come so suddenly and with such conviction and clarity there was no way to argue it. At the moment of the command—as if an order from somewhere inside me sounded in my head—I was scrubbing the life out of Tommy Lee Baker's shirt.

Tommy was a lonely child even though he had six brothers. He was a slight boy among a brood of larger guys. It was a family of boys and men who all thought of themselves as "guys," except for Tommy. Tommy did not fit the brood. He did not fit into any hand-me-downs that passed from brother to brother. He was different in many ways. Where his brothers' sounds and words were rough, Tommy's voice sang. Where the brothers were strong, with muscled arms and legs, Tommy was thin and weak. The brothers' breath could sway a branch like the wind. Tommy's breath barely moved him. At times he wheezed and coughed and turned colors. Sometimes his cheeks got bright red, other times his lips carried a gray-blue outline.

Most times his skin reminded me of milk in a glass to which I had added water on those days when there wasn't enough for my youngins to drink.

I shouldn't have been scrubbing the life out of Tommy's blue plaid shirt. It wasn't that dirty. It didn't need rough handling. He got enough of that at home. When I heard the command to "stop," I looked at the shirt. It was dripping wet, indistinguishable—no one would know what this piece of fabric was—and I began to cry. Slowly I lifted the shirt out of the washtub and carefully rinsed every bubble of soap out of it. Poor Tommy. Poor Tommy. Had I been scrubbing the life out of his shirt, or trying to scrub something fierce into it? Tommy needed fierceness. I could feel his gentle spirit succumbing to the world around him. Every time Tommy came by with his mother, his wince was still visible as they entered through my door. She walked at a pace he couldn't keep up with, so she often pulled him along. Sometimes she grabbed his shoulder, lifting one side of him off the ground and dragging the other. Yes, Tommy needed fierceness, but he never found it or maybe he chose not to let it in. I somehow felt it was too late for Tommy to take in or maintain a lion's disposition. To find a way to growl and prowl among the brood living in the farmhouse that was partially hidden by tall pines.

Brett was the oldest brother. He surprised us all when he cried at Tommy's funeral. In his last couple of weeks, Tommy wore his blue plaid shirt quite a few times. I caught glimpses of it among the trees, in the tall grass, peeking out from the side of his mother's frame, and turning the aisle at the grocery. Though I caught sight of a sleeve or the back of his shirt, I didn't see Tommy again. They sealed his coffin. I wonder what they dressed him in. One thing I knew was that I would not wash that plaid shirt ever again.

Another Chance

Considering I grew up on a farm this may be hard for you to believe, but once I got married to Harry, we never had any pets. No dogs. No cats. For a long time I wouldn't admit the reason. It was because I thought Harry would be cruel to them. Funny how things were. I didn't want pets because I didn't want them getting kicked or strangled or hit by him, but we had youngins. I guess I didn't want to believe that Harry would hurt youngins, even though I truly believed he could hurt animals. Sometimes he'd be mean to his horse. "Bud" was what he called him. But because he needed his horse, he always stopped short of doing anything that would make the horse fear him so much that he would turn on him. In Harry's eyes a work animal was different than a pet, which could easily be disposed of because it served no real purpose.

When Zak and Jeremy were little, I thought of getting them a dog. But then, whenever Harry would come home, I imagined the animal crossing his path at the wrong time and ending up in a burlap bag with a rope twisted around it and being dumped in a pond or, worse, just getting thrown into a hole and being covered with shovelfuls of earth. So each time the boys would plead with me to get a dog, I'd keep putting them off. Sometimes with excuses they could understand, like our not having enough food for us to eat so how could we feed another mouth. Sometimes with reasons that they couldn't understand, like I didn't want animal hair getting into all the clothes I washed.

They would say, "But Ma, if it gets on the clothes you can wash it off."

One day Jeremy came home holding this little scrawny mutt he got from a litter the Rosens' dog Yippie had. I'll never forget the look on Jeremy's face as he held the brown and white spotted puppy. Jeremy's eyes were big and begging of me to understand his need to have something he could hold and love and take care of. As Jeremy fiercely clung to the pup, it was licking his face, which had dirt all over it from playing in the sand. Jeremy wanted that dog so badly. But I couldn't stand the thought of Jeremy loving this dog and having to see it be mistreated when Harry came home. So, instead of hating Harry for hurting his pup, Jeremy ended up hating me for not letting him have the dog. He had even named him in those few minutes it took him to carry him home. He named him Whimper, 'cause the little thing just whined and whimpered.

"Ma, he needs me," Jeremy had said.

It broke my heart to say, "No. Go on now and bring him back where you got him."

He stood there for the longest time as if waiting for me to change my mind. But I wouldn't. I couldn't. So finally, tears streaming down his smudged cheeks, he stomped his foot and brought the pup back to the Rosens' place. He wouldn't look at me the rest of the day and would hardly eat anything that whole week. A couple of days later, I watched him playing with a caterpillar he found on the front porch. He was talking to it. Saying how he wished it could grow big enough to be a pet. Telling it that he was afraid, it being so little and all, that he might lose it, or worse, step on it and squish it by accident.

As little as Jeremy was, he knew enough about what he could handle. I know he would have taken real good care of the dog. And maybe if I had said "yes," maybe he never would have been playing with the marbles. Maybe he would have been romping somewhere in the meadow with his dog Whimper. And maybe if Harry had had a dog to be cruel to he wouldn't have killed his own son. But those things I'll never know because Jeremy never had a pet. As quickly as he had picked a name for the pup he wanted, I just as quickly said "no." I wonder how long it took him to forget about that dog that so dearly licked his hope-filled face that day. I wonder how long it took him to stop hating me for saying "no."

The reason I started telling this story is because when I was staying with Isabelle, her beautiful, long-haired gray cat had a litter. One day her husband brought all the kittens into her bedroom and let the five of them onto Isabelle's bed. Oh, how she responded to them scampering around her. Her eyes just lit up and the little extra movement she had gained in her arm seemed devoted to touching every one of those tiny kittens. Before she got too tired out, she pointed to one and then touched my hand. At first I picked it up and brought it closer to her thinking that she wanted to see it better. The more I did this, the more bothered she got.

I knew when Isabelle was upset. She would start trying to get her idea across, and not being able to talk, she would get frustrated. The more she tried to move her lips, the more spit would drool out of the side of her mouth, and her face would get really red. The doctor had warned us about the danger of her having another stroke if she got too excited. So after a few minutes of this, I just stopped trying to give her the kitten and I placed him in my lap. It was a sweet little thing. It was gray like its mother but had a white nose and white front paws. It was the smallest of the bunch and it had two different colored eyes. One blue and the other green. Once the kitten settled in my lap, Isabelle calmed right down. It was then that I understood what she was trying to tell me. She wanted me to have the kitten. She was giving it to me.

"Isabelle, are you trying to tell me that you want me to have this kitten?" I asked.

There was that slight lift to the side of her mouth. I

knew her answer was "yes."

What was I going to do with a kitten that would soon grow into a cat? But not wanting to upset Isabelle, I just smiled while thinking that when the time came for me to leave I would talk to her husband and explain how I just couldn't keep this animal.

"For the time being, I will make Isabelle happy," I decided as I gently stroked the little clump of fur nestled in my lap.

When the maid came in with the basket to gather up all the kittens and bring them back to wherever it was that they were kept, I picked this one up. While putting him into the basket I said, "Time to go back, Stranger."

I should have realized right then and there that, having given him a name, a part of me was already loving him. Already owning him. He was mine whether or not I was willing to consider it.

The Comfort of the Cavern

"No, Daddy. Don't, Daddy."

One simple, unfinished sentence that haunted me throughout my life. Some nights I would bolt upright in my bed. Sweat soaking through my nightgown. Those words slipping off my lips, which felt ice cold. Cold enough that if I spit, the spittle would form into an icicle. Odd how my lips were so very, very cold while the rest of me felt so hot and flushed, as if blasted by a cloud of hot air. There was never anything else. Never a dream with pictures that would give a clue to those words. Never anything but a sense of dread. A dread so great that all I could do with it was make it disappear. There was nowhere else for it to go. Nowhere else. I never woke up with those words coming out of my mouth when Harry was around. It was only when I was alone. Alone in my bed. Alone in my sleep. Alone in my dread. Afterwards, my head would ache so. Even my hair would hurt. It was like the feeling of hurt that comes when hair is let loose after having been tightly braided for days. Sometimes I would wonder what it all meant. Other times I would just pull the quilt up to my chin and squeeze my eyes tight. Forcing sleep. That was something I had learned to do when I was a youngin.

There was a time when Lilly and Lydia and I slept in the same bed. The two of them, being older and closer in age, would start yakking about things I had no mind for or didn't want to have anything to do with. Laying between them, their knees and elbows poking into me, their pillows crowding my head, I would force myself to fall into a place I called sleep. Though sometimes I wondered if it really was sleep. I would stop hearing my sisters' voices. I would stop feeling their bones. I would disappear into a dark cavern that held nothing but an emptiness. An emptiness that allowed me some peace. I called it sleep, but after they quieted down and fell into their own dreams, I would find myself lying there with my eyes once again opened. It was only then, in the quiet of the night, that I would be able to really fall asleep. No longer needing the help of my cavern. Eventually I got my own bed, but I never had a room to myself until Harry and I moved to Chapel Ridge and he began going away.

At first I didn't know what to do without having someone else's voice traveling through the room or someone else's bones clicking against mine or someone else's skin so close to mine our sweat mixed together. But as with all things, I got used to the changes. Less and less I needed the cavern for rest. Except of course on those nights that my lips turned ice cold. Then sometimes I would remember the cavern. So dark. So endless. So still.

So empty. And yet so comforting.

When I was about twelve I wrote a poem about that special, secret place of mine. I don't know if I can recall it now. That was so very long ago. I had been in school and we had been reading poems in class. The teacher, Miss Parker, liked poetry and always tried to make the youngins in her class like it too. The poem I wrote went like this.

A cavern dark, a cavern deep
Hid behind a grove of sleep
Hard to find unless you hold
The secret of...

I can't remember the rest of it. The teacher was nice and said it had potential, though she didn't quite understand what it was saying. One of the boys in the class grabbed it from me and made fun of my words. I got all red in the face and decided right then and there that sharing special things was not something to do. At least not something to do unless the other person understood that it was special.

Growing up I had one best friend. He was a boy. My sisters would often tease the living daylights out of me about him. But when it came to our friendship I stood firm as a rock. His name was Jake, but I called him Dimples. That was my secret name for him. I never called him that in front of anyone else 'cause I knew that as much as he liked me, he would have forgotten I was his best friend and walloped me. But when we were alone together he would let me call him that, 'cause he knew it meant he was very special to me. Jake and I shared the same birthday. And so every year that we were together we would either give each other something special or do something special for the other one. One year he found a perfect, heart-shaped rock and proudly put it in my hand. That was the year that he also planted a quick kiss on my cheek before running off to his house. I remember standing there and not quite believing he had done that. It did make me feel real special.

We were like "two peas in a pod" as my pa would say. Oh, we had other friends and there were times when he'd go off with his friends and I'd sit around playing dolls with my sisters. But sometimes the two of us, Jake and Hattie, or Dimples and Silly, which is what he called me, well, we'd just hook together and there'd be nothing that could separate us. Jake had dreams of being a writer, and he would sit with me under a tree and fill my head with his stories. His pa was in the newspaper business, and Jake always said that one day he himself would own the biggest newspaper around. Though I believed he would, I told him that newspapers were kind of flimsy things. People read them but then turned them into whatever they needed them for or just burned them up. I told him that he should put his words into a book that would be read over and over again. A book that would be kept safe on a shelf so that different eyes could, year after year, enjoy the words.

Jake made me feel that words meant something. He listened to me and heard most everything I said. He even understood my cavern poem and said that someday, when he owned his newspaper, he would print anything I wrote. Soon after we turned thirteen, Jake's family moved away. His father sold the paper business he was in and took Jake away to a place called New York. Just like that I lost the best friend I ever had.

Snippet

You may wonder why such simple stories are important. By the time my life came to an end, I think that just as Jake and I had a way of hooking together and weaving in and out of each other's days, parts of my life hooked together and made some sense. Funny how in one moment everything manages to fall into a place, like the cavern I would fall into, and be held together.

Something to Remember

The day I left Miss Jean's home, after I had finished cleaning up all the blood, I took something of hers with me. I thought about what I was doing and decided it was something I had to do. I guess another person would have called it stealing, but I had to take something of Miss Jean's. Something that would help me remember all those hours I sat with her. All those hours I spent helping her while at the same time helping myself. Giving myself a rest from the aloneness I felt. An aloneness that, day after day, moved about my house with me. Even though I would have written her letters for her whether or not she paid me, Miss Jean paid me well for the time I spent with her. Being kindly and able to pay, she insisted I take the money that she said was "well earned." No, I didn't steal money from her. What I took after Miss Jean was killed had little value to anyone but me.

I knew her things would soon be packed up and sent off to wherever her sister Isabelle intended them to go. So there was really no time to think about what I was doing. Anyway, the day that I finished washing up the stains of blood, I walked over to where Miss Jean kept all her beautiful stationery. Before getting to know her, I had never known paper could be so pretty. Her sheets of paper had a fine gold line running across the top of each sheet and a single gold rose stamped into it. No, I didn't take the stationery except for one sheet. What I did take was the writing pen I used all those days I sat with Miss Jean. It was a handsome ivory-handled pen. It always felt so light and yet so firm in my fingers. I also took the bottle of ink. I had no money to buy ink, and since a pen without ink or a bottle of ink without a pen would be of no use, I took them both.

Maybe I should have felt guilty over doing this. But I didn't. I knew in my heart that if Miss Jean could have given me permission to take the pen and ink she would have wholeheartedly given me her blessing.

A Circle of Women

During the time I lived at Isabelle's home several women came to visit her. Sometimes they would come alone, but most of the time they came in pairs or in a group. They were fancy women who must have had a lot of free time on their hands. They would come with their little calling cards that they would give to the maid who answered the door. Isabelle's husband introduced me to all of them. Though they were polite, I would catch that look in their eyes that questioned my being. That questioned what I was doing there. One of them mistook me for hired help and, not so kindly, asked me to fetch her a glass of water. Not that I wouldn't get a glass of water for anyone who asked, because when thirst is overwhelming, when the throat is itching from dryness and calling for something to soothe it, a cold drink is deserved. But it was the way she demanded it from me that showed, both in her tone of voice and in her eyes, I was not an equal. I was a servant. Thank goodness that Isabelle's maid Lenora was nearby. Having heard the request, she quickly came back with a pitcher of lemonade for all of us who were gathered around the bed. I helped Lenora serve the drinks. It helped her and it helped me because I felt myself caught in a place of tension. A place where I needed to say something about who I was to these women. Women who thought they knew something about me when what they knew was how to judge others, sometimes unkindly.

"I am a guest of Isabelle's and I am also a human being who treats others kindheartedly. And I know how to walk the bridge between different types of people and not be stuck at either end." I wanted to say this as I poured the lemonade, being careful to fill each glass to the same level.

Anyway, what I learned about these women was that they would meet often and sit around drinking tea while talking about many things.

"We have intelligent discussions," is how one of them put it.

They would share their opinions about what they read in the newspapers or whatever news was traveling through the city. I learned that when they talked about the city they meant the section they lived in. Some of what they talked about sounded like gossip to me. But it seemed that when one had an education, a rich life, and used fancy words, then gossip was not considered gossip. Instead it was called an intelligent discussion. As time wore on these women came by less and less. They didn't seem to know how to be with Isabelle now that she had no voice with which to join their conversations. Once in a while, as this group of women sat around Isabelle, I would hear snippets of thoughts passing through Isabelle's head. Enough to understand at least some of what she thought of each of them. I was glad that I could sometimes hear Isabelle's unspoken words, for it allowed us to understand each other in a very special and unusual way.

I found this idea of a women's discussion group both curious and interesting. Not that I would have wanted to be a part of such a discussion group. At least not with this group of women. In fact, I wondered what Isabelle had been like when she had her voice and sat elegantly within the company of these women, sharing conversations and ideas. In some way she must have fit in, and yet she was different than they were. Maybe she also found herself traveling the bridge between different ways of being.

All this got me to wondering about my own opinions and ideas. And what they were. I imagined myself sitting in a circle of women and voicing my thoughts. Each time Isabelle's friends brought up a subject, I would in my mind—keeping it to myself—say what I thought or felt about it. It seemed that these women had a whole lot of feelings inside them that were not finding their way out through the fancy, polite, and rather rigid words they spoke. Words that sometimes came out of their mouths like spurts of water out of a clogged pump rather than flowing in a fluid stream.

One afternoon they got to talking about relationships with men. Silently I joined in and thought, "Though it would have been better if he picked a tree trunk, even the best man can carve his initials in your heart and forget how deeply he carved. Forget that the heart feels pain. Most men will cause some pain, but only the men who we let into our heart have the ability to carve into it. If you expose your heart to a man, just hope he uses a pocketknife and not a hatchet. And pray that you have enough strips of cloth to bandage the wounds."

Just as I had a hard time understanding some of what they were saying, I believe that if these words of mine had been spoken aloud these women may have looked at me in an odd way. Isabelle, though, must have heard my silent words. As I finished my thought I glanced up at her. She was looking at me with an intense look and that little smile. Then, with her right eye, she winked at me and I knew she had heard me.

When the conversation switched to mothering, these women all seemed to be experts on the newest methods that a mother should use in bringing up her children. I wondered how they knew so much since most of them had servant help in raising their youngins. Once again I had my own advice to give.

"Mothering is the most difficult thing you will ever do. Hold hands with the earth and the sky when you take this job, for you will need the earth to stand on firmly and you will need the sky to be able to scream into. Not that mothering holds only anguish, but one doesn't need advice on handling joy. One needs advice on what to do about those things that make us scream. When a woman doesn't have any other choices, then screaming is about all that's left. And instead of yelling into our children's ears we should scream at the sky. It can hold a lot of sounds. But be careful if it thunders back to you. Because then it's telling you, you got to stop screaming for a while. It's time to remember the earth that you are standing upon."

During one visit from this group of women, the conversation was about the obituaries. Della, one of the women, brought the newspaper and pointed out that so-and-so's husband had died. "He left her a widow. What is she going to do?" she asked, adding, "I always said that she should have had children. Now, without him, she's all alone."

Being alone. Now there's something I've known. If I could have, I would have sought this widow out and told her that I have been without a husband and without children for a long time. I would have given her my opinion.

"When one is alone you get to be friends with a type of quiet that only those who live alone learn. You learn to talk to yourself and talk to objects in the house. You can choose to ignore your aloneness or talk to it. You learn that when you look at yourself in the mirror, you're looking at what you alone see. When you lay in your bed, you can choose to be angry that no one is there with you or you can be glad for it. Living alone is knowing that you open the door for yourself and there is no need to keep it open after you pass through it. Living alone can be life or death. It all depends on how you are with yourself. And it can be life one day and feel like death the next. But you just keep going. You just keep talking to yourself, knowing that someone hears you even if it's just you and the spirits of others gone before."

Maybe I wouldn't have said this to the widow after all. She'd probably think I was a bit crazy.

It was amusing to watch these women talk about private things. One of them had recently been to a doctor who was a gynecologist. She found the whole experience, as she put it, "appalling and embarrassing, though, of course, necessary." This managed to draw the conversation around to the subject of "those duties we as wives have." As they talked in mostly unfinished sentences, they all had a hard time looking into each other's eyes. There were more red cheeks in the room than I'd seen in a long time. Each woman kept clearing her throat until finally one of them asked for another pitcher of iced tea. The tea not only soothed their dry mouths but also brought an end to this most uncomfortable discussion. I myself felt uneasy and wished there was some way we could have all just relaxed.

I won't claim to know a whole lot on the subject of sexual intercourse, or "fornication," as Dolores referred to it. Dolores was the tallest in this group of women and she was very slender. Her thin lips would squeeze together into a tight line whenever she disapproved of something someone was saying. Even though I rarely spoke during these gatherings, I did at times say a word here or there, or smile, and sometimes I even nodded in approval. But this afternoon I dared not utter a word. As the women talked about wifely duties, I couldn't help but think of Harry and of Sam. And I didn't like having both of them in my head at the same time. They were such different men. And so as Dolores disapprovingly and with disgust said we shouldn't be talking about fornication and tightly squeezed her lips, I squeezed Sam out of the picture. That left me with Harry's face looming large in my head. Fornication to me was an ugly word. I may have heard it in the past, but that afternoon when Dolores spoke it, it grabbed my attention. From that day on, when thoughts of Harry found their way to my head, I thought of that word and it reminded me of the ugly man he had been. It was a strange thing to need that reminder. Sometimes, even knowing everything I knew about Harry and what he had done to me and to my youngins, I would try to make him into a better man than he was.

Later on that day I did think about sex, and what I might have said about it had we as women been able to speak openly. What I would have said is this, "What I know is to love it when it's something you want. Hate it when it's forced on you. Learn to feel the pleasure of your body through your own hands. And don't feel badly about filling your needs." Then I thought about Sam. With Sam, sex became lovemaking. And none of it was ugly or made me feel ashamed. None of it.

Had I shared any of my thoughts, ideas, and opinions with most of these women, who sat prim and proper and often with an air of arrogance, I believe I would have been politely listened to since I was Isabelle's guest, and then laughed at and scorned once they were outside the door. Just as I saw in them that which I had difficulty understanding, I know they saw in me that which they did not understand. Had I spoken more, I believe they would have found me downright strange. Yet I wonder had I spoken more maybe they would have understood me better. It is hard to know what I should have done.

The more I thought about women and talk, the more I began to imagine a group of us women, women who I loved—Adelphia, my friend Maggie from long ago, Isabelle, myself, maybe my sisters, and even Ellie, had she had the chance to grow into a woman—sitting together, talking, and sharing our lives and our selves. Not just listening, but really hearing all that was being said and felt. Appreciating the meaning of each other's words. I believe we could have spent many afternoons of inspiring and exciting conversations that would have moved us to tears, to laughter, and to feeling our hearts.

I didn't imagine these city women, who sat stiffly in their chairs, unable to do more than peck Isabelle hello on her pale cheek before moving as far away from her as they could without making the distance too obvious, sharing a flush of joy on their faces, or an unbridled laugh, or a stream of tears during their intelligent discussions. They had something I'm glad I did not. They had a long list of rules of proper behavior that in a way kept them as paralyzed as Isabelle was.

Meet You by the Stream

I am so glad that I had the pleasure of meeting Isabelle's niece Miss Margaret, who one day came to visit. She was in Philadelphia on business. She worked in the garment industry. I liked her right off. She was spry and she paid me no mind. By that I mean that she didn't pay any attention to the difference of my clothes or to the way I talked. She treated me no differently than she treated anyone else. She talked to everyone in the household, including the hired help, in a welcoming way. She did talk a lot though. Words and words just poured out of her mouth with barely a breath in-between. Her uncle described her as "having gumption" and being a woman who one day was going to get into trouble for what she said. I often paired gumption and trouble together after that.

Miss Margaret was always moving her arms and hands about as she talked. While my arms were solid and muscular and rather heavy to carry, hers were thin and light and fluttered about like a butterfly's wings. I was in her company only that one afternoon, and what an afternoon it turned out to be! Except for the few minutes that she requested to be alone with her aunt, she seemed to enjoy having others around. So I spent a good part of that visit in her company. I could tell that Isabelle was getting some life from Margaret. It's as if all that flutter of words and limbs was just about lifting her out of the bed and out of her stilled state. Her cheeks got rosy, her eyes were so very alert, and the side of her mouth kept lifting. Had she been able to laugh, I think her laugh would have been, instead of as one might say "a sight for sore eyes," "a sound for sore ears."

When in the company of people I didn't know, I rarely said much. Instead of talking, I would often be doing something to remind them and myself I was still in the room. That day I moved about, fluffing Isabelle's pillow, getting us liquid refreshments which, by the way, no one had demanded, and squirming quite a bit. Even when sitting in the chair next to the bed and next to Margaret, who had also moved her chair in very close to Isabelle, close enough that she could not only talk to her but also touch her, I couldn't sit still. I was more fidgety that day than usual.

Suddenly I heard Margaret saying something that made me think I must have heard wrong. For one who didn't say much, I became unusually outspoken. Up to that point I hadn't uttered more than a word or two in response to what Margaret had said.

At that moment I surprised and startled not only them but myself with my voice.

"Miss Margaret. What did you just say?" I asked rather loudly, not hiding my obvious curiosity about what she had started to tell her aunt.

Margaret repeated herself. "I said that Jake Harland has a new book out."

I had heard right. Yet the name Jake Harland made me feel like I was imagining the words that were spoken. It seemed impossible. It couldn't be the Jake I knew, could it? I was feeling stunned as I struggled to put together another question.

"Jake Harland?" I asked. "Do you know where he's from?"

Margaret, who seemed pleased with my apparent interest, answered, "All I know is that he lives in New York. His father used to be a prominent man in the newspaper business. Now he's in publishing."

Then Margaret got this look of pleasure on her face, as if enjoying a cool breeze on a hot day, and added. "Jake writes the most wonderful stories and poems. His new book is called *By the Stream*. It's a collection of short stories and poetry that he says was inspired by his childhood experiences. It's all right here in this article," she said as she reached into her satchel and pulled out a newspaper.

Earlier she had said that the only way she managed some privacy while riding the train was to immerse her head in a newspaper. Margaret was a very attractive woman. From what she said, she had far too many interruptions from men who sought out attractive women. Though she admitted to enjoying the company of men, especially in interesting conversations, she quickly added, "I can take them or leave them. Unfortunately for them, most of the time I leave them."

Even though she laughed when she said this, I could tell she was quite serious. This was a woman who apparently had managed to find that part of her self that didn't need a man to show her who she was. I admired that in her. She didn't need a man. Maybe that was because she knew that she didn't want a man in her life.

"Would you like to see the article, Hattie?" she asked as she handed me the newspaper.

I pulled my glasses out of my skirt pocket. I had to reach deep because I had sewn these pockets very large. They reached down almost to where my knees were. I had made this skirt years ago for a reason I can't quite recall now. All I know is that I had needed to make the pockets deep. The skirt was pleated and rather full. That way, even with many things in the pockets, you wouldn't notice much bulging. When Jeremy and Zak were little, I would sometimes put a long, strong stick into a pocket like this one. They always knew that if Mama had her misbehaving stick with her it meant they had to be on their best behavior. I rarely used that stick against their little bones. It was one of them things that they feared but rarely knew. In a way it brought us all a peace of mind because it helped avoid trouble. But this day there was no stick in my pocket. There were only the eyeglasses that I struggled to find. They had dropped way down to the bottom.

A bit embarrassed, I stood up, explaining that I was reaching for my glasses. As Margaret and Isabelle watched with amusement, I stretched my left arm deep into the pocket of my skirt while with my right I hiked the skirt up, bringing the glasses a bit closer to my searching fingers. Finally they grasped the metal frame.

I sighed with relief as I said, "These pockets are very deep."

Margaret, in her bold way, said, "Oh, but Hattie, all the more you can hide in them."

Then she laughed and added, "I must get myself a skirt with pockets like that. Then, instead of hiding my face in a newspaper, I could just crawl into my pocket and not be disturbed."

Apparently Margaret had a sense of humor and a rather strange imagination. This made me like her all the more. I wondered if she also had silly thoughts like I did. She would be a wonderful addition to that women's group I had imagined. Adelphia, Maggie, Isabelle, Ellie, myself, and Margaret. What a wonderful circle of women that would have been. But I've started getting away from the subject at hand, which, of course, was Jake Harland.

Could this really be my Jake? My dear friend from so long ago, I wondered.

As I began to read the article, Margaret suggested I read it aloud so "Auntie," as she called Isabelle, could hear it. It wasn't a very long article. One single column running down half of the page. It was an article about Jake and not by him. It was written by someone named Scottsberger. It mentioned a couple of other books Jake Harland had written, and it said that this one was by far his best work.

It quoted Jake as saying, "*By the Stream* goes back to a time in my life when life was simple, and in that simplicity it was magical. Many of the stories and poetry I've written had their beginnings back in those days."

This was my Jake. I knew it in my heart. One of the things he and I would do was to sit by a stream that ran between our properties. We would often, after school, holler to each other as we raced home, "Meet you by the stream."

"I know him. I know Jake Harland," I said rather quietly when I finished reading the article. Margaret's unexpected silence allowed me to continue talking.

"We lost touch with each other after he moved to New York. Jake Harland was my best friend. And I sat by that stream with him! I loved listening to his stories. I even told him he should write books."

Margaret, better able than I to express her excitement, a feeling I was also having but didn't know what to do with it, took her excitement and hooked it into mine. It was as if she was leading me in a dance that I didn't know the steps to.

"My goodness, Hattie." she exclaimed getting up from her chair.

"This is so wonderful. Can you believe this, Auntie? And you didn't know he became so successful a writer? Do you think he'd remember you? Oh, of course he would! I can't believe this. I mean I do believe you, but this is just such a surprise. And so exciting that you know him! That you were there with him when he got his inspirations."

She was talking so fast that I couldn't answer any of her questions. As she talked, her hand gripped my arm while her other hand fluttered about her face and waved through the air around us. She couldn't keep still. All this excitement danced around us while I just sat in the chair and smiled. Though I sat there rather quietly, in my mind I was twirling around and feeling my feet lifting right off the floor. I was learning a new dance and loving every minute of it. Relishing this moment that was truly one of those fine moments in life that cannot be erased.

Surprisingly, as quickly as Margaret's flutter began, it as quickly stopped. The sudden stillness startled me and brought a pause to what I was feeling. I looked at her. I could see that some thought had caught her attention and detoured the excitement. This sudden change, just as I was catching on to this dance she was teaching me, brought me to a standstill. To a place of not knowing whether I was coming or going. Then once again, as quickly as she had paused, Margaret started up again. This time I didn't join in. I decided to just watch her.

"Do I have a surprise for you," she said as she jumped out of her chair again.

She ran out of the room yelling, "Wait. Just wait."

I watched her dress disappear out the open bedroom door. I could hear her heels clattering loudly down the hallway, then down each step before the sound quieted. Isabelle and I both looked at each other questioningly.

All I could say was, "My word. Where does she get her energy?"

After a few minutes of waiting, during which I gently rubbed Isabelle's hand while my face still beamed from this discovery about Jake, the sound of Margaret's shoes returned. She was again hurrying and ran into the room out of breath holding a wrapped package. Only rich people could afford such beautiful wrapping paper. It had bouquets of flowers all over it in many different colors with gold ribbons running between them. Margaret stood in place for a moment as if deciding what to do next. Then she sat down. Again she was so close to Isabelle and me that one of her knees was right up against my leg while the other nestled up against the bed.

"Auntie," she said. "I think you'll understand what I'm about to do. I bought this present for you. But considering the circumstances, I would like to give it to Hattie."

Isabelle, who I could see was quite tired yet determined to stay awake, gently nodded her head. It seemed that she knew what this was all about. Maybe she and Margaret also shared silent thoughts.

"Well then, now that that's settled. Here Hattie, open it," Margaret squealed in anticipation.

I should have known what it was, but I didn't. I was still thinking about what had happened and wasn't ready for more surprises. As I unwrapped the parcel, I saw it was a book. It was then, before looking at it, that I knew I was holding *By the Stream*. At that moment I wasn't sure what to do first, so I hugged the book to my chest. I wanted so to read it, but I could see that the excitement of the afternoon had taken its toll on Isabelle. So, after a brief moment of the three of us glancing at the book, I gave Margaret a big hug and thanked her with all my heart for this precious gift.

"I hope we see each other again, Hattie," she said and I believed she meant it. Since she was going to be leaving soon, this was our goodbye.

"Maybe I can get you to make me one of those big pocketed skirts," she added as she squeezed me hard.

After again fluffing Isabelle's pillow, I left the room and went to my bedroom.

I sat on the bed holding Jake's book and I began to cry. The tears took me completely by surprise. I wasn't even sure if I was crying because I was happy or sad or what. I was so glad, at this moment, not to have my mother nearby, because I would have heard her usual "Stop your blubbering" command. Instead I sat there and cried and laughed and cried and laughed until I felt ready to stop.

It wasn't easy to open up the book and start reading. I didn't know what it would be like. I was actually kind of nervous and scared. What if I didn't like it? What if I liked it too much? I didn't know if I was ready to feel a whole lot more than I was already feeling. I had felt so much that day that I was tired from it. Tired from excitement and joy and surprises. I never thought those things could be so wearing. It was all wonderful, and I had had so much fun with Margaret and Isabelle, yet now I was feeling afraid. This didn't make much sense to me. The tiredness must have taken over. Instead of opening up the book, I lay down on the bed, holding the book tight, and fell asleep. A deep, sound sleep. I missed supper because of this sleep. When I awoke, the rest of the house was quiet and dark. I looked out my window. There, as if just outside the pane of glass, was a full moon. Shining bright. It appeared so close that I could wrap my arms around it and bring it into my room. I stood there looking at it.

"So close and yet so far away," I said to it. Then I turned on the light and opened the book.

"*By the Stream,* by Jake Harland," I read the words aloud. I liked the sound of them. It really was a lovely title. I turned the page and read on.

I dedicate this book to all the people who, throughout the years, encouraged my writing. I also wish to extend special

gratitude to Hattie, my dear friend from long ago, who lis-
tened to my stories by the stream.

I gasped. Then I actually stopped breathing long enough to feel myself getting faint. I sat there so quiet that I almost forgot I was there. Then I let myself say the words.

"He remembered me!"

Though still feeling lightheaded, I had the urge to run through the halls like Margaret would have done, yelling, "You won't believe this. Jake Harland dedicated his book to me. To me!"

But I didn't. Instead, I sat on the edge of the bed, my heart beating fast, while indescribable joy rushed through me in every which way. After a few minutes, or maybe it was more than a few minutes, after a while, the rampaging joy settled down, allowing me to move off the bed without feeling like parts of me would scatter in different directions. Holding the book, I went over to the window and again looked out at the moon. As my looking turned into gazing, I remembered so clearly the look that would come over Jake's face and the sparkle that would appear in his eyes when he was telling me his stories. I couldn't recall ever again seeing such passion and determination in anyone else.

"Thank you, my friend," I whispered.

Then, still in my clothes, I curled up in bed and read the book cover to cover. As the rest of the house slept, once again I cried and laughed and cried and laughed some more. Finally, late into the night, with Jake's book securely tucked into my skirt pocket, I fell asleep.

Snippet

Who would have wanted to listen to me? To my tellings? To my stories? To all those things that were a part of my life? When words or sounds lodged on the rim of my lips, I would usually scoop them up with my tongue and bring them back into my mouth. Send them back down to my voice box. I used to feel it was not worth the effort to let words out. So I kept them in most of the time.

Then, as I started reading books and as I heard other people talking, things changed. I heard things that weren't petty. I heard things that began to make sense of some of those words inside me. Words that had gotten all jumbled up. That happens when one tries to stuff too many things together. Things get all mixed up and don't make any sense. Then the effort to try to sort what feels like one big mess becomes much greater than the effort it may have taken to just let things out here and there in bits and pieces.

My Dear Sweet Man

By the time I was ready to seek Sam out, several years had passed from that day when Sam and his mule strolled away from me. I have to honestly say that, after I decided to say goodbye to Isabelle, it took a lot of courage for me to head toward Willow Grove.

I guess that Isabelle was nearer to life than to death when I first arrived at her home. I say this because she did not die while I was with her and, by the time I left, there were no indications that she was going to leave this earth any time soon. In fact, by that time she was spending moments outdoors in her real garden instead of in the garden of her bedroom. Her husband would carry her outside and lay her down on a lounge he had purchased for the patio. We spent many of our last days together outdoors, which made our shared moments all the more lovely.

Willow Grove was not all that far from Philadelphia, and Isabelle's husband ignored my reluctance to accept his kindness and hired a man with a buggy to get me there. Fortunately, this arrangement also allowed me to take Stranger with me. I must admit, by then I had become very attached to the little critter and probably would have had difficulty parting with him. I had been with Isabelle for well over four months. In that time, my belongings had outgrown the one bag I arrived with in Philadelphia nearly a year ago. Isabelle's husband, saying that it was a thank-you gift for all the time I had spent with Isabelle and for the roses I helped put back in her cheeks, bought me three dresses, a new hat, and even a pair of shoes. And such fine shoes they were. They truly made my feet forget that I was wearing shoes. He would have bought me more things, but I politely put my foot down and said, "Enough is enough." I also left with an extra travel bag that belonged to Isabelle. Her husband, rightfully so, said that she wouldn't be needing it any longer.

I had Jake's book. I also had a beautiful ring that Isabelle had somehow managed to get off her finger. Since her right hand had not regained very much strength or movement, I imagine it must have been quite a struggle for her to remove that ring. It had been on her right middle finger, which must have meant that she worked her thumb and other fingers pretty hard to slip that black onyx ring off. One day, when I as usual took her hand upon greeting her, she gently placed the ring into my palm. At first, I didn't know what to say. It was such an expensive gift. But I knew she wanted me to have it. So I bent down, my face close to hers, and as I kissed her on her cheek, I told her I would cherish it always.

Though it was a beautiful ring that I would keep forever, I

was convinced that, my hands and fingers being the size they were, I would not be able to wear it. But it fit! Somehow, and with the help of a little soap, I was able to get it on my little finger, which made both Isabelle and me smile. How did she know that from all the rings she wore I admired that one the most? I ask such a silly question forgetting the way she and I shared some of our thoughts.

When I made the decision to go to find Sam, I thought of sending a telegram first. I decided against it. I was afraid that I might get a telegram back telling me he wasn't there, or that he was dead, or that I shouldn't come. Whatever awaited me, I wanted to get as far as Willow Grove to see what it was. I knew that there was a good chance that things may have changed in Sam's life. Our letters to each other had been infrequent. I had not written him at all in nearly two years. I also knew that he might not want me any longer. There. I said it. If that was to be the outcome, I didn't want to read it in a telegram. I wanted to go where Sam had gone and in that place discover whatever was meant to be.

You would think that, spending all that time with Isabelle, I would have shared certain things with her. But as much as I had wanted to, or dreamt of doing it, in the end I didn't tell her much about my life. I told her about Ellie. I told her a little bit about Sam. I told her even less about Harry and the boys. I told her about Jake and some things about my sisters. Mostly we sat with each other in a quiet haven of sorts. Often I read to her, which, of course, I loved to do. Once, just once, I came so close to telling her about Jeremy but something sealed my lips. I blamed the tears flowing out of my eyes on my sadness over her condition and my upcoming departure. It helped that Isabelle couldn't ask me too many questions because if she had, her voice might have been able to pry something out of me. Made me make a noise like a board makes as one pulls a long, thick, rusty nail out of it. But she never pried and I never made a groaning sound.

I remember when my pa was once fixing the front steps and he started pulling up nails with his hammer. Oh the sound they made! It got our dogs barking and they wouldn't stop until Pa stopped. Pa hadn't finished yet, but Ma was so bothered by all the noise, especially the dogs yipping and barking, that she just put a stop to the whole thing. Told my pa that if he couldn't stop making such a racket he'd just have to wait on fixing those steps. Pa did just what she said. He stopped and left the steps as they were—missing boards and all. He left them alone for so long that Ma finally asked him to finish up the job because she was tired of being careful not to fall and break her neck each time she used them. In the end, Pa finished what he had started.

I don't know if things would have been different if Isabelle had been able to talk with me in a normal way.

Maybe I'm blaming her silence for the talking I wouldn't have done whether or not she had her voice 'cause it was mine that still stayed plugged up.

I could tell you that I spent days, weeks, months thinking about Sam, about Willow Grove, about us. But that's not how it was. Almost the whole time I was at Isabelle's I didn't know what I was going to do. I did think about Sam, but not in a way that included planning to see him. I thought of him in the ways I had known him. I thought of the past. I did a lot of remembering. Then came another one of those days when Isabelle and I had a "joining of the minds" as I started to call it. By then we had both realized that sometimes this happened between us, and we accepted it.

We were sitting out in the garden. I kept fanning bugs off of and away from Isabelle. Stranger was curled up near my feet, which were, as usual, bare. Once I began to feel at ease in the Sanderses' home, I began taking my shoes off here and there until I realized I had them off more than on. Going barefoot in a fine home was something I maybe shouldn't have done. But no one seemed to mind, and so my feet touched the earth again. Anyway, there we sat in the garden. Isabelle's eyes were open wide. It's like she didn't want to miss one movement of life out there. Actually, I think the bugs bothered me more than her. She would just look at them crawling on the blanket spread over her legs or buzzing around her head. I, on the other hand, did not have a fondness for crawling things or buzzing things that were close enough to touch. So back and forth I waved the fan, which otherwise stayed close at hand, tucked underneath the seat of my dress.

As Isabelle looked about, I heard her silent voice say, "Oh Hattie. What I regret the most about being sick is not being able to fulfill some of the dreams I still hold. All I can hope for now is that others will reach their dreams and tell me about them."

When she said this, I looked over at her. She knew I heard what she said, though I didn't respond. I hardly moved an inch. I even forgot about fanning away the bugs.

Then she asked, "Are there things that you dream about? Are there things that you wish would happen in your life?"

Being as I was, I admit I still had trouble thinking or feeling that good things could be looked forward to. I was always fearing that if I hoped for something, I would then have to deal with the sorrow of it not happening. Or of it happening in such a way that it brought me pain and tears instead of joy. Hoping for joy was an unknown thing to me. Yet when Isabelle asked me that question, I knew I had an answer for her.

"I'd like to try and find Sam. I'd like to see him again," I said with a determination that surprised me.

Her response to what I said was clear and simple. It was also true.

"Then that's what you should do," she said, her eyes twinkling a spark of life, hope, and adventure that mine were afraid to show. Or maybe mine just didn't know how to show it.

Soon after that I asked Isabelle's husband if he had a map I could look at. There I found, in small print, the name Willow Grove. To my surprise it was not too far from Philadelphia. It was close enough that I could not use distance as an excuse for not seeking Sam out. Yet it was far enough away that to go there would be a journey. Funny how words can mean different things. A walk I could take any old time. A visit meant still being able to go between two places in a short span of time. But a journey was not to be taken lightly. It meant preparation. It meant paying attention to detail. It meant having and holding feelings for a longer span of time. So I prepared. And with the help of Isabelle's husband, the preparation was not as difficult as I maybe had hoped. You see, in some way I kept hoping that something would rear its ugly head and stop me from reaching for this dream. But the ease with which the travel plans unfolded denied me an excuse not to do this. Everything pushed me in Sam's direction. I was really going to try to find Sam.

I arrived in Willow Grove, a town smaller than Chapel Ridge, late in the afternoon. The buggy ride had been bumpy at times, and Stranger was a bit out of sorts, mewing and unable to find a comfortable spot for any length of time. I, though, didn't mind the bumps and the grinding sounds the wheels made. They kept me from slipping too deeply into my dreams, into my feelings, into my hopes. You may wonder what it was exactly that I was hoping for. I was hoping Sam still loved me. I was hoping he still wanted to share a life with me. Most of all, I was hoping that he was still alive, for I had learned how quickly and unexpectedly death can move into one's life.

That evening I settled into a room at the local rooming house. Upon my arrival, I was going to ask Theresa, the woman who ran the rooming house and who welcomed me in a polite though somewhat cool way—I think she was a bit annoyed that I had a kitten with me—if she knew of a man named Sam. But I decided to wait. Waiting can be a terrible thing if one wants something right then and there. To tell you the truth, I needed to wait. As much as I wanted to find out about Sam, I also wanted to just be in this new place first. I have to admit that as we entered Willow Grove I liked it right off. There were many trees along the road, and the youngins I saw playing between them were laughing and running about in a manner that told me they had more smiles than tears in their lives.

I slept well that night. I awoke to a thunderstorm, passing over quickly, that left small puddles in the street. Patches of water that at one moment were there but then a few minutes later were nearly gone. That morning I asked

Theresa if she had any scraps of food and a little dish of milk that I could give to Stranger. I told her I was willing to pay. She offered me some pieces of leftover chicken and some cream without wanting money for it. I think she may have had a change of heart about Stranger. She even offered me the use of a fenced in spot in her backyard, which used to be a garden plot, so that Stranger could enjoy the outside without running off. As we chatted, I asked her if she knew a man named Sam who lived in Willow Grove. I tried to describe him as best as I could from how I knew him.

After I got to how tall he was, but before I got to the color of his hair, she said, "I don't know anyone by the name of Sam."

She then explained that she herself was new to the town, having moved here just a few months ago.

She also added, "I'm the sort that keeps to myself more than most people. I don't really know many of the folks living here."

I found it odd that someone like Theresa, who kept to herself, would want to run a rooming house. But the more I thought about it, it did make sense. No matter how she felt about her boarders—whether she liked them or not—sooner or later they moved on.

"You may want to check over there," she said, parting the lace curtains and pointing across the street at a blue building. "That's where the post office is. If anyone knows,

Tom will. He runs the place."

Just then, I became so afraid of the possibility of receiving bad news when I went across the street, I didn't go. I went back up to my room and sat on the edge of the bed. I could feel the fear shaking me. I had to loudly remind myself that I was here to stay. At least for as long as it took me to find or not find Sam. Only then, if the news was bad, would I figure a way out. The buggy was long gone. The driver had turned around after I got off and headed back to Philadelphia. Here I was, once again back to depending on my own two feet for getting me anywhere.

"What am I doing here?" I asked myself.

I began to feel an inside shiver that crept out over my skin causing goose bumps to appear. But then I was also feeling hot and flushed. I was really scared. And I was really excited. I was such a jumble of feelings that I must have stilled for a while. Next thing I knew, I was hearing a knocking at my door and Theresa was calling my name.

"Hattie," she called, "Hattie, are you in there?"

I got off the bed and smoothed the dress I was wearing. It was a simple cotton dress, beige with tiny red roses covering it. So tiny that one had to look real close to see that the flowers were roses. But once you looked close, there was no denying that's what they were. It had short sleeves and a scooped neckline and it held my bosom and waist in a way that said I was a woman. What do I mean by that? Well, it made me feel I was a woman that was not hiding herself. This was something I practiced during the months I lived with Isabelle. I also learned to style—a word the ladies in Philadelphia used—my hair in ways that helped do the same for me. Though I still often put my hair up, I now also fixed it in ways that allowed some of it to stay puffed and some of it to be flowing, rather than it all being tightly bound in a bun.

I went to the door and opened it. For a minute, Theresa just stood there looking at me. Then she said, "It's lunch time Hattie. Do you want something to eat?"

I still had the taste of breakfast in my mouth, and my stomach felt full. The eggs, sausages, and biscuits had been very good. But for some reason, the food just sat in my stomach. It sat there as still and unmoving as I had sat in the hours between breakfast and Theresa's knock on the door. Though I had no desire to eat, a cold drink and a bit of conversation with Theresa would probably do me some good. So I accepted her offer and followed her down to the kitchen.

"Do you mind if I keep my shoes off," I asked her, not wanting to seem impolite.

"Not at all. My floors are always clean," she answered.

"You may want to check on Stranger while I set the table," she added, reminding me that the kitten had been outside all morning.

I could see that she was avoiding my gaze. Once again I thought she was a little annoyed with me. Probably because

I had been neglectful of Stranger after having disappeared up to my room for the whole morning. The fenced-in area I had put Stranger into, near a group of trees that shed some shade over the spot, was at the back of the yard. As I passed by the kitchen window, I glanced out and noticed a young boy and man standing back there. The boy was holding on to the man's hand while both were peering down into the pen.

Must be a couple of the other boarders, I thought.

I stepped outside and began walking to where Stranger waited for me. I still get somewhat shy when approaching people I don't know. As I walked, my eyes were looking at the earth and at my feet. I was purposely pushing my feet into the grass. Enjoying the feel of the blades of grass and clover as they slipped between my toes.

As I got closer, I heard the child's laughter, such a sweet sound, and then I heard the man's voice saying to Stranger, "Hey there, little one. Aren't you a pretty little thing."

My imagination was starting to get the better of me, for the man's voice sounded so much like Sam's.

"Oh Sam," I said to myself in barely a whisper, feeling my longing for him. "What will I do if I don't find him?" I asked myself, my eyes still following the blades of grass as they appeared and disappeared, slipping in and out from between my toes. As I neared Stranger, I looked up and there he was. There was Sam holding Stranger and smiling the biggest smile as his hands gently moved over the kitten's fur, going between smoothing it and ruffling it, while Stranger purred loudly.

Do you hear what I'm saying? Sam, my Sam, was standing right there. There was no time to feel surprised. There was no time to wonder what he was doing here. There was no time for anything but what was happening.

"Hattie. My dear Hattie," was all Sam said as he moved toward me, still holding Stranger.

I must have run to him, 'cause the next thing I knew I was up against him. My arms wrapped around his neck. My face up against his shirt collar. And poor Stranger rather tightly squeezed between us. Sam's free arm wrapped around my waist and I felt my feet lifting off the ground as he pulled me closer and closer. His mouth, talking and kissing at the same time, slipped words and kisses over my lips and face. I felt a gentle rain flowing over us, and then I realized both of us were crying.

In that moment, everything I had feared washed away. All that remained was my love for this man. I didn't want to stop holding him, feeling his body so close to mine, smelling him, and tasting his salty skin, but Stranger's meowing muffled by our bodies reminded me he needed air.

As I released my hold on Sam, and between crying and laughing, I said, "I guess we could all use a deep breath."

I stepped back, just one step mind you, as I didn't want to move any further away from this man, and my eyes took in his face. Sam's skin was a rich color from the sun. His brown, almost black, eyes were opened, deeply welcoming. I say that because I remembered how, when Sam and I lived together, a couple of times Sam's eyes, even though they would look at me, into me, would not allow me to gaze deeply into them. It was as if a door closed inside of him, not letting me enter beyond what could be seen. At those times I would feel a distance that I couldn't explain and one that Sam denied, saying he was just preoccupied and busy with other things. But this had rarely happened and was definitely not happening now.

The passage of several years had not changed him. He looked very much the same as I remembered him. I took my hand and brought it up to his face. I held it up against his cheek. My body was weak from the joy I was feeling. There was so much that was wanting to be said, too much really, so instead of talking I was saying hardly anything.

"My dear, sweet man," was all I whispered. That's all my voice could manage to do.

With that, he once again drew me to him, not caring about the kitten's meowing, and kissed me so tenderly, so passionately, so long, that I could feel the heat rising in places I had almost forgotten about.

Then he made me blush by saying, "You feel even more wonderful than I remember."

And then, though I would have said that it was not possible, he pulled me even closer. I felt his passion rising hard against my body. I wanted him so. But there was a time and place for everything, and Theresa's back yard was not suited for what we were feeling. So with Stranger's persistent meowing, and the hot sun making our clothes damp from sweat, we let go of each other. Just as we did this, a sudden gentle breeze passed between us. It cooled the moisture that clung to our clothes, our skin, our bodies. Hand in hand, we walked over to a shady spot beneath a cluster of trees. There, upon the earth, we sat and talked.

At one point, I ran back to the house to apologize to Theresa for forgetting about lunch. Before I could say anything, she asked, "He's the fellow you were asking about, isn't he?"

I knew then that, even as she knocked on the door of my room waking me out of whatever place I had drifted off to, she had known that Sam was out there waiting for me. It was at that moment, as I was talking to Theresa, that I remembered what I had first seen when I glanced out the kitchen window. I had seen Sam and a young boy. I went back outside to Sam, who was quite involved in playing with Stranger. He was swishing a long weed over the grass while Stranger, scampering and jumping around, tried to catch it.

"Sam?" I asked, as I got nearer to where he sat. "The little boy that was standing with you. Who was he? Where did he disappear to?"

Sam looked up at me questioningly as I lowered myself to the grass, into a space between us that quickly disappeared as his left side and my right side came together. The sleeve of his shirt, blue like the color of sky, touched my dress. The tiny roses now appeared to be a deeper red than they had ever been before.

"What boy?" he asked, totally unaware of what I was talking about.

I explained that, before I realized it was him standing out there, I had seen a little boy standing next to him.

"He was holding your hand, Sam," I said, knowing I had seen what I had seen.

But when he insisted that there had been no boy, saying, "I was alone except for this kitten of yours," I could see that he was also saying the truth.

"What had happened?" I asked silently.

Odd how we can suddenly just know about something. It was just like that I felt it. Felt the knowing. And then, as Sam started telling me about that morning, he said something that helped me to understand what I saw and what I was knowing.

When he came into town that day, he heard that a lady had arrived the night before. Hearing that, he walked right over to the boarding house figuring he'd ask about the new visitor. He said he kept hoping beyond hope that it was me. He said that the people talking had said that this new woman had walked straight and tall, as if the sky was meant to touch her head, but that her arms were bent in an odd way. Sam said that, as much as he knew it couldn't be anyone but me, he didn't want to have his hopes dashed again. He said that when he left Chapel Ridge, at first, month after month, he kept believing that I would come to him. Then, after some time passed, he tried not to hope so much. Still, every time he heard someone new had come into town he would inquire as to who it was. Eventually, he stopped asking and just waited. Waited without hoping too much. Waited while he kept busy. After a while, it was only at night, as he lay in bed in the house he had built for us, that he allowed himself to dream about me.

Anyway, what he said, in response to my mentioning the boy, was that as he stood there in the yard, a thought of having a child with me had suddenly entered his mind. He said it took him totally by surprise. It was as if the leaves of the branches above his head parted, and this thought, like a bird flying out of the concealing thickness of the tree, suddenly appeared. He said that as much as he had, in the past, thought that we might have children together, it was not something that had crossed his mind in the last couple of years.

As he talked, I knew that the boy I had seen had been real enough for me to see him. Apparently though, he was only meant to be seen by my eyes. I felt a shiver run through my body. It left a tingling sensation over my skin. From the deepest part of me, I knew who the little child was. The little boy I saw had been Steven. If only for the briefest of moments, like a guardian angel, our son had come into our world. His spirit had come and touched Sam and allowed me see him and hear him. For the briefest of moments, the three of us had been brought together. I knew then that it was time to tell Sam about Steven. He had the right to know. He was Steven's father. And so I started to tell. Sam listened without interrupting the streams of sentences that came out of my mouth. Oh, how it broke my heart to see, after his initial surprise, the shadow of sadness spread over his face. His eyes changed then and I could feel that door closing inside of him. When I was done talking I waited, thinking that any second now he would say something. But, avoiding my eyes, he stayed quiet for a long time. His fingers kept pulling out blades of grass that, one by one, he dropped on top of each other. They were quickly growing into a little mound that Stranger was eyeing and getting ready to pounce on. But just as something kept Sam from saying anything, so Stranger, crouched and ready to lunge, did not do it.

"Why? Why didn't you tell me?" finally escaped Sam's mouth.

I could feel the sadness and the anger that he was struggling with at my not having told him sooner, and for the loss of a son. I got scared then because I thought he would hate me for this. I started to cry. I couldn't stop it. Uncontrolled sobs gurgled up through my throat. I didn't want everything to fall apart. It had just come together.

"I'm sorry. I'm sorry," I tried to say, but the words were

submerged beneath the sobs.

He reached for me then. He took my face in his hands, and I could see that his eyes were again opening up to me.

"Hattie," he said, as he wiped the tears off my face with his fingers, "I am so sorry for both of us. But what happened, happened. We can't change that."

Then, tenderly, he pulled me to him and whispered, "I love you, and I'm thankful that my son had you as his mother. As short as his life was, I'm glad that it was spent with you. I know you took good care of him."

And then Sam cried. It was not a loud cry, for men didn't do that, at least not that I had seen, but a cry that lowered Sam's head into his bent knees, which were pulled up close to his chest, and shook his body.

All I could do was gently run my hand through his hair as I whispered, "Oh Sam, I love you so. My dear, sweet man, I love you so."

And the Wind Blew

Settling into Willow Grove was the easiest thing I'd ever done. I have to say that I loved this place. I loved most everything about it including the little chapel that Sam and I were married in, just two days after I arrived. Nothing fancy. Just the minister and Sam and me and a few townsfolk who, for whatever reason, wanted to be there. Theresa was there, as were the Liftons, a couple Sam had become close friends with. Afterwards, the Liftons threw a party for us at their home. As the sun set and the stars, one by one, appeared, a small group of us sat on their porch and talked about what a beautiful day it had been.

And so I found myself living with Sam and Stranger and Hatfield, Sam's dog, who, in a roundabout way, was named after me. Sam tried explaining how he came about the dog's name, and I tried to follow his train of thought. It was not easy and it made me laugh, though I tried not to because I could see that Sam was being serious. He said that he kept thinking about our time together and his having, as he put it, "felt Hattie." When he finally settled into Willow Grove was when he began to feel his loneliness. That's when he got this dog. He said he was missing me something terrible. He thought the dog could keep him company in my absence. He said he considered different names, including Heartfelt, but that name absolutely did not fit this dog. Too sissy sounding. He thought of Felthat, but it sounded rather ridiculous. Then he switched it around to Hatfelt, which led him to Hatfield. "Hat" coming from Hattie and "field" because for Sam a huge open field allowed all kinds of possibilities. Once he got the name figured out, Sam said that every time he called the dog's name he thought of me. He made sure, when he was telling me this story, that I knew he meant me no disrespect. That he was in no way comparing me to a dog.

To tell you the truth, I had a hard enough time following what he was saying. The idea of disrespect never entered my mind. From this story I understood how hard it was for Sam to wait for me. He may have forgotten me had he not had Hatfield as a constant reminder. That thought should have made me sad. But it didn't. I knew what it was like to forget that which is hard to remember, or that which is hard to believe in. The more Sam talked, the more he said. He admitted that he was afraid I was going to fade from his memory. He was afraid he was going to forget me and in forgetting me he would let me go. He was afraid that in trying not to feel the heartache of missing me, he would start losing hope. Hatfield helped him to not forget.

I didn't take to the dog right off, even though he was lovable enough. He was a rich brown color, and his skin, soft to the touch, hung loose over his body. What I didn't like was that when he came up to give me one of his affectionate licks, he would slobber over me. There was always drool hanging from his mouth and dripping about the house. He and Stranger, though, got along fine. Hatfield, so many times bigger than Stranger, always gave in to the cat. At night they would sleep together, Stranger curled up against the wrinkled skin of Hatfield's belly.

With ease, Sam and I settled in. We truly, kindly, gently, and passionately loved each other. So I ask myself why it was that I didn't tell Sam some of the secrets I held. I never told Sam about how Jerry died. I never told Sam about Harry and Zak. I never told him about the many dark periods I had. There were things about me and my life that Sam did not know. Would never know. And it's not like I was waiting for the right time to tell him. I didn't have any intentions of sharing most of those things with him. When it came to talking about days gone by it was a choice between saying, "I don't want to talk about it," or just saying, "I don't remember." And either or both, at any given time, were true. Some things I had held inside me so tightly that they just grew into me. There was no sense of separation. There was no more chance of letting go of them than there was cutting off an arm or a leg. And many of those things I just didn't want to think about anymore.

For the first time in many years, I was feeling joy. And not just in sparse moments that quickly slipped away. Every day I was happy. I didn't want anything to make that happiness, the peace and rest I was feeling, go away. Except for an occasional bad dream that would remind me of old pains and terrors, there was little meddling from my past into the life Sam and I had together. Whatever remembering I did, I did alone.

Sam had done all right for himself in Willow Grove. Besides doing some farming—growing all kinds of vegetables that he sold in town—he was also a fix-it man. He could do just about anything anyone needed done. For some reason there were quite a few widows in this town. Women who needed things done around the house. Jobs that their husbands had done when they were still alive. Sam kind of fell into doing these things for them. Each week he would make the rounds between different widows' homes. He would fix what needed fixing, and for the following week he'd make a list of the odd jobs needing to be done. I offered to help him, but he said that for once in my life I deserved to be a lady of leisure. As long as he managed to bring in enough money to support us, he said, he didn't want me straining myself. If I hadn't gotten somewhat used to the leisurely life I had at Isabelle's, I may have argued about this. But I actually looked forward to having time to tend to our home and to our needs. And to just enjoy this life.

One thing that Sam and I loved doing was going on long walks. He would show me all the different places around Willow Grove that one would miss if they were just passing through and not looking for those hardly visible paths between trees or winding through fields. We would walk those paths. We would sit by streams. Sometimes he would fish, other times we'd just throw rocks into the water and watch the circles of ripples grow until they disappeared at the edge where the water and earth came together. Sam loved fishing and showed me a beautiful pond that I, on the spot, claimed as my own. Silly thing to do since it was not mine to own. But from the first day I laid eyes on it, I called it my lake. Sam said it was a pond, but because of its size—to me it seemed huge—I insisted it was a lake. For some reason it brought me the same kind of feelings I had when I would sit in the meadow where Ellie and Steven were buried. It felt like I was blending into it. It was a peaceful, glorious spot. What was interesting about it was the way the earth and the water came together. One side of the lake had a small, nearly flat bank of sand that let you step into the water and just wet your feet if that's all you wanted to do. Across the far side it was very different. There was a fairly steep bank that rose high from the water's edge. Along that side there were many trees, including one enormous tree. Or maybe it just looked enormous because the other trees were smaller. From far away it was hard to tell. This tree's branches spread out wide. One of them reached way out over the water.

Once, just once, because it was really quite a hike

around the water, Sam led me through a densely over-grown path to that far side of the lake. When we got there I could see that the trees were not as close to each other as they seemed from a distance. We walked as far as that huge tree. There, in an open space of earth, Sam and I sat and rested. This tree had leaves on it that were rather long and thin, much like a weeping willow's leaves. But it was different. It wasn't a weeping willow. Its branches and leaves didn't droop downward. This tree stood tall. And its branches, like arms, reached out, stretching to their full-est. I had never seen a tree like this one. I could imag-ine one of those leaves being a good tickling leaf. I could imagine some mama sitting with her youngins under this tree, grabbing one of those leaves and running it over their little, near-naked bodies, and the youngins laughing and running about. I could imagine the youngins playing with the acorns that were scattered around the tree. Picking them up and throwing them into the water.

I liked this tree. I liked this spot. I liked it very much. I didn't mind that the walk was a bit difficult. Sam, though, preferred the other side. "Easier to get to and better to fish from," was his reason. I asked him why it was called Wil-low Pond. He said he didn't know except that it was part of Willow Grove. I didn't know why the town had the name it did, either. As far as I could see, it's not like there were a whole lot of weeping willows around this town. No more, anyway, than any other tree. Then I had the silly thought that, considering there were probably more widows than willows in this town, it should be called Widow's Grove. But who knows why places get given their names. And I should be the last one talking about these things, considering how I picked Zak's name.

One day Sam came home with a surprise for me. He had bought me a sewing machine and reams of different fabrics I had admired. After that, I spent many a day sewing. I made curtains for the house, I made Sam a couple of shirts, and I made myself a couple of dresses. After so many years, it was a change for me not to be washing or cleaning for others. Not that I missed that old washtub, but after a while there was only so much cleaning and cooking and baking and gardening I could do for just Sam and Hattie. Sitting at that sewing machine I was able to soothe an old ache in my crooked arms in a way that none of the other chores were able to do. Here in Willow Grove, I again noticed the ache that I didn't think much about when I was with Isabelle. I don't know why that was. There, like here, my arms did not have to work hard. They did little at Isabelle's, except for propping her up on her pillows, straightening her covers, and holding all those different books I would read to her.

Eventually, as with many things, there was nothing else I could think of sewing for us. The sewing was different than when I had been a washwoman. Then there was never an end in sight with the washing because the people in town had needed me to wash their clothes clean, and it would have gone on for the rest of their lives and the rest of my life had I not left. Here in Willow Grove I could have thought to start sewing for others, but I didn't want them needing me and I didn't want myself needing them. And so, once there was nothing else to sew for Sam and me, I have to admit that I was bored. Not always, just some days. Days when Sam was off working and I was not inclined to visiting with Theresa or socializing with some of the widows who were often too temperamental for me. I was never sure how they would welcome me. It was rather strange and confusing.

Sometimes when they saw me they would say, "Hello Hattie," and smile and be friendly. Other times, as I approached them, especially if there were two or three of them standing together and talking, I would overhear them saying, in a tone that told me I was imposing on them, "Here comes Sam's wife." Sometimes, though I'm embarrassed to say it, I felt like they were jealous of me for being Sam's wife.

One day I almost said to them, "I was a widow once." But then I changed my mind. To tell you the truth, even after finding out about Harry's death, I never felt like a widow. As far as Harry went, at first I just felt like I had been left, and then I began to feel fortunate that I had been left. So as much as I was tempted to show these women that we had something in common, I realized it wouldn't have made a difference. Often they would start talking about their dead husbands with a reverence I couldn't understand. I reckon, from the way these men were described and honored, if they hadn't died, if they had all lived, this would have been known as a great town instead of just a good one.

There was a cemetery off one of the side roads and I would often see one of the widows walking to it holding a bunch of flowers. One day I took a walk to that cemetery. I'm not sure what brought me there. Maybe it was curiosity. Maybe it was the boredom. Maybe it was just a day to walk into the cemetery. As I found my way among the gravestones, I noticed that there were also children buried there. One little baby named Mary died at nine months. Another child, a little boy named John, was taken by the Lord at the age of five. The more I walked about, the more I saw that besides all the men I heard about, not only were there many youngins buried in this cemetery, but there were also women lying under those gravestones. It puzzled me that all I heard about was the menfolk who had died. Men who, in their wives' minds, were destined to be great men had they not died so young. But what of the women and children?

Then I noticed a fairly new stone that caught my eye because it had two names carved into it. I scooted down in front of it and read the inscription.

Margaret and Samuel Harding
Both taken by the Lord
on the seventh day of April

"Just two years ago," I whispered, as my eyes blurred from tears.

Mother and son, both taken up to heaven at the same moment. That thought moved me in ways I can't describe. The image of both their spirits flying together into that world beyond struck me as a beautiful moment. There at their grave I knelt, feeling both a sadness and a joy. Holding that image and not wiping away the tears, I slowly walked home. As the tears slipped into my mouth, I tasted them and realized I was feeling envy. This woman had been able to take flight with her baby. Had been able to take care of her little one even in death.

That evening, as Sam and I sat having supper, I said to him, "I took a walk today into the cemetery and—"

At that moment, suddenly like a flash of lightning, why I hadn't thought of it earlier I don't know, I realized that Margaret and Samuel had the same last name as Sam and I did.

What an odd coincidence, I thought for the briefest of moments, until I saw the look on Sam's face.

Before he could say anything, I felt the flash of lightning turn into a sharp blinding bolt that found its way right into my heart. From the look on Sam's face, I knew this was no coincidence. I knew that Margaret and Samuel had been his.

I couldn't talk. I couldn't do anything. I started to get up from the table because I felt I would vomit the food already in my stomach, or choke on what was still in my mouth.

Sam reached across the table for my hand.

"Hattie. Wait—" he started to say.

But the noise in my head, like an endless rumble of thunder, turned into a roar and made everything a blur. I felt hot. I felt cold. I felt like the world around me was disappearing. Disappearing into an empty space. A place that I was falling into.

"Help me," I silently pleaded.

Suddenly Sam was there at my side. Holding me so tight that I knew he wouldn't let me fall any deeper than I had already fallen.

We stayed like that for a long time. A time during which many things and voices screamed and howled inside my head, even though the expression on my face didn't change. My mouth didn't move. The clump of chewed food stayed pocketed in my cheek. My eyes stared at the carved roast that sat in a puddle of its bloody juices, and at the spoon sticking out of the center of the bowl of mashed potatoes. It was stuck in there so firmly that it never moved in all the time I stared. Oh, how questions screamed inside me. Yet as quickly as each began, every scream was silenced with an answer.

"How could he have lied to me?"

"You lied too, Hattie," a voice answered.

"Why didn't he tell me? Why?"

"Why didn't you tell him things? Why?"

"He said he would wait for me forever."

"You're with him now. Aren't you?"

This argument could have continued indefinitely. Maybe because of that, the anger softened and the screams quieted.

At some point, possibly for the hundredth time, Sam said, "Hattie?"

I turned my face to him and away from the jelled, bloody juices and the cold, hardened potatoes. I was too tired to speak. I didn't have anything I wanted to say. The roaring sound in my head, a sound I imagined a tornado making, had subsided. I didn't want to move. I didn't want to speak. I could barely swallow the food lodged in my cheek. The only thing I felt capable to do was to listen, though I didn't know if I could hear.

Sam began telling his story. He said that he had waited for me for such a long time and then, even though he had tried so hard not to, he began losing hope. One day he met Margaret, who had recently lost her ailing father, a man she had nursed for a very long time. He said that Margaret came out of the world of the dead into the world of the living with a desperation to experience all that she had missed. The simplest things made her happy. He said that, unlike many of the women in the town who were empty of feelings, Margaret was a wonderful woman. Margaret, he said, was in some ways like me. It was when Margaret discovered she was carrying his child that they married. He said that with her he found some happiness and also a comfort to the loneliness that was difficult to bear. When she died in childbirth giving birth to a son who was born dead, he nearly died, too, from sorrow and loneliness. He not only had to grieve the loss of a wife and dear friend, but also that of a son who he had no opportunity to know. After their deaths, he was once again reminded of not having me in his life.

I listened. I heard. I can't say I understood. At that point, everything seemed foreign to me. And selfishly, I couldn't help but think of myself.

"I thought you loved me. I thought you wanted to share your life with me," I said.

"Hattie, I loved you from the moment we met. I never stopped loving you. I don't know how these things happen. I loved you and I also loved Margaret. I loved Margaret and I also loved you. I can't explain it any differently. That's just how it was."

That night I laid in the bed, not knowing whether or not I wanted to nestle up against Sam in our usual fashion. My chest against his back. My arms around his chest. Both of us cradled into each other. Our breaths moving at the same pace. In and out. In and out. I laid in bed thinking about Sam. Thinking about me. And I laid there thinking about Margaret. I had no feelings of hate or jealousy toward her. Odd as it may seem, I was feeling a kinship with her. I also had no feelings of hate for Sam. And though I was so terribly hurt by his not telling me sooner, I believed that at some point he would have told me. I could now understand why some people in the town looked at me in an odd way. Or became quiet in their conversations when I approached.

That night, as he had earlier, Sam begged my forgiveness. But what was there to forgive? I, more than many, understood the keeping of secrets. Surprisingly, finding out about Sam's marriage did not in any way encourage or inspire me to divulge my own burdens. If anything, now that I knew how deeply one could be struck when truths were told, I held onto them even more fiercely. Though I didn't say this to Sam, I knew that after this I would always wonder if he had really wanted me back in his life.

From that day forward, a week didn't pass that I didn't go to the cemetery and lay flowers on Margaret and Samuel's grave. Or if not flowers, then something else that I gathered. Sometimes it was a small branch full of green leaves. Sometimes a pretty rock. Once I even took a swatch from a shirt of Sam's that had been worn thin beyond repair, and placed it on the grave. Always I brought something. All this stirred up a lot of things in me. One day

I decided to do something that I told no one about. I made four crosses. I used small branches and held them together with twine. Using a small but very sharp knife, one by one I carved the names of my four children on the crosses—Ellie, Jeremy, Steven, and Zak. I went far into the woods beyond the back of our house. It was a spot that I knew Sam would probably not venture into. There I made my own little cemetery. There I went many a day. There I would lay flowers. There I watched toadstools grow. There I smelled the damp leaves. There I searched for streams of sunlight that would find their way through the thickness of the trees that were so full with leaves. There I would let myself remember. And there, each time I walked away, I would leave what I remembered.

One day I asked Sam if he had anything of Margaret's in the house. He didn't ask why I was asking. He went into the cellar and brought up a wooden box. As he opened it, he told me it was a jewelry box that had belonged to Margaret. In the box were a pair of baby booties that she had knit for the baby, Sam and Margaret's marriage certificate, and a picture of Margaret that had been taken a few years before they met. I asked Sam if I could touch those things. He nodded. I found myself lifting them out with a gentleness I didn't know I still had. I brought the booties up to my face and, knowing that Margaret had held them, I smelled them hoping to get a whiff of her. I don't know why. I ran my fingers over the photograph, over her pretty though serious face. In a way I was sorry I did not have an opportunity to know her. I knew I would have liked this woman. This other woman who Sam loved.

In time, Sam and I were able to find our balance again. This had not changed our love for each other. Yet though it changed little between us, it did change me. I don't know why, but after that spending time alone became less boring and more enjoyable. I found a pleasure in being alone during those times when Sam was off working. I stopped feeling like I had to fill my alone time with chores. And sometimes even when he was home I chose to go off and just be with myself.

I also began to write. Not in the way I wrote for Miss Jean, but in a new way. One day I sat under a willow tree and decided to begin writing. I didn't know what, and I didn't know how, but the urge—the calling from inside—was strong. I decided to write a letter to my youngins. I also called them my children. My language had changed over the years. Maybe it was because of all the reading I had done. Maybe it was because of Jake Harland's book. Maybe it was something I had held within me without knowing. All I know was that I had stopped feeling stupid and had decided I was no worse than any of those people that I had lived with all my life. I still couldn't say I was better. That was because I didn't know what better meant, but I had learned what worse meant.

I started writing a letter to my children—my angels, as I called them, because I knew they were in heaven.

My dear children, your ma has been granted a longer life than any of you knew. But longer only means longer, it doesn't mean better. It just means having more time to feel things, to learn things. I have often wondered why me and not you. I don't have the answers to that.

After that I began to write more, and I began to write poetry. Or at least I tried to. Sam got used to coming home and finding me sitting at the table. Scraps of paper strewn about. He would come in, sit down next to me, and ask if I had written any new poems. I appreciated his interest and his not reminding me of other things that needed doing. Some poems I readily shared with him. Others I tucked away in the drawer beneath my undergarments and night-clothes. Sometimes I wrote things quickly and then just as quickly tore them up. Sometimes it took me days to write just one short thing, and even then I often crumpled it up and threw it aside. Sometimes, though, I would go back, unravel it, and keep what I had written.

While I was staying with Isabelle, I owned up to taking Miss Jean's pen and explained why I had done that. I asked Isabelle if she wanted it. I had pulled it out of my bag to show it to her. As I held it out to her, she wrapped her frail hand around my fingers that held the pen, and she squeezed them, telling me the pen was mine.

When writing, I found myself holding that pen with a vigor I had not known before. I would sit for hours and think and write and feel and write. Sometimes I wrote things I felt no one would ever understand. Sometimes I wrote things even I didn't understand. My writing captured my attention and held me through hours of time that I would have otherwise worked many chores to fill.

One day I decided to go back to the spot by the lake where the huge tree with the tickling leaves stood. I woke up early, packed my satchel with paper, my pen and ink, pencils, a blanket, and a few pieces of fruit in case I got hungry. Though the path was overgrown and rough in spots, I managed through it by myself, without Sam's help. When I got to where I was going, I spread the blanket on the ground and started to write. I wrote about Ellie and all my youngins. I wrote about Sam and me. I even wrote about things that I usually chose not to remember. As I sat and wrote, the pile of papers grew. All the while the tree stood there. Its thick trunk so close that I could easily, as I sat writing, reach out and touch its gray-black bark. So I did. I reached out and ran my hand along the bark that had many rough cracks running through it. Then I decided to write a poem about that tree.

Oh tree that I touch and yearn to be
So constant in your daily stance

While over the water your shadows dance.
Standing tall and standing strong
Even when fierce winds attempt to break your boughs.

As I wrote about the tree, I found myself examining it more closely. Before I even finished the poem, I was so drawn to this tree that I stopped writing and got up. I walked around it. My hands running over the trunk. Its coarseness felt surprisingly pleasing against my skin. My fingers ran along the crevices within the bark and felt tiny bits of tree breaking away. It was during this closer look that I noticed how low some of the branches were to where I stood.

Now, let me tell you, it had been a long time since I had climbed anything but stairs. Yet as I came closer and closer to this tree, reaching up, almost touching the branches, I got closer and closer to that young girl I had been. A girl who, though she couldn't run very fast, could climb trees better than anyone. I remembered the day when Lilly had been teasing me about being such a slowpoke. She was saying my spindly legs weren't worth much and other mean things. I had burst into tears and walked away from her and the group of youngins who were playing tag. I had walked into the apple orchard. There I looked for and found the biggest tree, and, after a bit of a struggle, I managed to climb that tree. I climbed it and stayed in it, even when it started getting dark. I stayed in it, even though

I heard Lilly calling my name. I stayed in it, even when I heard her crying as she called, "Hattie. Hattie. Where are you? Please come home." I stayed in it until I heard my ma's yell. Only then did I climb down and go back to the house. The strapping I got from my ma, as my pa sat in the parlor, his head hidden behind the newspaper, was worth my knowing I had done something that I knew Lilly couldn't do.

So, anyway, there I stood alongside this impressive tree, feeling my body able to climb. "You're really crazy, Hattie," I said to myself, as I started pulling off the dress I was wearing. Though I may have been a bit crazy and filled with the determination of a young girl, one thing I knew was that I couldn't have folds of clothing getting in my way as I climbed. I found a big rock and dragged it over to the tree. Then I got another one and put it on top of the first. This gave me the added inches I needed to grab hold of the branch. Though wobbly, the rocks held together as I stepped on them and reached up. My crooked arms grabbed tight. My bare feet found footing against the bark of the tree's trunk. And then I felt myself hoisting this woman's body into the arms of the tree. I won't say it was easy, but I didn't mind it being hard.

As I struggled, I felt my whole body moving closer and closer to the branch. Pulling myself into it with an embrace and strength I didn't know I had in me, I found myself wedged into the space where the branch and trunk joined.

From there it was easy, though I did take a few minutes to rest and feel my heart beating stronger and faster than I had felt it in a while. Then I shimmied my behind over the branch, not caring that my underclothes were probably getting mighty soiled and maybe torn. I got halfway across the branch, which was quite thick, nearly half the size of the main trunk, and I looked down. All I saw below me was the water of the lake. Its surface glistening in the afternoon sun. I sat there, straddling the branch, looking out over the lake and feeling joy.

"I did it!" I said proudly. Then I laughed. Not because anything was funny, but because I was so happy. There I was, a woman in her late forties, sitting in this huge tree. I sat there, feeling the breeze that had gently started to blow through the long, thin leaves, making them go in different directions. I sat there watching the water ripple as an occasional fish swam to the surface searching for some unsuspecting bug.

Sam's wrong, I thought to myself. This side of the lake is much better than the other side.

I plucked a couple of leaves off the tree and dropped them down to the lake. They drifted down until they reached the water, where for a moment they clung to the surface, but then rather quickly disappeared. I moved out along the branch. The further I went, the thinner it became. I was feeling a bit nervous. I didn't doubt its ability to hold me but, to tell you the truth, I was getting somewhat sore between my legs from all the straddling. Carefully I leaned back and, holding tightly onto the branch, I swung my right leg over it. That felt much better, as I sat dangling my legs and swinging them back and forth.

Suddenly the wind picked up. I held tight as I felt the branch sway ever so slightly. I glanced down to the water and then looked over to where my blanket lay. Pieces of paper, all those pages I had written, were being blown around. Being lifted and carried off into different directions.

"Oh no," I cried out and moved my arms as if I could somehow stop my poems and stories from being whisked away by the gusts of wind.

Then I was no longer feeling the tree. In my left hand I held a few leaves that I must have grabbed at as I slipped off the branch. I heard the splash. I felt the lake. So wet. So cold. I felt the water surrounding me. As I gasped from the surprise of my fall, the water entered my mouth and went up my nose. Then I was under it. Or was I? It all happened so fast that I thought I might still be sitting in that tree and letting my imagination run away from me. I loved trees. I knew how to climb them. I couldn't run very fast, and I didn't know how to swim, but I could climb trees. Silly the things a woman will think when she realizes she's drowning. As my arms slapped at the water and my head broke through the surface, I remembered the beautiful lady who had so long ago pulled me out of the icy pond. I looked for her outstretched hand to save me. It wasn't there.

"Why now?" whispered through me as I struggled for one last gulp of air.

Sam found my dress and scattered writings. The talk in town was that I had drowned on purpose. I could see Sam shaking his head, not knowing what to believe. He was again alone and lost. So one night I went to him. I met him in one of his dreams. I told him how it happened. I told him that I loved him and that I had never been happier than when I was with him. I told him that I didn't kill myself. I wouldn't do that. I don't know if he remembered the dream, but after that I could see that Sam gained a calmness that helped ease the pain in his soul.

Snippet

During the span of my life, I felt like I had died many times. The difference was that each time I thought I died, I woke up to find my body still alive, somehow managing to pull me back into it. It amazed me that no matter how much my heart broke, it didn't kill me. It amazed me that as often as my mind felt on the brink of insanity, it didn't remove me from the body that somehow refused to stop. And even when the body seemed to stop, when it came so near to stillness that I felt myself dancing with death, it kept going with the smallest of breaths.

The notion that an accident or an error in judgment would end this seemingly endless life of mine had never crossed my mind. I gather now that I was meant to think that, or should I say not think it. Had I been too careful or too afraid, then I would not have gone where I went. Seen what I saw. Felt what I felt. Found what I found. And to just focus on the misfortune that ended my life is to ignore all the paths that led me to that point in my life. I guess my life was destined to end with an element of surprise. And it did.

THE END

About the Author

Anna **Bozena Bowen** is a poet, writer, and holistic nurse. She was the first American-born child to her Polish immigrant parents and was raised in a Polish community in Holyoke, Massachusetts. Bowen's holistic approach to life and connection to spirit are evidenced in *HATTIE,* her first novel. "*HATTIE* is a testament to the multidimensional aspects of our human and spiritual lives," says Bowen.

Her twenty-five years of nursing, mostly in critical care and mental health, her personal healing journey, and Bowen's work with adult survivors of childhood abuse "privileged me to hear many stories. I witnessed the resilience of spirit and the freeing of one's soul that occurs with finding one's voice," she says. Bowen was a contributing author to *Take Back Your Life: Recovering from Cults and Other Abusive Relationships* (2006). She is a member of the International Women's Writing Guild and the American Holistic Nurses Association.

In the late 1980s, Bowen reached a turning point. "As much as I loved being a nurse, I felt something was missing. I started with one summer course—The Short Story—at Holyoke Community College, fell in love with writing, poetry, and literature, and began writing *HATTIE*." In 1990, Bowen was one of ten recipients of the *USA Today* Distinguished Student Scholar award. She also had the privilege of reading her poetry alongside Pulitzer Prize-winning poet Maxine Kumin. Bowen went on to receive a BA in English and Women's Studies from UMass Amherst.

Bowen enjoys cooking, sharing meaningful conversations, collaging, and traveling. She lives in Western Massachusetts with Doug, her husband of thirty-six years. They have two grown children, Michael and Mary. "I love this journey that I am on," says Bowen.

Acknowledgments

I wonder if it is even possible to recall all the people who over a span of more than twenty years made a difference in *HATTIE* and in my writing life. I may not remember everyone, but I will try.

No one deserves more appreciation and recognition than my husband, my lifelong companion, and my best friend, Doug. Thank you for believing in me, loving me, and supporting my endeavors. The optimism you offered during times of discouragement helped more than you know. I would not be enjoying this accomplishment if it weren't for your steadfast devotion to me and this life that we share. To my daughter, Mary, you were the youngest woman to read my novel. Your insight, questions, and comments helped me see Hattie from another valued perspective. To my son, Michael, thank you for your enthusiasm and support of my creative life. Both of you in your unique and special ways have expanded my life landscape and inspired me.

I am also grateful for and deeply value my dearest friend and fellow poet Suzanne Lumsden, who read *HATTIE* almost as many times as I did. You invested time and heart into this process. Our deep connection and many conversations were invaluable and led to profound insights and important revisions, and also nurtured my soul. Thank you to Janet Thomas. Way back when, our paths intersected at a significant time in our lives and a true bond was formed. Your commitment to your work and your spiritual journey continue and enrich others' lives, including mine. Your perceptive editing, guidance, and wisdom were essential to *HATTIE* being published. And thanks to my friend Deb Austin. Your questions and attention to fine details inspired the addition of the Conversation Guide.

Over the last ten years I have been blessed by the kindness, encouragement, and joy I received from many members of the

International Women's Writing Guild (IWWG), especially the "regulars" in the Poetry Critique workshops. Special thanks to Heather Cariou for generously taking the time with my manuscript, and thank you to Marlene Moore Gordon, Rainelle Burton, Nancy Denofio, Joyce Jacobson, Kate Gallagher, and Marj Hahne for all the connections and conversations that inspired and validated me as a writer.

When *HATTIE* was first coming into being, there were colleagues and teachers whose attention, comments, and guidance were significant to my writing practice. I am indebted to Professor Marion Copeland, my mentor at Holyoke Community College, who once said, "A scholar and poet, Anna has the potential to become an important writer." Your encouraging words fostered my journey. Thank you also to Professors Jim Dutcher (HCC) and Charles Kay Smith (UMass Amherst). You encouraged critical thinking with your challenging questions and helped draw out the seeker in me. Special thanks to Dick Poletunow, friend and colleague. From the beginning you understood Hattie. The emotional, spiritual, and psychological perspectives you offered validated her journey. Thank you, Grace Mayfield—I cherished our internet writers' connection. It was a gift from the universe at a time when I needed support in writing my novel.

I have been fortunate to have many remarkable and meaningful relationships with amazing women who believed in me and encouraged me to trust my intuition, my "knowings," and my connection to spirit on this soul journey. My heart is grateful for their presence in my life. In addition to all those friends already mentioned, thank you Lisa DeGrandpre, Mary Hollway, Ardy Schmidtchen, Reva Seybolt, Peggy Perri, and Janet Allen. And thank you to Andrea Fiske—your insights helped me to understand so many things.

Lastly, I want to thank my publishers, Trisha Thompson and Fred Levine, and graphic designer Kristen Sund, for giving *HATTIE* a beautiful physical form.

HATTIE

a novel by

ANNA BOZENA BOWEN

This conversation guide is intended to enhance both
the individual reading experience and the experience
that unfolds when we share our thoughts, questions, and
feelings about what we have read with others.

Questions for Discussion

1. This novel opens with Hattie saying, "It's funny how the world can be as small as the flesh around you or as large as the winds your voice travels upon." Since this is Hattie's initial connection with the reader, what is she telling us to pay attention to? How relevant are these words to Hattie's journey, to the novel, and ultimately to you, the reader?

2. Hattie tells her stories not in chronological order but guided by her emotional and spiritual needs. She shifts in and out of different ways of being, exposing and expressing different parts of self. What does this tell us about Hattie? How does this affect the reader's experience?

3. Hattie takes pride in being able to "get any stain out," and her talents as a washwoman are valued. Although her washtub provides her with a livelihood, Hattie's relationship to it is conflicted. What does the washtub represent in Hattie's life? And why does Hattie make a conscious decision to stop being a washwoman? At one point Hattie says, "as much as it [the washtub] had helped some, it had damaged me enough." What does she mean by this?

4. The author doesn't focus on certain specifics; she never states exactly when or where this novel takes place. Why do you think this information is left out?

5. When Hattie visits Ada, the soothsayer, she steps into a realm of the in-between and beyond what is visible and tangible. What does the purging of the vines represent? How does this encounter influence the rest of Hattie's life and her search for truth?

6. "Voice" is a running motif in the novel. Hattie talks about not having a voice, finding a voice, having a silent voice, talking aloud to herself, and sharing nonverbal conversation with Isabelle. She also comments on the voices of others. How does Hattie discover her voice during her life and after her death? What insights about the importance of finding one's voice does *HATTIE* convey?

7. Hattie endures many losses in Chapel Ridge. She considers leaving several times, yet even when Sam wants her to go with him she doesn't leave. What finally leads her to leave Chapel Ridge? And why?

8. Why do Isabelle and Hattie have the relationship they do and an ability to read each other's thoughts? If Isabelle were able to speak and move, would she and Hattie still share an intuitive connection?

9. *HATTIE* is divided into three parts—In the Meadow, By the Stream, and Through the Woods. What themes does each section hold? What meaning do these titles hold in Hattie's journey?

10. On the train ride to Philadelphia, Hattie has a dream. In the dream each of the children holds a treasure—Ellie holds a pocket watch, Zak holds a thermometer, and Jeremy a cup of water. What do these objects symbolize? What does this dream represent in Hattie's search for freedom, and in her relationship with Harry and her children?

11. In the story "Food for Thought," Hattie saves Annie's cookbooks. We never learn what comes of this action. We don't know if Hattie ever sees Annie again, or what happens to the cookbooks. What meaning does this story about Annie bring to Hattie's story? To anyone's story?

12. In Willow Grove, Hattie creates a cemetery in the woods to honor all her children, a place she goes alone and tells no one about. What inspires her to do this? What does this tell us about

Hattie's journey? Had Hattie not died when she did, do you think she would have shared this special spot with Sam?

13. This novel explores healing and transformation and the effects of abuse and trauma on one's whole being—mind, body, heart, and spirit. What are some moments in Hattie's life when she seems to gain greater awareness and experiences healing and transformation?

14. As a young girl, Hattie slips through the ice and would have drowned had she not been saved by the lady who has an ethereal presence. When Hattie slips off the tree limb and falls into the lake, she looks to see if the "lady" is there to save her. She is not. How does this impact Hattie? How does it affect her response to her drowning?

15. There are unfinished stories in *HATTIE* and unanswered questions. What does this tell us about Hattie's life? What does this tell us about anyone's life journey?

16. If Hattie could join you in your discussion group, or sit with you one on one sharing a cup of tea, what would you ask her?

CPSIA information can be obtained at www.ICGtesting.com
Printed in the USA
BVOW070157041012

302100BV00001B/29/P